BROKEN DOWN

BROKEN DOWN

Susan Koefod

NORTH STAR PRESS OF ST. CLOUD, INC.

Saint Cloud, Minnesota

First Edition: September 2012

Printed in the United States of America

Published by
North Star Press of St. Cloud, Inc.
P.O. Box 451
St. Cloud, Minnesota 56302

www.northstarpress.com

DEDICATION

For Kurt, a man of discretion and patience. The world could use a few more of you!

ONE

NICK MCQUILLEN GATHERED taconite pellets from the railroad tracks near the river one morning in early April. The pellets had spilled from overfilled ore cars that regularly passed by on their way from Minnesota's vast iron range—a few hundred miles north of Nick's hometown of Somerset Hills—to the steel mills in the eastern US. Scattered amid the gravel, iron ore pellets were plentiful and highly sought after for slingshot use, but Nick had another idea for them that day. He loaded as many pellets as he could carry in his pockets, balancing some on each side, excited about the plan he had for them fifteen minutes hence.

He set his unicycle on the southbound rail of the train track, climbed onto the saddle, and began to pedal. It was still early and he knew he had plenty of time to take the long way to school. And he was taking the very long way that morning. The iron ore pellets shifted around in his pockets, but gradually settled and he proceeded on his route.

He'd learned to ride a unicycle when he was four so he'd been riding for over a decade now, and riding on top of a rail was nothing to him. For kicks he'd done it a couple of times with his eyes shut—just short distances—but far enough to impress his friends. Today he was alone, with no one to impress and plenty of time to kill. As he emerged from the woods, the full force of the morning sun hit him, absorbed by his black hoodie. He tossed his hood back, revealing the thick mane of damp white-blond hair, not yet dry after his hurried shower.

He caught his first glimpse of the river and saw that it was churning. Entire trees moved quickly by, their trunks stripped of bark by the surging current. The denuded forms bore a ghastly semblance to the human body, limbs awkwardly jutting out of the water like the arms and legs of drowning victims. Small islands and sandbars he knew were there had fully submerged, and although he had no time for newspapers and no patience for weather reports— he was a fifteen-year-old boy after all—he knew that record-level flood crests were predicted in a few weeks. Pleas for help sandbagging the low-lying residential neighborhoods had been posted at school.

Nick didn't need news reports and high school bulletins to inform his awareness of the river's dangers. His natural experience of growing up in a river town taught him everything he needed to know.

He'd learned, for instance, how much was enough ice to support a boy and a few friends, daring each other to walk out on the river, laughing at each other's fears. Still, the lesson never quite stuck until he learned how much ice was not enough to support a lone boy, and why it might be foolish to wander out on the river ice alone. He subsequently learned that he could survive not only breaking through the ice, but the long, freezing walk home in soaked clothes. This last lesson added new words to his vocabulary: "hypothermia" courtesy of his mother and a number of new expletives courtesy of his father.

But the ice was gone now, the water rising high because it was gone, and Nick had no plans to get close enough to check the temperature. In fact, this early April morning he planned a trip he had taken dozens of times before, the novelty never wearing off: a quick unicycle ride on the top level of the double-decker swing bridge that crossed the Mississippi and connected his hometown of Somerset Hills with Old Port.

He'd never thought too much about the possibility of slipping off a rail and winding up in the river. It hadn't happened yet, so he gave no thought to the idea of the potential danger. Besides, a narrow fence edged the upper level, and though it was not quite to his waist, it did offer some protection should he slip.

Still, he hadn't yet connected the wild excitement he felt—brought on by the prospect of his morning journey—with fear.

The century-old bridge looked like it had been constructed from a child's erector set. The metal girders had rusted long before Nick was born, and the creosote coating the wooden side rails gave the bridge a hazardous, noxious odor. Almost no one called the bridge by its official name: the Stone Island Swing Bridge. The wheezing, rattling, and clinking it made as cars drove across it gave rise to many creative names: some called it the Rickety Rack Bridge, others the Death Trap, still others had words for it they didn't use when polite company was around. It had the look and feel of a creepy ramshackle rollercoaster ride—driving across it one could feel the bridge sway and bounce from the weight of cars and trains, all in a great hurry to cross the thing as quickly as possible.

To calm their fearful children's nerves, parents said that if a train traveled on the top deck at the same time they were crossing on the bottom deck, any wish made would come true. The parents had a simple wish: to make it to the other side safely. The fact of the matter was that the bridge had been in operation for a hundred years, surviving after the interstate system came into being. While its appearance called into question its stability, it passed inspection after inspection, which was a good thing if you lived in Somerset Hills: most people were bound to cross it regularly. It was the quickest way to get to the state highway and the direct route to the city. Even the gangster John Dillinger was rumored to have used the bridge to make his getaway from town, disappearing into Mendota County's hilly roads far ahead of the hapless G-men chasing him.

For Somerset Hills' residents, it was the shortcut to Old Port, where the dangerous, grimy refinery jobs paid better than the dangerous, grimy stockyard work just north of town. Without the bridge, a long detour was necessary—the long way around to the interstate highway crossing ten miles down the road.

For Nick and every kid from Somerset Hills, bike riding across the swing bridge was a thrilling, adolescent rite of passage.

The auto level, treacherous as it was, was for beginners. Daredevil bikers had to avoid being side-swiped by passing cars, since there was hardly enough room for two-way auto traffic and the lighting was so dim—practically non-existent at night—that one was lucky to be seen. The challenge of beating barge traffic left the victorious panting, sweaty, and disheveled. Those less fortunate could be trapped on the far side, with hell to pay for being late to school or home. But it was so worth daring each other to race across the bridge and back, upping the stakes every time.

Nick stopped for a moment to assess how much time he needed, and listened carefully to determine whether any trains were coming. His plan was stop above the bridge operator's pilothouse and see if he could get a rise out of him by dropping the taconite pellets he had gathered onto the pilothouse roof. Then he'd hightail it back to the east bank and up the hill in time for school.

He looked downriver and upriver, but not a barge or towboat was in sight. Even if one came into view, he knew he would hear the tugboat's horn signaling a request to the swing-bridge operator to open the bridge, and allow passage. There would be plenty of time to pedal back to safety. He knew enough to check for rail traffic. Any idiot knew you had to do that. It only took him a few narrow escapes to have that precaution drilled into his head.

Nick set off, his unicycle wheel humming against the rail, and with the lightest thump, he knew he'd made the transition from solid ground to bridge deck. He adjusted his backpack slightly as a counterbalance against the wind, though there wasn't much to speak of. The cloudless morning sky hung like a stilled glass bell over the quiet river valley.

Nick heard the telltale rattle and clanking as a car or two passed by on the lower deck. In a short time, he pedaled close to the center of the bridge, just above the swing operator. He slowed the unicycle and hopped off. He stood quietly, taking in the view of the swiftly moving current a few hundred feet below, hauling its cargo of downed trees. The river's roiling silence mesmerized Nick—he felt its presence, its totemic hold on him, a boy of fifteen with two handfulls of iron ore and mischief on his mind. He held his arms out, his fists clenched around the taconite, and considered whether to wreck the swing bridge operator's morning after all. The river didn't exactly tell him not to—how could it?—but somehow his idea seemed silly now, almost sacrilegious, given the otherworldly power of the current passing under his legs.

Without warning, pigeons burst from their roost under the swing deck, startling Nick from his trance. Nick watched them scatter in frantic escape as if they were being shot at, though there was no reason for them to move. Then an engine roared to life and tires squealed below him. He looked over the edge of the railroad tracks to see a motorcycle speeding in the direction of Somerset Hills.

Next he heard, or rather felt, something he really didn't expect. A throbbing rose from deep within the bridge. The swing bridge was coming to life. No horns had sounded, either from the bridge or tugboats calling to it. The warning bells hadn't sounded either. "What the hell?" Nick said, letting the rest of the taconite slip through his hands.

The motorcycle was rapidly picking up speed below him. He calculated the remaining distance the cycle had, factored in the speed at which the swing span was opening, and admired the ballsyness of the driver below him. Nick liked math. He was good with numbers, especially numbers that, when multiplied and powered up to the nth degree, amounted to unbelievable awesomeness. He held his breath.

The motorcycle came to the end of the swing span, the open water below coursing through the visible wound of bridge. The cycle's engine raced as it hit the gap, the driver expertly jerking his machine up and around to navigate the angled opening. It miraculously landed on the opposite span, the driver pulling out of a slight skidding bounce. The cyclist momentarily stopped, swinging his machine around to watch the bridge open the rest of the way.

Nick almost thought he saw the helmet tip and angle in his direction, as if the guy saw him, but he couldn't be sure. A moment later the rider took off, revving his engine and accelerating quickly to an unthinkable speed. The vision of that machine imprinted itself in the boy's brain, along with the phrase, "Want that."

Once the swing bridge had completely opened, Nick heard the bridge engine automatically cut off. The rumbling stopped, and the pigeons felt safe enough to return to their roosts. Nick looked around, uncertain whether he should move or make his presence known. He waited for the swing span to close again, since there was no need for it to be open in the first place. But nothing happened.

Traffic began to build on either side of the swing section, cars honking with impatience, and a few spectators wandered onto the bridge from a nearby marina. No one seemed to be in the operator shed at all, judging from the random and dramatic opening of the swing. There was nothing left for Nick to do but make his way down a service ladder to the shed.

When he got to the pilothouse, the operator was nowhere to be seen. Nick heard the distant sound of squad car sirens. This was some serious trouble, he thought, and as he walked outside the control room he saw what remained of the operator.

The man's body was in two pieces, snapped in half at his waist, blood everywhere. It lay directly beneath one of the huge spools of cable involved in operating the bridge. Signs reading "DANGER" were prominently hung all around on the high fence that surrounded the bridge's mechanical core, but the ordinarily padlocked gate was wide open. Nick had seen plenty of dead bodies before, and he'd killed plenty of guys, but only on his Xbox. And even though this was a real dead man in front of him—a widening pool of blood beneath him and dripping from the cables— it seemed unreal. Was death really this silent? This still? Nick didn't particularly feel scared. He didn't feel a thing. Until a sickness suddenly erupted within him and he staggered off to throw up over the side of the bridge.

He looked across the open span to see police cars arriving. Ambulances and fire trucks screamed to the river crossing, then silenced their piercing sirens. A crowd of cops gathered at the edge of the span, their squad lights flashing. It was a thrilling display of authority completely powerless to do anything for the operator, let alone guide Nick.

Nick knew he had to make the next move. He turned away from the gruesome sight of the dead man and re-entered the control booth. Once inside he learned the dead man's name for the first time. Karl Lutz. The name appeared on a certification paper hanging on the wall, and on a label on his jacket, hanging on a peg behind the door.

Nick had known the guy all his life, since Karl had operated the bridge from a time long before Nick was born. Along with his friends, Nick had spent hours dreaming up ways to torment the guy, and the one day he thought of giving the guy a break, someone else had come along and killed him. Nick was sure of it. Until that moment, Karl had been an anonymous nobody, someone to irritate and best, like the thousands of goons Nick had chased in virtual reality.

The swing bridge operator was dead, but at the same time, Karl Lutz had never been more alive to Nick. A sense of unfairness rose inside Nick. It wasn't right that the guy had been killed. The pilothouse where Nick stood, and where Karl had in a sense lived, had the cozy feel of a tiny cabin. A home almost.

No it wasn't right at all that he'd been killed. Practically in his own home.

Nick stepped to the control panel. He had operated lawn mowers and boat motors, tinkered with mini-bike motors, and taken apart several household appliances, much to his parents' annoyance. He'd even rewired the school's PA system, happily accepting the weeks of detention for the stunt. It was worth it to be able to unleash chaos by announcing school was closing early. Operating a swing bridge couldn't be that tough. And Lutz was no genius. The only possible problem was that whatever killed Lutz also messed with the bridge controls, potentially rendering it inoperable. There was only one way to find out if that was the case.

Nick examined the swing bridge control panel, and quickly knew what to do. He competently pushed levers and pressed buttons as if he'd been operating the bridge as long as Lutz had. The engine came to life beneath him, and he carefully increased the speed, maneuvering the swing section slowly into place. After a few moments, the operation was complete, and he cut the engine, walking out of the pilothouse to an oncoming rush of police.

The first cop who got to him was Trudeau, the chief of the Somerset Hills Police Department. He saw an immediate look of recognition on Trudeau's face.

"McQuillen," Trudeau said, almost spitting his name. "Why am I not surprised? What the hell have you gotten yourself into this time?"

Nick shook with rage. "Me? Look. Before you jump all over me, you better see to the guy back there." He flashed on the memory of Lutz. So much blood. An imprint of horror remained on the guy's face. The clearly evident sense of doomed surprise was there as well.

Paramedics rushed past.

"They don't need to hurry," Nick said, apparently to no one, since they neither listened, nor slowed.

Trudeau took aim, and quickly peppered him with questions. Nick barely had time to form one-word answers to one question before Trudeau shot the next at him. Trudeau clearly had only one aim in mind: a long detention in juvie. Among the scattershot of inquisition, surely one would land a direct hit condemning Nick.

Other cops came by, and it seemed to Nick they were all asking the same series of questions. What was he doing on the bridge? Why wasn't he in school? Didn't he know it was illegal to ride on the train level? How had he vandalized the machinery? What axe did he have to grind with Karl?

Finally, the paramedics came by and pulled the cops off him. "The kid's in shock. You guys gotta lay off for now."

They escorted Nick to their ambulance, took his blood pressure, and gave him bottled water, which Nick held with hands he couldn't stop from shaking.

"Maybe we should just have you lie down for a moment," the taller, tanner one told him. Guy looked like he spent a lot of time in the gym, Nick thought, maybe too much. The smaller, fatter guy helped him in and put a blanket over him. The ambulance gurney was hard, but at the moment it was the most welcoming object he'd encountered. Of all the people with authority on the scene today, these were the first two people who looked at him without an accusation on their faces.

Not one of the cops had taken note of his bravery. What would have happened had he not been there to close the bridge? He was the only one who could tell them anything about what happened. He thought they would be amazed as he was about the motorcyclist. Instead, he had faced a wall of cold disbelief.

"Your parents are on their way here," the short one said.

Nick was surprised to find himself feeling relieved. His father would set everyone straight. Though his opinion of Nick had taken a nosedive over the past years—an accomplishment Nick recognized he'd amply contributed to—his father would quickly see that the cops were being assholes and point out that Nick had exhibited courage under pressure. He hoped his father drove his BMW and not his mother's mini-van. He'd seen the press. He wanted to be driven off in style. After all, he was a hero. Only he had been able to get the bridge closed.

"Oh, my god, oh, my god," he heard his mother say. "He's all right isn't he?"

The tall paramedic helped him out of the ambulance.

"You're fine, aren't you?" his mother said, and Nick let himself smile, though he hated seeing her chin quiver. God, he didn't need that. Why was it his responsibility to make her feel better? He was the one who had just been through hell.

He took a cautious look at his father. The sight of him working his jaw and saying nothing told him what he needed to know: as usual, he had been found immediately guilty.

Sheriff Ruud introduced himself to Nick's parents. "We'll need to talk to the boy," the sheriff said to his father.

"Of course you will," Nick's father said without looking at his son. That look meant *If you say a word, I'll strangle you.*

On their way back to the car, his father hurried them by the reporters.

"Am I going to school today?" Nick asked when they were inside the mini-van and driving away.

"It's not like you'd miss it," his father snapped.

"Dennis. Really. After what he's been through already?" his mother said.

"Right. What *he's* been through." His father shook his head. "Sure. Well it's either go to school or stay home, because you're grounded until school gets out."

His mother turned around in her seat to catch his reaction, but Nick looked away before she could see the resolute look in his eyes. He'd be damned if they were going to keep him under house arrest. He'd done nothing. If they weren't going to bother even trying to believe him, then he wasn't going to bother heeding their rules.

Nick felt in his pocket for the remaining pieces of taconite, and gripped the heavy pellets hard. He was done living by anyone's opinion but his own, he thought, clutching the handful of iron. He was done with them.

Two

ARVO THORSON WOKE IN AN UNFAMILIAR bed, with a not-too-unfamiliar headache. The familiar buzzing of his smartphone sounded from somewhere nearby, but when he reached for it on the nightstand, it wasn't there. The nightstand was cool and glass-smooth to the touch. He thought it seemed vaguely familiar to him. But then he remembered he no longer owned a nightstand, certainly not a glass-topped one. His ex-wife had taken everything with her when she left.

Arvo hadn't slept in a real bed for over a year and a half. He had forgotten how comfortable a bed could be. He no longer bothered to open out his sofa bed—the thin mattress left the forty-something Mendota County investigator with a backache. The couch itself was comfortable enough, but at loveseat-length, a bit cramping for his six-foot frame.

His eyes adjusted to the dim light in the room. Was he hung over? He couldn't yet remember what had happened the night before, how he'd ended up in the strange, yet somehow familiar, bed. His head pounded harder as he tried to focus.

A perfumed arm snaked around him. *That* perfume. Its sweetly noxious, narcotic aroma clung to the sheets and flooded the air around him with a unique signature of allure, excitement, and poison. By the time Helen began nibbling on his ear, the full weight of awareness finally set off his internal alarms.

He was in his ex-wife's bed.

Even after everything she'd done to him—her countless affairs and denials—he found her intoxicating. He turned to meet her lips, pressing himself against the petal-soft warmth of her breasts and the welcomed pressure of her inner thighs on his hips.

His passion surged, along with a growing undercurrent of anxiety. Within his consciousness, a weary voice told him he should stop, really he should.

He felt helpless.

As she tightened her legs around him, flashes of the prior evening came back to him. They'd run into each other at one of the local bars. Arvo had just finished meeting with an informant, and admirably had kept himself to just one whiskey sour. Helen sauntered by, newly on the prowl—as anyone, even Arvo, could see. Everyone in town knew that her latest rich boyfriend was otherwise occupied and unavailable to squire Helen around town. He'd just been sentenced for business crimes related to his massive—and now defunct—auto dealership empire. With four ex-wives and one current wife to support, that meant the mistress, Helen, was on her own. Rumor had it that the former multi-millionaire had stashed money with several of his women, but Helen hadn't seen a penny.

Despite Arvo's bitterness with regard to his ex, they struck up a friendly conversation, and even though he knew better—given her many years of yo-yoing his heart—they were in bed together just a few hours later. Arvo had ended up with enough liquor in him to put a cork in what was left of his common sense.

The Smartphone urgently buzzed again, and were it not for the headache, Arvo might have ignored his phone and took whatever else Helen wanted to offer of her luscious, toxic goods. He pushed away from her and stumbled out of the bed in the direction of the vibration, finally locating his phone in his pants pocket.

It was a text from Juney, the Mendota County Sheriff Department's clerk. He saw she'd texted more than once. "Get your butt down to the swing bridge. Ruud on the warpath." Ruud being Sheriff Bill Ruud of Mendota County. Obviously something big had happened or Juney wouldn't have bothered interrupting him, at least not before 11:00 a.m.

Christ, he thought. It was only nine. *This must really be bad.*

His brain started functioning. *Nine?* A glance at the phone confirmed it.

Tuesday was it? He took a deep breath. Yes, it was Tuesday.

Helen leaned on her elbow with an inviting look and he turned away. A thought had crossed his mind. Wasn't there something he'd planned to do on Tuesday morning? That is, aside from the tumble with his ex-wife? Which hadn't exactly been planned.

Of course for anyone else, it would have been as simple as checking a Smartphone to find out. But Arvo tolerated modern gadgets about as well as he tolerated needy informants. If it was up to him to spoon-feed information into some device, whether that was a phone or a sneak and all he got back was nuisance information, pointless alarms, and unnecessary reminders, then he called that a one-way relationship. He had to get far more out of that kind of relationship, as he was definitely not going to be ruled by technology or creeps.

He couldn't remember what it was that might have been planned, and the forgotten appointment scurried off to its lair, disappointed, setting off an alarm on someone else's phone on the other side of town.

Helen rose from the bed and stole near him, wrapping her arms around him once again. "Don't go," she whispered, kissing him on his neck, her hands caressing his thigh.

Arvo pushed her away. He knew it was entirely his fault to have succumbed to her again. It was almost as if the past eighteen months hadn't happened, their divorce hadn't happened, and her betrayals hadn't happened. He still wanted to climb back in bed and on top of her again, and it was that sense of his defeat—of his inability to detoxify from her completely—that finally drained enough of the remaining ardor out of him to allow him to function. But the unspent passion clung to him, as always, an aching reminder of wasted years of longing, an omen of lonely years yet to come.

He said nothing more as he pulled on his pants and shirt, and strapped his gun underneath his jacket. Before he left her, she slipped a house-key into his pants pocket, and whispered into his ear that he was welcome, any time.

ARVO ARRIVED AT THE SWING BRIDGE with a hangover gripping his head and churning his gut, all reminders of an evening he wished had never happened. The chaotic scene at the bridge complemented the sickening, tangled mess he feared his life might become again.

A long line of traffic had backed up on both sides of the bridge, and as Arvo made his way by the jam, he observed the expressions on drivers' faces, and saw it was clear that Karl Lutz's death amounted to nothing more than an irritating inconvenience to most. Closer to the bridge, the scene took on a garish, carnival-like appearance: the flashing lights from dozens of squads, the racket of TV satellite vans and roaming reporters, and the long, tangled cables snaking out of the vans and winding along the road. Microphone booms moved through the crowd like one-eyed freak-show giraffes.

Throngs of gawkers had come over from the marina and down from the trailer park. Since the only witness—and possible perpetrator—had left the scene, all the reporters could do was interview spectators. Of particular interest were longtime locals Muriel and Ed Rasmussen and their three-legged dachshund, Roxie. They had been the first to arrive on the scene, passing by on their morning walk to the gas station for Ed's snuff. It was Muriel who'd hurried back to the gas station to have someone call the police. Ed, who was getting more senile by the day, couldn't comment on what had happened that morning. However, he did have much to say about his time working for the CIA in Vietnam in the late fifties.

With the press swarming near the bridge entrance like blowflies crawling on a stinking corpse, it was only a matter of time before Arvo was spotted. Microphones were shoved in his open car window, and everyone was asking him about aspects of the accident that Arvo hadn't even begun to investigate. "Is it an accident?" "No comment." "Lutz was cut in two by the cables, do you have any suspects in custody?" *How the hell did they know that?* "No comment." "The bridge was inspected last two years ago, and given a poor, but passing grade. Did the bridge fail?" *How the hell did he know?* Arvo was about ready to punch the reporter who asked that question. He pushed the close button on his car window. He never made statements. Releasing anything at this stage would jeopardize the investigation, and it was his boss, Ruud, who got paid the big bucks to talk to the press, not him.

Arvo found the press beyond unnecessary. They were an impediment. He didn't need their dumbed-down armchair analysis of events, the way that they whipped up public sentiment into an "interest" that only gave his office work it didn't need. He didn't need the low quality "tips" that came through from the press, that were more often than not provided by clueless (and oftentimes crazy) members of the public who had nothing better to do than make crank calls to tip lines.

The local cops waved him through the barriers and he drove onto the narrow bridge. He glanced at the train deck above him, surprised at the nineteenth-century engineering that had given this bridge the ability to carry fully loaded freight trains and automobile traffic for more than a century. It didn't seem possible that the old structure could hold up to the heavy wear—yet it had, year after year.

Arvo nosed his car into an empty spot next to a waiting ambulance. He hated the sight of EMTs with nothing to do but kill time and empty ambulances with lights flashing pointlessly, but he knew they had to stand by while the scene was being processed. Everyone had to be accounted for, dead or alive. Apparently the crime scene was short at least one potential victim or hapless perpetrator.

"Arvo," Fritz Ferraro called out, ambling up and holding out his beefy hand. Fritz had a permanent surfer tan to match his body-builder physique. He worked hard at tanning and body-building, saying that surviving the harsh Minnesota winters required well-toned abs and extra UV.

"Fritz. What brings you out so early?" Arvo said, pumping Ferraro's hand.

"I was going to ask you the same. We don't usually see you up and about so early, Arvo." Fritz took a swig from his high-tech water bottle. "Got to keep hydrated."

"Well I thought I'd try to start getting up a little earlier, now that spring has finally arrived. You know, emerge from hibernation." Arvo saw his reflection in Fritz's shiny sunglasses. The dark circles under Arvo's eyes emphasized the unhealthy pallor of his complexion. He did not winter as well as Fritz did. "So how long have you been out here, 'hydrating'? "

"Oh, you know, we're really only the welcoming committee for the coroner," Fritz said. "Though Scott was hoping for a drowning victim to resuscitate. Maybe a pretty blond school boy."

"Shut up, Fritz," Scott said under his breath, clearly not happy with his pumped up, inappropriate partner. Scott was the opposite of Fritz, short, balding and soft where Fritz was tall, tressed and muscled. They'd been more than EMT partners for years, but rumor had it that Fritz had just dumped Scott for a cute, geeky ER nurse they'd both had the hots for.

"I heard that the kid left the scene. That leaves just Karl and he won't be needing your help," Arvo said. His headache began to ease once he started talking shop.

Scott spoke up. "A couple of cops talked to him. The kid swears a motorcyclist jumped the swing span gap."

Arvo whistled. "Well that would be a sight to see."

"Problem is no one in the vicinity reported a motorcyclist going by," Fritz said. "People keep an eye out for guys on motorcycles. Especially Scott. No one likes a guy on a bike more than he does."

"Shut up, Fritz."

"You said you can smell one coming," Fritz said, "If you get my drift."

Scott stalked off.

"Anyway," Fritz said dismissively, "If this supposed motorcycle driver didn't make it across the bridge when the bridge was swinging like a square dancer, then maybe the guy is in the water somewhere. Hence," he gestured, "We await."

"Okay, boys," Arvo said. "At ease. I'll see if I can find a way to get you out of here. Keep hydrating until then."

Arvo continued his walk on the bridge, the air getting noticeably chillier with every step. He walked along an empty gap of a couple of blocks, an area free of squads and ambulances: in the distance, he could see the sheriff's car near the pilothouse. He glanced over the edge of the bridge to the water below, noting the high, fast water and the accumulation of flood debris. Arvo knew very well how deadly that current was. He'd answered more calls than he wanted to remember and been on the scene as bodies were pulled from the river. Sometimes a stupid stunt claimed a life—but there were those who came to the river because of its power, fulfilling their sad destiny through use of it.

Arvo looked upriver, seeing that a good number of boats had reclaimed their marina spots, though traffic on the river was still restricted due to the dangerous current. Onlookers were watching from the marina as the one boat in the river, a Coast Guard vessel, combed along the shoreline and in the area beneath the swing-span.

If a motorcyclist had jumped the gap, simple gravity would have meant a quick nosedive into the deadly current below. Looking down, Arvo saw nothing but fast-moving water. Had the cycle dropped into the river, an oil leak might have marked where it hit the water, but the current likely already obliterated the evidence, if there was any. He knew the river wouldn't quickly—or perhaps even ever—relinquish what it witnessed of Karl's death.

He arrived in the area of the swing-span and saw there wasn't another investigator of his rank in sight. Apparently no one, thus far, had taken the boy seriously. It was hard to believe that anyone could jump across a gap of more than a few feet, so it was clear to see why the boy could be a suspect. It sounded like a story a fifteen-year-old in trouble might make up. Arvo examined the seam between the swing and fixed spans carefully. A motorcycle tire might make an impression, or a skid mark, depending upon how the machine landed and whether the driver sped off afterward. The whole area near the junction of swing-and fixed-spans was an incoherent mess of rutted roadway. Still, he wanted to make sure the area had been carefully scoured and photographed.

Sheriff Ruud approached him. The handshake he offered reminded Arvo that their years in the department together, which saw each of them helping the other through tough personal times, had at its bedrock their shared passion for the law. Their relationship was never on more solid ground than it was at the scene of a crime. Things fell apart only when personal business got too much emphasis, as they both learned when the sheriff once forced Arvo to take an unwanted medical leave. Arvo continued investigating despite orders to cease and solved the crime anyway.

The adrenaline rush of an active crime scene investigation and the sharply chilled air above the water erased the rest of Arvo's hangover headache.

"Has the area around the split been scoured and photographed yet?" Arvo asked his boss.

The sheriff waved over Somerset Hills Police Chief Larry Trudeau and relayed Arvo's question.

"I'll get someone on it right away," The police chief answered. Larry's hair was still jet-black after years on the force. Longevity ran in his family, his father just having turned 104. Larry's mother was a sprightly seventy-five year old who was still touring senior tennis circuits, accompanied by his old man. Larry had only recently married himself, even though he was pushing fifty-five.

"How's Yvonne?" Arvo said, asking about Larry's much younger wife. The joke around the department was that the French-Canadian-bred Trudeaus were late blooming studs in the bedroom. Larry's own father had married late as well and Larry was born just as his father turned fifty. It took a robust, young wife to keep up with them, and many years of sowing their oats before they settled down.

"She's great. The twins are due in a month."

"Twins! Glad to hear." Trudeau stud had struck again.

The police chief brought Arvo up to speed on the progress of the investigation. "Coroner is ready to remove the victim after you've had a chance to see the accident scene."

"What's the initial assessment?" Arvo asked.

"We're looking at a freak accident, maybe caused by this kid either accidentally or on purpose." Trudeau said. "Lutz seemed to have got caught in some cables that operate the bridge. Possibly he was trying to check something and the bridge began opening, pulling him into the machinery. The thing ripped him in half, right at the center of his torso."

"The Coast Guard hasn't seen any signs of a motorcycle in the river?" Arvo inquired.

"Well that could be consistent with what the kid's saying. That the driver jumped the gap." Trudeau scratched his head.

"He would've had to make his run at top speed to make the jump," the sheriff added.

"Anyone see any motorcycle tread marks at the scene?"

Trudeau and Ruud gave him the same discouraging look.

"I know," Arvo said. "The bridge is in horrible condition. Been on the condemned list for years. I still want every tread mark cataloged and photographed. I want every mark matched with a potential vehicle."

"If the kid's telling the truth, we need to find a motorcycle. If the kid's lying, we need solid proof of that." Arvo realized he was stating the obvious, but it obviously needed to be stated as no one had exactly checked into the kid's story until now.

"Understood," Larry said.

"And I have another request. Once the body is off the bridge and the area's been cleared. I want someone brought in who can reopen the bridge so photographs can be taken of the gap. If a cycle touched down on the fixed span, there might be some mark made by a tire on the edge of the swing span, under the roadbed. Is there a lip under there, maybe where the two parts come together?"

"We'll get on it later," the police chief said. "As I understand it, Karl is the only operator. Far as we know there's no one else who can run the damn thing."

"The boy did," Arvo pointed out. "Also this missing motor-cyclist maybe did. It really can't be that difficult, can it? I don't want the bridge reopened to traffic until we've made a thorough review of its operation.

"It's not reopening anyway," Larry said. "The engineers are shutting it down. Indefinitely."

"If the kid didn't cause the bridge to open, and the motorcycle driver is a phantom anyway, that leaves only one perpetrator," Bill reasoned. "The bridge malfunctioned." Bill spat on the roadway. "The thing should have been shut down long ago. No one would be surprised if Karl was killed by the bridge."

"That's an interesting possibility," Arvo said. "But I think no one should be jumping to premature conclusions. So far from what I've heard about the investigation, everyone's only looking for evidence that supports whatever they think happened."

Arvo realized exactly what needed to happen next. He regretted he hadn't immediately acted on the page he'd received an hour earlier. "I want everyone to start over. From the beginning. I want everyone to pretend they just got here. I want every assumption everyone's made so far, erased. Blank slate. Understood?"

"Understood," Larry said.

"Oh, and somebody tell Fritz that he and Scott can leave. Jesus Christ, no one else is going to turn up at this point that they can help." Arvo knew it seemed counterintuitive to his orders, but his gut told him to call off the EMT boys. The treacherous current would have carried any evidence far downstream from Somerset Hills.

Trudeau and Ruud hustled off to inform their teams, and Arvo heard his name muttered by more than one cop as he made his way to where the victim lay, in pieces, under the huge cable mechanism that muscled the bridge's operation for the past century.

A junior-level police photographer stood nearby the blood-drenched scene, gabbing on his cell phone, unaware of the speed at which Arvo was approaching. Arvo yanked the phone away from him and roughly hung up on the caller, jamming the phone back into the guy's hands.

"Now," Arvo said, his face close to the photographer's. "I don't want to know how many shots you've taken so far. You're with me for the next hour. Where I point, you shoot. Other than that, I want complete silence. Got it?"

"Yes, sir."

"Better yet," he said, "Hand me that thing. Only way it's going to be done right is if I do it myself. I'll tell you where to place the marks."

Arvo turned to face the ghastly scene, pointed his camera at the victim, and began to press the shutter.

THREE

I MISS WALTER CRONKITE" CLARE LUTZ said as she refilled her husband John's coffee cup in their tiny Somerset Hills kitchen. John sat at the table buttering his toast, while Clare stood at the counter simultaneously updating her grocery list, mixing batter for banana bread, and fussing over her husband.

"Oh, he's been gone a long time now," John asked. "When'd he die?"

"What are you talking about?" Clare said.

"Cronkite. You said you missed Walter Cronkite." John felt himself tear-up. He sort of missed the old CBS newscaster himself. He was surprised how easily he cried these days. He looked down at his toast, brushing the tear away when he was sure Clare wasn't looking.

"I said: we need to *water the lawn tonight.* Not *miss Walter Cronkite.*" Clare added a note to the to-do list she kept under her prized Obama 2008 fridge magnet. *Hearing test for John.* John kept his own list next to hers, under his McCain-Palin fridge magnet: *Write swing bridge opinion piece.*

"You were mumbling, again, Clare."

"You need to get your hearing checked," she said, pouring the banana bread batter in the pan

"Bah," he said, waving her off. "You need to speak up."

It was possibly the thousandth time they'd had the discussion. She'd scheduled a number of audiology appointments for him, all of which he promptly canceled.

She really did mumble, John thought to himself, crunching his whole-wheat toast. If she'd just enunciate, they'd never have these misunderstandings.

John and Clare Lutz had their portable kitchen TV tuned to the morning news, as always, while they ate breakfast in their three-bedroom 1950s-era rambler. They'd lived in Somerset Hills for over fifty years, moving there in the early years of their marriage.

John had first laid eyes on Somerset Hills by accident, when he took the River Road streetcar and fell asleep, missing his stop. He stumbled off the streetcar half awake, only to realize after the streetcar had begun its return trip to the city, without him, that he'd made a mistake. He was stranded at the intersection of River Road and Tenth Street for a half-hour. He saw enough during that half-hour to decide that Somerset Hills was the ideal place to raise a family. He found a new house in a subdivision on top of the bluff, and promptly moved there with his wife and five children (all under the age of five).

In the next five years things changed rapidly for John and the streetcar system that had delivered him to Somerset Hills. Six more children (a set of twins a surprise) were added to John's family, and the streetcar lines were deemed outdated, the cars shipped to other cities (Newark, New Jersey, and Mexico City among them). John's family thrived while the transportation system fell apart. The efficient, economical streetcar system was replaced by the environmentally wasteful bus system.

John felt betrayed by the loss, not that he had a lot of time to dwell on mass transportation in those days with a dozen mouths to feed. Still, it was clear to him that it was a bad idea to get rid of a working transportation system. The bus system never caught on because before the bus system was even in place, the politicians and planners were busy with the next thing: building highways. Because suburban growth (to John: sprawl) meant cars and cars needed highways. So in less than five years the streetcar line was gone and Somerset Hills, and the many other towns like it ringing the big city, bloomed (or sometimes festered, as John preferred to think) into suburban burgs of 20,000 inhabitants, to which John personally contributed a baker's dozen.

John's contemporaries were veterans of World War II (his oldest brother was killed in action). He himself had spent time as a GI in post-World War II Germany and Italy, though the only action he saw was in the saloons of the Italian Alps and the beer halls of Bavaria. He was old enough to have seen his parents scrimping to get by during the Depression. So it grieved him, to no end, to see the waste that was the American suburb, and it pained him that he had contributed to the excess.

In his retirement he'd become a man who opined on wastefulness. He abhorred litterers, polluters, democrats, welfare recipients, and young women who tailgated him in their fast red cars, wasting gas and irritating him to no end. People who were wasteful were always in a hurry, completely careless about their actions. He'd written letters to the editor (as often as daily) on each of these squanderers. But always in the back of his mind were the long vanished streetcars of his youth, given away to lesser cities without so much as a thought. John was horrified to learn some of the cars were burned for scrap. On principal, he never rode the bus, considering the system corrupt from the start.

Of his eleven children, the youngest remained at home. Though Karl hadn't made as much of himself as his other children, John found it satisfying that he had worked steadily as the swing bridge operator for the past twenty years. John was also more than satisfied that the bridge itself had outlasted everything in the area: the streetcars, the outdated and under-maintained interstate highways, and all the attempts politicians and planners had made to put it out of existence.

He wasn't too surprised to hear the bridge mentioned that morning as he was wiping away his tears for Walter Cronkite. He'd intended that very day to write another editorial speaking out against replacing the old bridge with a new river crossing some miles downriver.

Still, when he noticed his wife standing still in front of the tiny television set watching the news about the bridge being unsafe and outdated, he was surprised. He rarely witnessed her at rest. And she was never terribly interested in hearing him go on a rant about how the lobbyists were threatening a perfectly functional, double-duty river crossing. Replacing the bridge had nothing to do with safety: it was all about development and bloated government contracts and lining lobbyists' pockets.

She was so transfixed that she didn't immediately go to the front door to see who was there, urgently knocking. John was forced to get up and answer it himself, wondering whether it was his wife who was the one needing a visit to the audiologist.

He was stunned to see police officers standing at the door, their hats in hand, and not quite able to understand what they were saying. When his wife arrived at his side, she was crying. She placed a hand on John's arm as John asked the uniformed men to repeat what they said.

"There's been an accident on the bridge. We're very sorry to tell you that your son Karl did not survive."

FOUR

CHRISTINE IVORY EXAMINED HERSELF in the staff restroom mirror of the Mendota County Social Services department. *Mouse brown. Ugh.* She caught some loose strands in her fingers and examined them closely. She observed what looked like it might possibly be the start of a graying hair. Possibly. *Double-ugh.*

The reality was that her hair hadn't changed since she took that one last glance at it in her condo, just before heading out earlier in the morning for her breakfast date. She knew that. Nothing had changed at all about her appearance. The plum-colored lipstick, the light coating of foundation with a touch of blush, and the carefully applied mascara all gave just the perfectly subtle, and not overdone, touches to her naturally attractive appearance. This morning she thought she'd never looked better. And best of all was her hair.

She'd been leaving her hair uncolored for quite some time, after dying it back to her natural dark brown, and in that period without the harsh hair-dye chemicals, it had gained a luster she had forgotten it possessed. She couldn't have been more pleased with herself when she noticed that she didn't have a single gray hair. For a woman in her early forties, this was a remarkable achievement.

Now, less than an hour later, she could find nothing but fault with her looks, particularly her mouse-brown and now graying hair. Was it too late to declare it a bad hair day and head to the salon?

She was on the point of looking up the nearest salon on her Smartphone when it went off in her hands, its vibration sending a stinging sensation into her palms, irritating her even more. Most days she loved its hip presence in her life, how it contributed to her sense of well-being with its ability to efficiently organize everything. The Social Services department assistant, Sharon, had begrudgingly accepted that such devices were here to stay, though she felt she could do an even more efficient job of keeping everyone on track than some stupid, pocket-sized device.

Not to take anything away from Sharon—she was a godsend, Christine thought—but Sharon really needed an "off" switch, the Smartphone's one advantage over the hyper-efficient department administrative assistant. Still, Sharon had one key advantage the Smartphone didn't have. She might be irritating, but she could often anticipate a need, and applied that ability to keep the office well organized, though she also put her clairvoyant abilities to use in detrimental ways as well. Still, the device was far more discrete. She wondered whether Sharon was.

Christine was moments from flushing the electronic device down the toilet and telling Sharon to cancel everything. An acrid feeling gnawed in her empty stomach. No breakfast yet, other than the power bar she found in the dashboard compartment of her Volkswagen Passat.

The Smartphone reminder of her first appointment jarred her back to reality. There would be no emergency salon run today— her calendar was crammed full of appointments courtesy of Sharon. She deleted one that Sharon hadn't set up. An early morning "networking" meeting she'd scheduled with a coworker. Upriver from Somerset Hills, and past a ramshackle arrangement of aging houses, shabby apartment buildings, decrepit gas stations and abandoned storefronts lay a small café with a bold sign advertising simply, "GOOD FOOD." It was good, guilty-pleasure type food: biscuits and gravy, more bacon than anyone should ever consume, and huge portions of crispy hash browns, fried in loads of butter. But she'd been stood up. By Arvo Thorson.

She crashed into him in her aggravated walk to her sixth floor office.

"I've been looking for you," he said, with an apologetic grin.

"Since when?" she snapped. She pushed by him, but stopped short of heading into her office when a familiar scent hit her. It was perfume, coming from him. Overpowering perfume. The kind of perfume worn by clingy, money-grubbing ex-wives.

And the stale scent of alcohol.

She gave him a searing look. "Unbelievable."

"What," he said.

"Her? You were with Helen? Your ex-wife?"

"Lower your voice, Ivory." He touched her arm, but she slapped it away.

"Do *not* tell me what to do." Despite her best efforts, she felt tears, angry ones, stinging her eyes. Damn. The mascara had been her perfect armor, ringing her eyes in an irate fringe. Now even that was going to be ruined.

He took her arm, hustled her into an empty conference room, and slammed the door.

"What? So you're going to give me an explanation? Don't bother," she said.

"I won't. Look, Ivory, no one ever said we were exclusive. In fact, *you* were the one who insisted that the relationship remain that way, I recall."

A moment of confusion flittered in her type-A brain. Must. Stay. Furious. Easy: Helen. The bitch. Confusion evaporated.

"I don't care if you sleep around, Thorson. I don't care if you drink yourself to death." She knew both were lies. He stood in front of her, slouching, graying, hung-over, and she still wanted him to want only her. "But Helen?" she added. "You disgust me. Both of you. You always have."

He gave her a glittering smile—touched with anger. "Your opinion of me changes as fast as your hair color used to. What, sick of me, Christine? Again?"

She stalked away, entered her office, and walked right past Sharon without bothering to explain herself or take the urgent phone messages Sharon held out to her. She stepped into her office and slammed the door shut, breaking a nail when she threw herself into her chair.

Sharon quietly crept in, set down the messages and told her, "I can give you a half-hour, tops."

Why had she allowed herself to get involved with the man? For years, their work had occasionally thrown them together, and their relationship had maintained that carefully balanced spot between combative and professional. One recent case had required them to set aside their differences more than usual. As a result, sparks flew, and against her better judgment, Christine found herself closer to Arvo then she'd ever imagined herself. In fact she found herself actually liking the guy, practically in love with him, after all these years of despising him. But now Helen was back in the picture.

He'd been in Helen's clutches since the moment she'd first laid eyes on him in high school, when he was the handsome blond captain of the football team. His high school girlfriend Helen was the prom queen, whom he eventually married and had divorced just recently

In her more charitable moments Christine knew that Helen's cheating and Arvo's drinking were connected: the former causing the latter. But this was not one of those moments. She did not need to be the enabler in the middle of Arvo's lingering addictions, both to Helen and booze.

Nothing had changed since high school. She would always be the "smart girl"—then class valedictorian, now lead social worker in the Mendota County Social Services department. She easily handled crushing workloads, whether that was casework or homework—having coasted through her junior and senior year, mostly keeping to herself—her small circle of geeky losers and weirdoes gradually drifting away. She never let anyone come close enough to notice she was more than the poorly dressed, unpopular smart girl.

Arvo certainly had never given her a thought in those days— though he'd recently told her the opposite was true, that it was *she* who never gave *him* the time of day, recalling that she'd walked by him at Somerset Hills High with her nose in the air and the scent of her disdain advertising her disinterest.

"Oh, I noticed you," he'd said to her the past New Year's Eve, as they watched New Year's fireworks from her condominium balcony, champagne glasses in hand. He'd kissed her eyelids and caressed her soft, blemish-free skin. "You acted like you were too good for me." He ran his fingertips over her delicately curved lips.

"I still am," she said with a wicked, hungry smile, nevertheless letting him lead her back inside to the warmth of her bedroom.

Christine forced those thoughts from her head. They were through.

Sharon brought in a cup of Christine's favorite herbal tea and laid an armload of case files on her desk. Tall and rail-thin—Sharon's body had the unbendable, abrasive quality of a metal file. She could wear a person down in seconds.

Sharon said, "I needed to adjust your eleven o' clock. Some juvenile delinquent—"

"—Sharon. They are children. At-risk. Not delinquents."

"—He's fifteen years old," Sharon pointed out, "So not really much of a child, since these days a kid that age can easily be tried as an adult. Anyway, he was on the bridge this morning when that operator was killed."

"There was an accident?" Christine asked. "What happened?"

"You mean Arvo didn't tell you this morning?" Sharon said.

Despite her abrasive personality, Sharon was loyal and Christine counted on her to keep the details of her and Arvo's relationship secret from the department gossips. Not that they'd ever spoken openly about it. What made Sharon an excellent assistant was that she anticipated every department need. The downside was that anticipating everything meant she knew everything. She kept people's secrets to herself, Christine hoped, but Sharon hid nothing of her disapproval about their liaison.

"Oh," Sharon said. "You apparently haven't . . . spoken with the investigator yet today." She paused.

Christine felt another surge of irritation from her earlier exchange with Arvo. "I don't need the attitude this morning. Just give me the facts."

Sharon removed the eleven o' clock file from the enormous pile on Christine's desk.

"Nick McQuillen. He was the only person in the immediate vicinity when the swing bridge began to open, without warning. They found Karl Lutz, the operator, dead. You can call downstairs for the details, the full report hasn't made it to us yet. The delinq... I mean 'client' is a person of interest in the investigation."

"So they're saying this kid may have vandalized the bridge somehow, which resulted in the death of the operator?"

"That's a generous view of the situation. He may have just outright killed the guy."

"Sharon. Really." Christine found Sharon's callous judgment shocking. "That bridge is in such a state of disrepair that it's been an accident waiting to happen. The boy may be an innocent bystander."

"If you say so. I've got an open request to get the boy ready for an interview. You know what that means," Sharon said, a sort of triumph in her voice.

Yes. Christine knew.

"Need anything else from me now?"

Christine often wished she could find a way to fire the woman, but there was no one as brutally efficient as Sharon. "No. Thank you. That's it for now."

She did, however, wonder if Sharon had a little something to spike her tea. The morning's events meant she would have to face another person even more irritating to her than Sharon.

Arvo.

He'd be leading the investigation and with this boy as the only witness—and possibly the only suspect—they'd be together again far sooner than she hoped.

"So, HOW'S HELEN THESE DAYS?" Juney Janette asked. "Not that you'd know, what with you and her being divorced for—how long is it—almost two years now?" Arvo knew that Juney was fully aware of exactly how long he'd been divorced.

The Criminal Investigation Department's head clerk, Juney had worked for the department since she was nineteen. In addition to cataloging and filing the various criminal case records, physical evidence, photographs, recordings, and any other relevant material collected during investigations, Juney maintained encyclopedic knowledge in her head. More often than not, she was the one person in the county who could link seemingly unconnected crimes based on her knowledge of the materials locked away in the evidence room. She had a capacity for quickly recognizing patterns, for synthesizing vast quantities of material. More than once Arvo had told her that with her knowledge, she should be leading investigations, not playing such a background role. But she would never hear of it.

Now Juney had Arvo under scrutiny and was trying to not-so-subtly point out a pattern she'd quickly observed the moment the investigator arrived in the office. If anyone could sniff out a relapse, it was Juney.

"You know I don't have time for this," Arvo said. He sank into his chair, a sharp pain stabbing him in the side. He'd lost some weight in the past several months after making more regular visits to the gym. But last night's escapade with Helen made it clear that old habits die hard. He knew he looked worse than he had in a long time. Reluctantly he loosened his holster.

"You shouldn't have time for her," the tiny clerk said. "Arvo, I thought you'd cleaned up your act. For good." She tossed a file on his desk and stared down at him, impossibly imposing for a person of her stature.

"Three women on my case," Arvo said, "And it's not even noon yet."

"Ah, yes. The lovely Ms. Ivory. Well, you'll be getting cozy with her again soon enough. A fifteen-year-old kid and no one is quite sure whether he is only a witness or a suspect. Read up," she said, hammering the case file with her index finger. "Get your butt down to the crime scene, you need to interview the victim's elderly parents, and the sheriff wants your report today."

"For your information, I've already been there. In fact," he said perusing the file on his desk, "These are the preliminary reports, right?"

She nodded.

"I got down there, and it was a disaster. Ruud and Trudeau had lost control of the scene, Fritz and Scott had nothing much to do but quarrel, and they had the Coast Guard dragging the river for a possible drowning victim or perpetrator or who the hell knows, maybe the elusive monster sturgeon the old-timers claim is in the river."

He tossed the file into the trash. "I ordered a complete do-over."

Arvo saw Juney smile at him and relax, at least slightly. "You know this isn't your only case, Arvo, but for the foreseeable future it will be the number one case. Mendota County isn't as sleepy as we wish it was. Though frankly if we kept you busier maybe you'd have less time for ex-wives and angry girlfriends."

She left his office for a moment and then returned with a steaming cup of coffee and a paper plate holding an enormous, gooey caramel roll.

"Nichol dropped by with this on her way home from her shift at the restaurant. She said she wasn't the only one surprised not to see you this morning."

Nichol was Arvo's favorite waitress at his favorite, quiet breakfast joint the next town over, just outside of Mendota County jurisdiction. The place had become practically home to him since his divorce.

She'd delivered his roll and coffee every morning, his daily "caffeine, carbs, and protein," she'd quip, "the perfect breakfast: cures whatever ails you—hangovers, broken hearts, you name it."

"Where's the protein?" he'd said more than once, the sweet, yeasty aroma intoxicating. The rolls were always served with a side dish of creamy butter, a fork and a knife. Arvo often thought a bib should be included.

"Check out those meaty pecans," she answered. "I'll be back with your omelet in a few minutes."

A recovering alcoholic, not even thirty, Nichol had quietly kept Arvo supplied with "caffeine, carbs, and protein" and generous wisdom for such a young woman. He found her inspiring—a single mother of a toddler, Nichol had a full-time job and a full course load at Somerset Hills Community College. She was working even harder on her recovery. Arvo didn't think of himself as an alcoholic. He could manage, he thought, on his own, and he'd proved it by stopping drinking entirely for months now. Nichol had been nudging him to attend AA, not pushing him, but nudging. Arvo had declined every time

Now, staring at the caramel roll, he felt ashamed that Nichol already knew, not everything, but that there'd been a setback. The caramel roll was her response. She'd been there, and she'd be there for him again.

"Try not to get the files sticky, okay?" Juney said.

Arvo dug in, taking his first mouthful as he booted up his computer. The first order of business was to schedule two interviews, both of which would be excruciating for different reasons. Arvo considered which he should schedule first.

The victim's parents, John and Clare Lutz, would have to be questioned about their son. He didn't relish the fact that he'd have to practically accuse the victim of his own death, sorting out who might have had an axe to grind with the guy.

The other immediate interviewee was this kid. So far there was nothing else to go on. He was the only one on the scene around the time of Lutz's death. Arvo knew he could handle a kid, even a truant, confrontational fifteen-year-old.

Christine was another matter.

He wished she didn't have to be involved, but he knew that with kids, especially the types Christine handled, there was no one better to help him in the difficult cases both of them had worked on over the years. As pissed off as she was with him, he knew she would act like the professional she was when they got down to the business of solving the case. But she could also get in the way, and she often had in the past, making him wait for days before he could interview the kids who'd witnessed horrific crimes.

The boy would be arrogant and confrontational, he guessed, regardless of whether he was an innocent bystander or the killer. Arvo smiled. He remembered fifteen. He recalled that his dad's hair went gray during his teenage years, though the man offered him nothing in the way of "course correction." That came from his mother.

He was in for a fight. With Christine. She wouldn't go soft on this kid, but she wasn't going to give Arvo an inch until she was good and ready too.

He looked up a phone number, and dialed.

"Good morning," he said. "I'm Investigator Arvo Thorson of the Mendota County Sheriff's Department. Am I speaking to John Lutz?"

An elderly man answered him in the affirmative.

"Yes, Mr. Lutz. First, let me offer my deepest sympathy for your loss," Arvo said. "I apologize for having to talk to you at such a difficult time."

"I'd been told to expect a call from you," John Lutz said.

"I need to meet with you and Mrs. Lutz. As part of the investigation in sorting out what caused your son's death."

Arvo waited while John Lutz had a word with his wife, and he thought he heard her crying in the background.

"I can speak to you as soon as you'd like," Lutz said. "Though you may have to wait to chat with my wife. Where is the best place for us to meet?"

"Wherever you are most comfortable."

Arvo jotted down directions to the Lutz home. "Later this afternoon then? Thank you I'll see you then."

FIVE

M R. AND MRS. MCQUILLEN. Please come in." Christine Ivory ushered the couple into her office. She was surprised to see that Nick was not with his parents.

"Please, sit down," she said. "Can I get you a cup of coffee or tea?"

"Coffee would be fine," Mr. McQuillen answered for both.

Christine inventoried their appearance, much like she quickly sized-up a rack of clothes at a consignment shop. McQuillen's suit was ill-fitting for a man of his stature, which Christine estimated to be in the area of six-foot-eight. His sleeves were too short, the shoulders too tight, the fabric wrong for the season. Though he was by no means overweight, he looked unnecessarily padded, layered as if there was an extra sweater beneath the business jacket. He appeared overheated, and within moments he extracted a handkerchief and wiped the back of his neck. He breathed heavily, got up and asked to adjust Christine's blinds. "Warm in here," he said, "the sun must really heat the place up."

"Black?" Christine offered, giving Mrs. McQuillen a reassuring smile as the woman twisted her purse handles. Mrs. McQuillen was fragile next to her robust husband, swimming in her clothes: an oversized and unattractive sweater, layered on top of another thick sweater, over polyester pants that had gone out of fashion years earlier. Despite the youthful appearance of her face—bright eyes, a turned-up nose, and wide-set cheeks—her fine skin showed early signs of middle-age. The crow's feet and tiny fractures around her mouth were by no means laugh lines: the woman's smile sought approval and agreement. She squeezed her arms close to her body, huddled bent and submissive in her chair, and Christine feared the slightest touch might cause her to crumble.

"One moment," Christine said, leaving the mismatched pair in her office and walking Sharon to the break room. Sharon leaned on the counter and drummed her fingers impatiently on the Formica countertop.

"They wanted to have a word with you privately." Sharon said. "First. Why do you look surprised?"

Sharon didn't even attempt to hide her hostility from Christine, though Christine wasn't sure whom Sharon was more irritated with: their clientele or her.

"Our clients are the children." *Not the parents*, Christine's eyes said. "We really need to remember that."

"We?" Sharon said, giving a bored, challenging look. "I'm told someone is bringing the boy from school."

"When?" Christine asked as neutrally as possible. *Damn it*, her clenched jaw ached to say.

"Later." The finger drumming continued, percolating raw tension into the atmosphere.

The day had started with a confrontation with Arvo. These parents were already in her face on a case she had barely looked into, the over-sized father suffocating; the mother one crisis short of a nervous breakdown. And now Sharon was getting on her nerves, more than usual. Was it time for Christine to tell Sharon to start looking elsewhere? For a new job?

Christine knew the discussion was long overdue. As much as she sometimes hated working with Sharon, the thought of training in someone new was nightmarish. She remembered the summer that a temp filled in for Sharon, who had taken the summer off with almost no notice, mentioning an unspecified medical condition of a relative Christine had never heard of.

Christine began filling two Styrofoam cups with coffee from the break room machine. The coffee smelled vinegary, and it looked like it was not much more than hot, tan water. She dumped what remained of it and tossed the cups. She knew better than to ask Sharon to make another pot, so she dumped the old grounds and got a fresh pot brewing.

"Will you let me know when the new pot is ready?"

Sharon sighed in answer, her glasses sliding down her nose.

Good gracious, Christine thought. Maybe she would send the long list of complaints she'd quietly tallied over the years to Human Resources and start to work through the laborious process of firing her after all.

That she had never done this yet spoke volumes. The woman was bristly but competent. Maybe Christine was the one who should get a job elsewhere. With both Sharon and Arvo constantly getting on her nerves, a fresh start might be just the thing.

She made her way back to her office. "Just got a fresh pot going. It shouldn't be long." She hoped Sharon would, for once, be the assistant her job description called her to be.

"Is he in trouble?" Mrs. McQuillen said. "Nick, I mean?" She smiled once again, exposing the small gap between her two front teeth. She pulled her cardigan together, buttoning it with shaking hands.

"Correction," Mr. McQuillen said. "How *much* trouble is he in?"

"Dennis, please. You *always* think the worst," his wife said. Julie had managed to miss a button, leaving a gaping hole in one area and the two sides askew.

"Julie, you know I always turn out to be right." Dennis pulled himself up in his chair. "But let's not quarrel in front of Ms. Ivory. We haven't even had a proper introduction yet."

"I apologize for that," Christine said, extending a hand. Dennis gave her a sure handshake.

Next she took Julie's hand, which was shockingly cold. "I'm sorry," she said, "I'm never warm enough. I'm sure it's poor circulation." She shivered.

"Let me go grab that coffee." She hustled out, trying to give Sharon a look, but the woman was gone, as usual, probably gossiping with her friends in the Property Tax department. "Hopefully this will help warm you up."

"We understand you want to talk to Nick. And we wanted to tell you about our son. He's a sensitive boy," Julie said.

"HAH!" Dennis broke in.

"Dennis, you promised you'd let me speak. Without comment."

"You're right, dear. I did say that. I apologize, Ms. Ivory, for that outburst."

"No problem," Christine said, frankly entertained by the discussion. For once, she wasn't the only person at whom irritation was directed. The attention was off her.

Mrs. McQuillen continued. "Nick is sensitive, despite what his father might chose to believe. I agree, the boy has his challenges as well—"

"He's hyperactive on his best days. Which are few and far between—" Dennis interjected.

"He means well, but has trouble staying focused—" Julie said.

"I wasn't at all surprised to hear about this escapade. In fact, I was relieved. I'd been waiting for something like this to happen—" Dennis said.

"He's a good kid, he just needs a little more time, than most. And the right person to bring along his gifts—" Julie said.

"Like a prison warden."

"Dennis!" Julie shivered.

"Dear, I'm just trying to be honest with Ms. Ivory. Are you finished?" he asked his wife.

Julie nodded sheepishly.

"Ms. Ivory—" Dennis said.

"Please, call me Christine."

Dennis cleared his throat. "Christine then. We've done everything we can possibly think of for that boy. Yes, he's our son and will always be our son, but I faced the truth about him long ago. We are good people, but we've been able to do nothing to stop him from the path he's on. We've grounded him, we've cut off his allowance, and we've taken away everything we can possibly take away from him. But it's made no difference. He's failing ninth grade now."

Julie started weeping.

Dennis put a hand on his wife's arm. "The boy will give you a load of bullshit excuses. Just like he has to us. His mother," he said, "has given him far too much sympathy. And that did nothing but give him permission to continue along the road he's taking."

"I'm warning you—" he said to Christine, "just once. The only gift that boy has is a talent for lying. Don't be taken in by him. He's been telling stories since he could first talk, mostly just finding elaborate ways to blame anyone but himself for the trouble he's caused."

Julie looked up from her tears. "Dennis is being too harsh."

Dennis softened and took his wife's hand. "Julie, you know I'm not. We've been through this."

"I just want him to be treated fairly. That's all," Julie said through her tears.

"Your office will get full access to his records, medical and crime-related," Dennis told Christine. "I want you to proceed, knowing the truth about our son. The worst thing that could possibly happen . . ." he stopped, his voice quavering slightly.

Christine knew she should offer nothing more than her patience, waiting for Mr. McQuillen to regain control of his emotions. It surprised her to see that he had them, and perhaps he hadn't completely lost faith in his child.

He continued, "The worst thing that could possibly happen is that someone could be hurt by an action of our son's. I can't have that happening. I can't have that on my conscience. Do you understand?"

"Yes," Christine said.

"I'm counting on you to find out exactly what my son has done. I must insist that he receive no special treatment. He needs to be forced to face up to who he is, and how his actions have consequences, even when the results are unintended ones." Mr. McQuillen's eyes had reddened. "Do you understand," he commanded, rather than questioned.

"Yes," Christine answered once again. "I understand completely."

SIX

S AM BANACH DROPPED BY ARVO'S desk with a case file in hand. "Is that latest bridge inspection in here?" Arvo asked, rifling through the pages.

"Kieran's just locating it now," Sam said. Sam had been hired on as an intern a few months earlier. Just finishing up his criminology degree at the U, Sam was a slight, hunched young man with a wide smile and a button nose, a sci-fi geek who had read that genre's cannon. Arvo wasn't sure they needed a department expert on extraterrestrials as UFOs were rarely sighted in their part of the country. Sam said that sci-fi wasn't all about space aliens, it was about the future and technology and expanding the confines of present time and space. Even though Arvo preferred the past and analog and the confines of Mendota County, he could see Sam had the makings of a fine investigator. He didn't settle for the obvious, it was clear he knew that there was more than met the eye.

Sam led Arvo down the hall to a cramped, dank basement room where the computer lab was housed. "Kieran," Sam called to a reed-thin, redheaded young man with thick glasses. Kieran glanced up for a moment. "Oh, hey, Arvo. Sam." Even though Kieran preferred the fantasy world of Tolkien over the alternative worlds of Phillip K. Dick, Kieran and Sam had already struck up a friendship over their shared guilty pleasure: Weird Al Yankovic.

Kieran loved all things code—languages, software programs, technical manuals—he was a crack researcher with an ability to locate anything you needed in thirty seconds or less, usually faster. Translating to English took him extra time, but not often a lot. The more obscure the language, the better, as far as he was concerned. With his language skills, he could have gone anywhere in the world, but he was a homebody. He liked to say he preferred traveling in his mind, preferably to Middle-earth.

"I believe you're looking for this," Kieran said, handing Arvo the bridge inspection report. "Last inspected a year ago. Was downgraded from its previous rating. It's classified as structurally deficient."

"And it's still open?" Arvo said. "I've been avoiding crossing that death trap for years."

"It's one of thousands rated in that category across the country, believe it or not." Kieran said, "According to this U.S. Department of Transportation report I found, of the country's 600,000 bridges, twenty-six percent were found structurally deficient or 'functionally obsolete,' meaning they're aging or unable to accommodate modern vehicle weights and traffic volume." Kieran had obviously already read up on all the available materials and sounded like an expert.

Not to be outdone, Sam chimed in. "There's no money in the county budget to fix it, and no one's willing to shut the thing down. Rerouting the trains would cost a fortune to the refinery."

Kieran gave him a look, the neat cleft in his chin marking his expression with a sharp period.

"I see you might have some competition at last, Kieran."

"Fine with me," Kieran said. Competition was not his thing.

"So I guess no one's suggested that Northoco help fund the repairs then?" Arvo pointed out, "Since they have the most to benefit from keeping it open."

Northoco ran the gasoline refinery on the Old Port side of the bridge. It employed many from the area, and the gasoline it refined went to hundreds of gas stations in the region.

Sam piped up. "They said it's the county's problem. It's the county's bridge."

"Yet strangely every time the county threatens to close it down, Northoco heads off to court to file some protest," Kieran said. "The company is working to get a new pipeline running that will increase production and potentially quadruple output. It says here that they are planning to hold a stake in the pipeline and sell other shares to investors."

"Well, you think that would help them to cough up the cash to fix the bridge. Of course I'm a non-technical layman, so maybe the obvious solution isn't that obvious," Arvo said.

"Well that is not too far off from what some people think, if you read *InqSquid* and *The Compass Jerk*," Kieran said.

Arvo rolled his eyes.

"You don't read blogs, do you?" Kieran said. "My friends write them. Everyone on the local alternative scene follows them."

"I'm not very alternative, as you know," Arvo answered. "I prefer my news on paper. Call me old-fashioned."

Kieran leaned forward. "Well your—ahem—newspapers as you call them, regularly check *InqSquid* and *The Compass Jerk* when they want sources that know what's really going on. Check them out and get informed. Maybe it would give you some street cred. At least with the alternative crowd."

"Sure, right, Kieran. First thing." Arvo flipped through the report. "I'm not sure I can make anything of this engineering speak. I don't have your head for jargon. Looks like good bedtime reading to me."

"You look like you could use some sleep-inducing engineering reports, Arvo." Kieran said. "You look like you haven't slept in days."

Thoughts of Helen flashed through Arvo's head, though now memories of her past treachery had hardened his resolve and were successfully blocking the pleasurable memories of her curves. He didn't know how he'd managed to let her so easily seduce him. He knew he would have had a better chance of staying away from her without the booze. If he could just refrain from the one bad habit, he could cure himself of the other.

"Thanks for the sympathy," Arvo said, grabbing the report and adding it to the rest of the case file.

"By the way," Arvo said to Sam, "Has he told you yet whether Kieran is his first or last name?"

Sam said, "Kieran doesn't bother with labels. Too limiting."

Kieran had managed to get by with just that one name, rewriting his own history with a couple clicks of a button as a teen. He had entered employment with Mendota County with the single name. He'd passed through all the security checks with no problem. As far as anyone knew, it was just "Kieran."

Arvo headed off to the Mendota County cafeteria to read the pile of material and grab a quick lunch.

Christine was there when he arrived, heating up her lunch, something that smelled both delicious and rancid.

"Sure that's still edible?" Arvo asked as he punched the selection buttons for the turkey sandwich in the vending machine.

"It's Indian food. From the best place in the city. Not like you'd know, with your taste for garbage." She walked away from him.

"Ah, so you're talking to me again," he said, following her to her table.

He sat down across from her.

"Did I ask for your company?" she said.

"Sure you did," he said, smiling. "We have business to attend to."

He watched her licking her lips, knowing that the desire for him was still there. "Hungry today, are we?"

"Frankly I lost my appetite the moment you came in the room." She dug in anyway.

Arvo wasn't sure he wanted to offer anything more by way of apology. She'd vocalized her disinterest in him, though she gave signs to the opposite. Things were fine as long as she could decide and maintain the distance in the relationship, controlling how close he was allowed. At all times.

She was the opposite of faithless Helen, who had no boundaries at all, whether she was married or not. Of course that also presented problems. Particularly if you were her husband. Now that he was her ex-husband, Arvo refused to become another of her laissez-faire boyfriends, men who had no problem spending time and money on her just to buy an evening in bed with her. This of course made him more of a challenge than he'd ever been to Helen, and he was sure she would find some way to gloat that she'd managed to seduce him. That time would come as soon as her next alimony check was due.

Christine was just plain not being fair with her ridiculous system of rules, both professional and personal. So screw her, he thought. When had he ever bothered with rules? He'd never really liked her anyway, no matter how coolly beautiful she was. She was probably the kind of broad Sam Banach read about in his futuristic novels: cold, spiteful, and entirely alien to Arvo's world.

He took a bite of his sandwich and decided to contribute to her irritation by talking with his mouth full.

"Case files," he said, jabbing his index finger on the pile next to him and spitting slightly, "For the bridge murder."

"Oh, so it's a murder is it? Not an accident anymore?"

"This kid, this—" he flipped to the first page, reading and drooling, "—Nick McQuillen. You're seeing him when exactly? Next month?"

She tried not to roll her eyes. They rolled.

"Meaning I'll be able to talk to him a year from now?"

"You know very well how the process works. No one gets to talk to the kids until they are cleared through my department. You will be informed when that occurs."

Arvo kept his eyes on her, "Of course I'm very well aware of your department's rules. I've already been in touch with your assistant, and she told me that the boy's coming in this afternoon at three. I want to see him tomorrow morning, first thing."

The mention of Sharon caused Christine to nearly spit out whatever the brownish substance was she was eating. He knew it galled her that he got on better with her assistant than she did. Then again, Arvo had a great working relationship with nearly everyone in the county. Except for Christine.

"I don't know why you bother talking to me. I need to complete my assessment of him."

"So assess away. Everything I'm told says the kid either knows nothing or is the main suspect in Karl's death. If it's the latter, I don't want him to have a lot of time to come up with phony alibis I'll have to spend months chasing down."

"So you think I'm going to go soft on him?" she said with fire in her eyes.

"Did I say that? No, I did not. Though you clearly have a soft spot for derelicts." Arvo felt mustard dribbling down the side of his face. He saw that Christine had spotted it and made a face. She handed him a napkin and he set it aside.

"For your information, and in case you've forgotten, I don't take sides," she pointed out. "That's for your department."

"Right. Like you didn't take sides with that *supposed* witness in that first-degree murder case. The kid who had never known his criminal father and had been abandoned. Lived quietly with his poor, elderly grandmother," Arvo said, taking another bite. "Supposedly some other guy he was 'acquainted with' but barely knew ransacked a random stranger's house, stole a worthless handful of coins that he managed to pawn for nine bucks, and tried to burn the guy alive. Nearly succeeded in killing the guy. No, this 'witness' knew nothing, was an innocent bystander. Such nonsense."

"You always misread my objectivity as going too soft," Christine said.

Arvo swallowed, setting down his sandwich. He had a case to make. Against her. "I spent days tracking down and interviewing this kid's senile grandmother. She kept asking me who I was, who the kid was. Her own grandson! Meanwhile, all of his gang friends got together on his alibi. If we hadn't been able to plea bargain with one of his friends, and gotten him to snitch, that criminal would have been set loose on the streets and maybe the next time he'd succeed in murdering someone. I'm told the jury was close to hung trying to decide that case. All because of what your department did in 'processing' him."

"You know the way the system works," Christine said. "You remember, don't you, what happened when my office wasn't brought in on the Williams murder. The perpetrator's younger brother refused to cooperate, even though he'd been there when the murder happened. If I recall correctly, the DA told you there wasn't enough to bring a case against his brother, without the younger boy's testimony. Maybe if you'd let us do our work, and not rush someone to be interviewed when they weren't ready, there would have been a chance."

Arvo swallowed hard. The perpetrator had been released from bail on a technicality. The next week, an eleven-year-old girl was caught in the crossfire. They had enough evidence then, but it was far too late. He had attempted to attend the girl's funeral, but her family made him leave.

"Mistakes were made. I agree. But the release was engineered from a legal technicality that the public defender basically made up. Not anyone trying to slip something by your department. Give it a rest, Christine."

"Technicality—not properly conducting a search. One of several 'technicalities' in that case. Arvo, you should know better than anyone that procedures only help you. They don't hinder justice. You can't act like a vigilante. You have to remember that we are only working with a small sector in society, not everyone who comes in here is the bad guy. This is the definition of remaining objective. You'll find others in the US Constitution and the Bill of Rights."

Christine stood up and gathered her lunch things. "If you'll excuse me, I have clients waiting for me."

"I'll be at your office tomorrow morning, first thing," he said again.

"You will get my report when it's ready."

"I'll get it before it's ready. Count on it." He watched her stalk away. He couldn't help noticing how well her skirt hugged her hips, but considered her attractiveness an irritation, now that their verbal skirmish left him wanting to strangle her. She was right and he knew it. Everyone had to do their best to go by the book, or there were consequences. She'd better get moving, though, or there might be other consequences. Arvo wanted to avoid at least one of them: too many run-ins with Christine could become an excuse for a drink. And one drink always led to another. And another.

SEVEN

ARVO MISPLACED THE LUTZ'S ADDRESS. He realized that as he was driving past the King of Spades, a strip club on the road that led by the swing bridge, so he pulled into the club's parking lot to locate the address. Since the place opened late in the afternoon and didn't close until the middle of the night, the lot was deserted except for the club owner's Lincoln Town Car. Vern Eide was tending to his business somewhere within the premises.

It seemed fitting that the strip club was located in a part of town that catered to industrialized hungers. On its side of the river, the club processed unsavory desires into a sexy, mostly legal quencher for any thirst you might have. On the other bank, the refinery processed crude liquid energy into gasoline, filling tanks and fueling transit for an entire region. Between the refinery and the strip club, one of the world's most powerful rivers flowed by, carrying loads of cargo not as the servant to human commerce, but the master. Despite the series of locks and dams, the Mississippi River was never completely under control, much to the vexation of the Corps of Engineers. It consented to human need only when it wished, and demanded respect and allegiance for the majesty it was. The raw power of the river trumped the ingenuity of humans, always. This year would be no exception; the river was running higher and faster than ever, surging without regard to any whims but its own.

As Arvo was dialing the office to ask Juney to run down the misplaced address, he heard a knock on his car window.

It was Vern Eide. "Something I can do for you, Arvo?" he asked.

Arvo had often found it his duty and pleasure to attend to detective business at the club. The place was a convenient location

51

to meet informants and have dinner and drinks, compliments of the house. He and Vern maintained a professional relationship as both benefited from their association. Vern kept a few off-duty cops well paid to mind the premises and act as bouncers, and those cops kept the department informed of illegal goings-on and the whereabouts of informants and suspects. Beyond their professional association, they maintained the kind of long-standing personal relationship that arises between public servants who witness human behavior at its most base.

Arvo offered his hand, and Vern held out what remained of his bad arm in return. He had lost most of it in Bosnia during the ninties. Arvo shook it in warm greeting as always.

"Nothing at the moment, just sitting here while I make a call," Arvo answered. "How's the family?"

Vern's beautiful wife, Sarrah, was the main attraction of the club. An exotic African mixture with a coal-black river of hair that accentuated her perfectly endowed, sensual frame, Sarrah's languid, seductive movements entranced, no matter whether she was dancing on the main stage or walking to her car. Hearing tales of a beautiful black dancer—said to be the reincarnation of the legendary American-born Parisian dancer Josephine Baker—the wealthy, the powerful, and the perverted from all parts of the country and all walks of life made their way to the King of Spades to see her.

Sarrah received many attractive offers from visitors passing through the club. Some offered her fabulous wealth, far more prestige, and an amazing life away from the unknown, and somewhat disreputable area of Somerset Hills. Others pressed forward merely for a touch of her soft, enticing hand. But Sarrah wanted nothing more than what she had: a place at her husband's side, and a way to express her unusual, sensual art. She was the shimmering, haunting gem set in tarnished, shoddy tin.

"The family is well," Vern remarked. "We haven't seen you lately at the club. Sarrah has a new revue that I know you would find enjoyable."

Arvo smiled. "I'll be there within the week."

"We'll be expecting you." Vern nodded.

"Say, come to think of it. Maybe you can help me with something." Arvo leaned an elbow on his car window. "That accident on the bridge—"

"Terrible. The operator got killed, I understand. The club, as I know you know," he emphasized, "was closed at the time." Vern wanted to make it clear that the club would not be implicated in whatever investigation was being conducted. Even if there was a connection.

"You have my word that your club is not being investigated as part of this matter. But will you keep your ears open?" Arvo asked.

"Of course, as always. As you know, we like to remain on good terms with the county."

"And you always do," Arvo said warmly. "I'm told there may have been a motorcyclist in the area?"

"I haven't heard anything about a motorcyclist. I heard that a boy was the only witness? A juvenile delinquent?" Vern and Arvo had both had their days of truancy, Vern's in another state, Arvo's right in Somerset Hills. They'd swapped stories of their own escapades and both had marveled that they managed to survive to adulthood.

"Yes, he may have had a few run-ins already with us. Nothing major. Mostly stupid stunts." Arvo grinned to acknowledge he'd pulled a few stunts of his own. "At this point, it's not clear whether he actually caused the problem, or was just there when it happened. This is going to take some time to sort out. I appreciate anything you can pass along."

"Of course," Vern said.

"Oh, and one other thing. Do you entertain the people from Northoco here? Execs or corporate insiders?"

"Of course. We're an equal opportunity strip joint."

Arvo laughed.

"We have something for everyone here," Vern added, ever the marketer. "And that includes anyone from Northoco. What in particular are you interested in?"

"I just had an inquiry from the Cities. A friend of mine has an ongoing corporate investigation, whistle-blower thing involving, I don't know, some supplier, I think it was a trucking company. You know, I find those kinds of cases pretty boring, so I don't know really know what all the details are."

"We'll keep our ears open for you. No problem." Vern said.

"Appreciate it."

"Please remember," Vern emphasized, "and this invitation comes directly from Sarrah: you have a standing VIP reservation, you don't need to come here just on business." He knocked his one knuckle against the door, to seal the invitation. "Bring that pretty woman we saw here a while back. Lovely, slender thing, wore her dress like it was a second skin."

Arvo knew exactly whom Vern was referring to. Christine. Arvo had intimate knowledge of what lay beneath Christine's well-fitting clothes.

"We hadn't seen her around here before, but we'd certainly love to have her back," Vern said.

It wasn't a place Christine would have frequented except for Arvo. They had wound up there one night while Arvo was investigating a case that involved one of Christine's clients, a fragile young girl.

"She was attracting stares from my customers. Even Sarrah was taken by her 'uncommonly beautiful eyes' as she put it. I don't think it was her eyes that got my regulars' attention, if you know what I mean."

Yes, he knew. And that Sarrah, who had uncommonly beautiful everything, admired Christine's beautiful eyes said a lot. He wondered what Christine would think of Sarrah's praise. He remembered being jealous when other guys had begun hitting on Christine.

Arvo thought Christine was overdue for a shock to her system again.

"Why don't you put me down for Friday?" She was also due for a reality check on her own appetites, which lay hidden within her. Since she insisted on being cool and in control, he would insist on turning up her thermostat. For even Christine had succumbed to Sarrah's charms, and might be drawn out of her safe, secure, boring condo by a chance to see Sarrah dance again. Even if it meant she had to rely on Arvo to bring her to the club.

"Of course. We'll have a private room ready for you."

"Take care, Vern. Tell Sarrah I'm looking forward to seeing her on Friday."

AFTER A LENGTHY SCOLDING OVER THE PHONE ("Why can't you get yourself organized, Arvo? For once!"), Juney quickly located the address Arvo needed and he drove up the river bluff to where the Lutz's home was located. As he drove through the town's oldest suburban subdivision, he saw a scene that he knew had been mostly unchanged—except for the maturing of trees—for the past half-century. Cul-de-sacs had not yet become fashionable when the Somerset Grove subdivision was built, so the streets were mostly straight, ordered by number or alphabet, and easily navigable, with no dead-ends that might confuse passersby. Small, single-leveled ranch-style homes with detached garages were evenly spaced through the subdivision's wide streets, and most had not been remodeled.

Occasionally the original cedar-shake siding of the homes had been replaced with aluminum, but except for that there was rarely anything to distinguished one house from the next. Most were painted in bland beiges and grays. Small, well-kept lawns and carefully manicured hedges were the rule. Each yard contained either a maple or an oak, sometimes both. Lilac trees formed borders between some of the yards and would soon be breaking into bloom.

Arvo parked in front of the Lutz home and noted that it did not especially stand out from the rest, except that it seemed even tidier. The driveway had been recently recoated with asphalt. The snow had only completely melted in the past weeks, and already the lawn had been raked once and possibly twice. A soon-to-flower crab apple tree adorned the front yard, and a well cared for American flag waved next to the front door. Arvo judged that Mr. Lutz was a veteran, the kind who took pains to respectfully bring the flag in every night at sunset.

He knocked at the front door and was quickly welcomed by Mr. Lutz, who though in his early eighties, still had a full head of silver hair styled in a mid-length crew cut. His silver goatee had been neatly trimmed.

John ushered him inside and let Arvo know that his wife had left for the afternoon in the company of her friend. They were off to buy a suit for Karl to wear in his casket. "Not sure why," Mr. Lutz said. "Karl never wore a suit in his life. He'd probably be more comfortable in overalls."

"I'm so sorry for your loss, Mr. Lutz, " Arvo said.

"Thank you. Please call me John, Officer Thorson."

"And please call me Arvo."

"Certainly. Thorson, that's Norwegian?"

"Swedish. My dad's family came from Sweden. My mother's side is Finnish. Arvo is a family name on her side. All the sons get named Arvo."

"Ah, the Finns. Then of course I can offer you some coffee?"

Arvo knew that accepting hospitality under these circumstances was practically a job requirement. Even if he didn't like what was offered, he accepted it graciously and choked it down. But his Finnish-Swedish heritage bred in him a special love of coffee. The stronger the better. And black.

"I'd love some if it isn't too much trouble."

"Come, join me in the kitchen. Mrs. Lutz despises coffee and so she never makes it strong enough. I'll brew up a strong pot that meets Finnish standards."

Arvo was ushered to a seat at the Lutz's counter and watched as the old man filled a small drip coffee pot with coffee and water, and hit the switch. "I served with a Finn at the end of WWII. Man named Hakala. He loved good dark coffee. In fact, he looked something like a younger, blonder version of you. He attracted a lot of female attention, as I recall," Lutz said, giving Arvo an appraising look as if to say, *and I am sure you do as well.*

Framed photograph collages lined one of the kitchen walls. Arvo spotted one that showed a thirty-year-old man, his wife, and what appeared to be at least a dozen children.

"That would be a Lutz family portrait, circa 1970," John said, noting the focus of his gaze. "And yes, we had quite the brood. Eleven total. Karl's the youngest boy there."

"I'm impressed," Arvo said.

"By my excessive contribution to the baby boom?" John paused to catch Arvo's response.

"I apologize, I meant it must have been something to manage that many children."

"No offense taken," John said. "I regularly ponder the excess of my generation: our need for space, our unmanaged development of the suburbs. Maybe you've read my opinion pieces in the paper? About the demise of the streetcars? The impending condemnation of the swing bridge? We waste too much, and I, for one, have been equally guilty. I'll be damned if I see that go on."

Arvo rarely read the paper. On purpose. He knew the intimate details behind what the papers packaged up and sold as the truth, but was in fact pure fantasy. Crime news was featured on most pages and he had no desire to read beyond those pages. He didn't find the funny pages funny, kept up with sports on his radio, and had no interest in the soft feature columns, which he had determined were written by whiny types he did his best to avoid.

On the occasions that he had read a paper, he always found the reporting inaccurate and one-sided, despite the journalists' claims that they'd gotten insider perspectives and wrote objective, fact-based stories. Arvo knew that they ignored the facts in favor of attention-grabbing headlines and sensational opening paragraphs. People rarely read the full story, and if they did, they formed judgments based on a provocative manipulation of reality into a prominently placed feature story.

Real facts were boring, tedious, and rarely sold newspapers. He had never consented to being interviewed, because he didn't trust the media to get the story straight and feared any repercussions on ongoing investigations.

To Mr. Lutz he said, "I seem to have missed your pieces."

"Then you don't read the paper, at least not the opinion pages, since I have a letter or column published almost every week."

Mr. Lutz was that kind of crank. Arvo could see he might have to be cautious with what he told Lutz.

"I see more than a few graduation photos, and now grandchildren?" Arvo said, trying to return to more neutral topics.

"Yes," John said, clearing his throat. "Well, they owe any success they've had to Mrs. Lutz. I do feel that I gave her more to do than she needed, but she said she wanted lots of children. She was an only child and didn't want her children to feel as lonely as she did, growing up. Still, a half-dozen should have been plenty. But it was nothing to have that many children back in those days. You could support a houseful on one person's salary, that's how easy we had it. Every house in this neighborhood was full of children. Mine had to sleep three or four to a room. "

"Kids these days are completely spoiled, coddled by their parents," John went on. "My grandchildren complain if they don't have their own room, complete with a TV, a computer, and stereo equipment. Mrs. Lutz doesn't like to take me out in good society, as she says, since I can't keep my mouth shut when I see a spoiled brat misbehaving."

"Mine were taught to behave," he continued. "Or else. These days people are given grief, sometimes charged with crimes, for disciplining their children. I also showed mine what hard work looked like and what it could do. So, yes, we had a good number of them graduate from college and several have master's degrees. They were, in fact, the first in my family to graduate with four-year college degrees. But that's not what you came to talk about exactly. The others. You want to hear about Karl." He reached into a cupboard for a pair of coffee cups.

"Mr. Lutz. I meant, John. I'm sorry that I have to come to you on a day like this, but I do need some information about Karl. I need to tape our conversation. Just so we both have a record of exactly what you told me. I don't know about you, but my mind isn't as sharp as it used to be. But beyond that, I need an official record."

John poured out a cup of coffee for Arvo. "Go ahead. But can you tell me why they sent an investigator out? To my house? Karl was killed in an industrial accident, if I understand what I've been told."

"I'll explain more in a moment. With your permission?" Arvo said, gesturing to the recorder.

"Of course," John answered.

Arvo switched on a small recorder and identified himself, the date, where he was, and whom he was speaking to. "We need to investigate why he died on that bridge. It's possible it was just a terrible accident. It's possible that there were circumstances that led to the accident—"

"Such as?"

"Well such as someone tampering with the bridge."

"You mean that someone might have actually caused my son's death? Caused the bridge to malfunction?"

"That's a possibility we are looking at," Arvo answered.

"Why would anyone want to do that? Unless, that kid who was on the bridge caused the accident. Maybe it was just garden-variety vandalism."

"Yes," Arvo said. "It could possibly be garden-variety vandalism. That could lead to a charge of manslaughter, or possibly murder."

Arvo paused to gauge the effect of his words on John Lutz. The possibility of murder would change everything for John and his surviving family. It was as if in ending Karl's life, a new person came into the Lutz family: the murderer. This threatening, and unwanted, new family member with the potential to haunt the family forever.

The murderer joined the victim's family in a single moment, with a bloody act not of birth, but of terror and death. An unwanted child, it had as its destiny the destruction of everything the victim's family knew about itself. In the murderer's wake there was more than one victim, and a whole network of fractured family bonds. Marriages sometimes ended when a child was murdered. Family members who had been on good terms no longer remained so; the chaos of emotional and mental stress unleashed by the victim's death saw to that.

"That boy probably had parents who were too soft," John said, dismissively, the ire growing. "Too tolerant. Not one of my boys would ever have come close to causing something like this."

"I need to ask you some questions, John. About Karl. Some are going to be rather personal. I apologize for that, but I need to investigate every possible angle."

John nodded, giving him the go ahead. Arvo asked a few rudimentary questions establishing demographics about Karl. His age, schooling, job history.

John patiently answered, though he did point out that a resume wasn't going to explain what happened. Arvo smiled and said that sifting through information was tedious. John said that the questions didn't seem overly personal. Arvo told him that he hadn't even gotten to the ones that would likely make him uncomfortable. A moment later he did.

"Did Karl like to gamble? Have any debts?"

"Of course not. Why would you even ask that?"

"If he owed someone money, perhaps lots of money, and Karl had no way of paying what he owed, maybe someone was extracting punishment." Arvo knew he was causing some pain, but he had to.

"I see. Well, my wife, were she here, might understand your line of questioning," John said, the tone of his voice sharpening.

"Why's that?"

"Oh, she's into all these TV detective shows. You know. *Murder She Wrote?* Loves that one."

Arvo doubted Clare could even begin to understand why he asked what he did, if all she had to go on was some eighties detective show.

Arvo asked the next question as neutrally as he could. "Do you know if Karl was seeing any prostitutes?"

"What? Unbelievable!" John's face began to redden.

"Do you know?" Arvo said, unblinking.

"First of all, I can't even imagine he was," John said, almost spitting. "Secondly, if he was, I can't ever imagine he'd tell me."

Arvo heard a car driving into the Lutz's driveway. John looked out the window. "That would be Clare." To Arvo he said, "Are you finished with the personal questions?"

"Mostly." He switched off the recorder while John helped Clare into the house, introducing Arvo to her. Clare was a tiny woman, not more than five feet tall, with eyes that looked like they typically sparkled with vitality. Now they were red from grief. It hurt to look into her face.

"Mrs. Lutz, I'm very sorry for your loss. I've been speaking to your husband as part of the ongoing investigation."

"He's trying to figure out if our son had unsavory tastes." John immediately blurted out.

A look of anger and shock came over Clare's face.

Arvo decided he might have to end the interview earlier than he'd intended. With the amount of trouble Mr. Lutz had in answering the questions, he knew it would be impossible for Mrs. Lutz. He prepared to leave the Lutz's house, unplugging his recorder and shoving his small notebook in a breast pocket. But before he could leave, Clare gripped his arm so fiercely that he thought she was going to amputate him on the spot.

"Wait just a minute there. Am I going to be interviewed?" Clare said, bitterly. "Aren't you going to ask me if my son, who is the victim here, is responsible? Why is my son being accused of crimes? Why aren't you trying to figure out what happened? Learn who might have killed him?"

"Ma'am, with all due respect. I'm not accusing your son of anything."

"I suppose next you'll want to know how much he cried as a baby. When he was potty trained. Try to figure out whether I was a decent mother." She turned to her husband "John, what have you been telling this man?"

"I have, of course, told him that our son was a model citizen. As all our children were." John looked from his distraught wife into Arvo's unreadable face. Now John needed to back pedal, Arvo realized. Arvo could leave, but John would need to spend the rest of the day explaining himself. Even though he'd given Arvo practically nothing to go on.

"Dear," he said. "Karl may have associated with less than model citizens, of course, but not on purpose. I believe the detective is trying to sort out what happened and who might have been involved. That is, if it wasn't just an accident." He turned on her, ever so slightly. "You're the one who watches all those TV murder mysteries. Don't they do this sort of thing all the time?"

"John. For Pete's sake. That's television. No one would even begin to think any of that is the way it works in real life. Is it, Detective?"

"Oh, I wouldn't know," Arvo said, stepping out of the middle of the quarrel. "I don't really keep up with those shows."

"Well, you don't know a thing about my Karl," Claire sniffed.

Arvo knew that was the truth. Of course he didn't want to remind them that was exactly why he had come to talk to the

Lutzes. He needed to know far more about Karl, and that, apparently, was not going to happen anytime soon.

"My husband regularly contributes to the opinion pages of the newspaper. The moment you leave our house, I'm going to insist that he write a letter to the editor complaining about the tone this investigation has taken," Claire complained.

Arvo could see the headline. "Victim Blamed for His Tragic Death." He'd seen it before. Of course he wasn't at all trying to pin Karl's death on his own lifestyle. On the other hand, he was often the one who ended up breaking the news to wives and parents that their spouses or children had not been the perfect angels they'd been led to believe they were. The worse cases of turning a blind eye involved those where family members had been victimized, in some cases brutally and violently beaten or murdered, by someone who, from all accounts, was a quiet, upstanding citizen. Parental and spousal crime and abuse were more common than the Lutzes knew.

So in fact, it was possible that Karl had contributed to his own death. And the Lutzes were unwilling, or just blind, to anything that might suggest that.

Arvo finally extracted himself from Mrs. Lutz's grip.

"I'll leave my card," he said. "In case you do think of something else that might be of help." He almost regretted making the offer. If anything, it was likely the sheriff would be on the receiving end of the John Lutz's letters. Complaining about Arvo.

Thankfully he had taped the complete conversation and knew he had strictly followed procedure. It wasn't his memory that was diminishing with age, but his faith in his fellow citizens. The closer the relationship, the blinder it was. Neighbors were shocked to learn that the churchgoing assistant scoutmaster had a sizable child porn collection that continued to grow. Husbands had no idea that what their wives most intimately desired was a multiple-speed vibrator, or a fling with the cute grocery bagger, not a new blender. Mothers had no clue as to their sons' gambling addiction, that mother was not on their mind as they headed out for an evening of drugs and sex. Being honest about their loved ones' flaws meant they had to be honest about themselves, because having the capacity for a good hard look inward was required in order for an honest appraisal to be made of anyone else.

Arvo drove away from the Lutz's house, through the streets of the tidy, respectable and nondescript aging suburb. The houses that lined the streets—with their closed drapes and locked doors— offered no clue about what secrets lay hidden within. Arvo considered his own failings, which he knew were many, but always found himself incapable of applying personal insights that might guide him away from dangers. He had no clue how to avoid being tripped up by Helen, and how to settle on Christine as the healthier option.

Christine insisted on something Helen never did, something he was apparently incapable of: accountability in his personal life. That there were consequences, eventually, of bad choices. Arvo *understood* that. He had, after all, witnessed the consequences of bad choices every day in his professional life. But somehow it never sank in that the same rules applied to him. He seemed to go on, in spite of it, like the river running over the same course, century after century, never ceasing. Gradually it wore down the obstacles until their sharp defining edges were unrecognizable. Arvo thought maybe he could do the same, wear down the obstacles around him, versus being defeated by them.

With that thought in mind he planned his next interaction with Christine, the chief obstacle in his personal life at the moment. He had time to return to his office, update the case files and review any other material that had come in. Then he'd head up to her office and see what she learned from the boy, before insisting she accompany him on Friday night, to the club. He'd wear her down, he knew. Like he always did.

EIGHT

CHRISTINE CHECKED HER CALENDAR half a dozen times and wondered aloud, "It was today, wasn't it?" Three o'clock had come and gone without any sign of Nick McQuillen or his parents. *Yes, here it is: 3:30. He should have been here.* The thirty minutes she'd waited had gone painfully by, each second pricking her, each minute scornful of her attempts to ignore their urgent and persistent chattering of idleness. Another thirty minutes passed, even more slowly than the previous half-hour of fretted seconds, clotted minutes. That meant that an hour had passed with no client to attend to and nothing but unending irritation that showed no sign of letting up. She could have done so much in an hour, had she been able to plan for it. But an hour spent waiting was an eternity: she was unable to begin any other task for fear of being interrupted. She hated interruptions about as much as she hated waiting. So there wasn't anything she could do except fret and grow more impatient with each passing minute.

Ordinarily, she didn't let a client get to her. She didn't let a patient's parents get to her. But this one client and his entire family had quickly gotten on her nerves, far too soon.

For the past year, things had been running smoothly, much more than they had for years. Sharon still got on her nerves, yes. The occasional client proved frustrating. But for the longest period ever, life in the county social services department didn't seem too bad.

Now, everything had changed for the worse, and all at once. Arvo had fallen back on his twin bad habits, this new client was vexing, and Sharon seemed worse than ever. So Christine fell into a few old obsessions of her own, withdrawing to the safety of coping mechanisms that really didn't ease her frustration but at least occupied a fraction of the time. She rearranged the small pieces of art on top of her credenza and reorganized the top of her desk, then moved things back to where they had been, even though their placement had been unsatisfying. Imperfection was everywhere, and no matter how hard she tried to fine-tune her environment, nothing worked.

It was the most beautiful day of the spring, thus far. She knew that on an intellectual level only, tapping her foot impatiently as she took in the sweeping view out her sixth floor office without any solace or comfort that winter had finally let go of its death hold on the landscape. Just downriver from the town of Somerset Hills, the Mendota County building occupied prime real estate on the top of the river bluff, and her department had snagged the best offices on the very top floor. She had to be thankful to Sharon for arranging that.

The building lay at the intersection of three distinct landscapes: the boreal woodlands of the upper Mississippi River Valley, the fertile Great Plains, and a small stubborn area that had resisted the last glaciers. Known as the driftless area, the deeply dissected valleys, rushing trout streams and thickly forested hills arranged a mathematical problem too complex to be solved by agriculture. Therefore, the driftless area remained mostly unfarmed, and a welcoming place only for the hikers, fishing enthusiasts, or backwoods types bent on escaping the modern world.

Most days, the tranquil view could be a godsend for her troubled clientele. For the young victims of abuse and the young witnesses of crimes—some of whom who'd seen their own parents die at the hands of an abusive spouse—the scene far below her window could often be put to use as a distancing device, allowing her fragile patients a place where they felt safe. In this safe setting, Christine could carefully probe, far deeper than any of her colleagues, and set her clients on a path to a better future, one that did not at all seem possible in the hours and days before they came to Christine's office. The view offered a glimpse at other possible futures, a place where the horrors they'd seen could turn into a distant, untroubled memory.

She did not have a similar power over her own trajectory. And today was one of those days where it was becoming ever more difficult to retain the essential perspective she needed.

Christine was about to ask Sharon to call the boy's parents, when she saw him standing at her door, his mother mouthing an apology from the waiting room.

"Come in, please," she said to the boy, acknowledging his mother.

The boy stepped inside her office a few feet, attempting a subdued stance in the unfamiliar setting, but he was like a clipped eagle tied to a post: in the unaccustomed and obviously affected pose, he was full of wild movement, his eyes darting around the room looking both for prey and escape. Christine could sense him straining against his nature to stand quietly. But she knew that the last thing he wanted was her pity.

He'd clearly been coached countless times by one parent or another to behave himself in Ms. Ivory's office. Christine had expected that movement would be Nick's natural state, judging from the records the school had provided. The boy had been placed in special classrooms due to his inability to sit quietly and avoid distracting other children. Attention deficit disorder had been written in a number of places, and based on what she'd heard from his parents, he was not being medicated for it. His mother said she didn't like medicine, and his father had acquiesced to her desire to not go that route, though it was clear he wished they had.

Nick would quickly need a focal point for his energy, or nothing would be accomplished. She saw him look towards the window, and she hoped that the view might provide an opening for a discussion, but unlike many of her other patients, he didn't seem the least interested in what lay outside the glass. It was off limits to him for as long as he needed to be cooped up inside the county building. Pretty views meant nothing to a boy whose only interest was full-on interaction with reality, both the virtual and the physical kind. You couldn't do anything with a picture-window view.

A small, ornate wooden box sat on Christine's credenza, and she noticed the boy looking at it. Christine had just moved it to a prominent place on her credenza in the hour that she had awaited the boy. Perhaps she'd sensed that he'd need it.

"Go ahead," she said to him.

Nick picked up the small box and examined the intricate pattern of black and white geometric designs on its sides. The repeating patterns formed a puzzle of their own, with bird-like designs morphing into fish, and then back again.

"It's a Japanese puzzle box," she told him, watching how he ran his fingers along the smooth sides of the box. "Do you know what that is?"

He shook his head.

"You have to find the right combination of moves to open the box. This one requires nine moves."

She saw him slide one panel up.

"I've heard there are some that require as many as 200 moves to get the box open," she pointed out.

He turned the box over and found another panel to slide to one side.

She wondered if the puzzle would frustrate him. She'd replaced one of her boxes already when a client wound up throwing the original on the floor and stomping on it until it opened.

Nick seemed mesmerized.

"Do you like puzzles?"

He didn't answer, but kept turning the box over in his hands.

She was free to examine him. The boy at fifteen was already a few inches taller than she, thin but strong, sinewy. He looked like he'd easily get to six feet or more, and Christine remembered how his father towered over his mother. A thatch of thick, unruly white-blond hair shot out of his head in all different directions. She admired the color, having dyed parts of her hair that color on occasion. For the moment, his unblemished face was free of stubble. She wondered if he'd begun shaving yet.

He wore a striped, sports-theme-free t-shirt and clean, neat jeans that were devoid of rips—whether fashionably placed or otherwise. He appeared not to have adopted any of the urban or street styles favored by a number of suburban Somerset Hills youth. She doubted the boy had been influenced in any way by his parents to dress in such a plain style. A daredevil rider of unicycles would need clothes that fit—no sagging pants and exposed boxers for this boy. Such fashions might cause a disastrous spill from the unicycle.

She wondered how long Somerset Hills would contain him. There couldn't possibly be enough here to absorb him here for long. In fact, something better grab his attention, fast. She hoped that there was a mentor out there who could get a hold of him and set him straight.

He sat in her side chair seemingly lost in the puzzle, then as quickly as it had captured his attention, it lost him. He set it aside and looked directly at her, surprising her with a placid look from his piercing gray eyes. The look in his eyes told her he had been waiting for her to begin.

She was stumped. She had no idea what to ask him. How many moves would it take to solve the puzzle he presented? She did not know.

"Can I get you something to drink? A glass of water?"

"No thanks," he said, startling her with the directness of his statement. "Can we just get started?"

"Sure," she said, "right away. Let me start by explaining why you're here."

"I think I know that. I saw a dead guy and now people are wondering if I'm going to be whacked out by it. You're going to heal me and then I can 'function in normal society' or some bullshit like that."

His gaze remained placid and she was sure he was gauging the effect of his words, and in particular, her adult reaction to his use of profanity. A wrong move or response from her would close him down.

She smiled. "Something like that, but slightly different."

"Aren't you a doctor?" he asked.

"No. I'm a social worker."

"Don't I need a real doctor?" he challenged.

She knew it was best to keep a firm neutral tone. "Some people experience exactly what you've gone through, even worse, and do completely fine without any medical help at all. Others wouldn't be able to recover without medical help. Some get help for years and never recover. It really depends on the circumstances and the person."

"I saw a guy cut in half by the cables that operate the bridge. He was lying in a pool of his own blood. That's pretty horrible."

She knew he was trying to shock her. She wouldn't take the bait. "Yes," she said flatly. "It is."

"I'm not really bothered by that, so I don't need any help." He kept his eyes on her.

"Fine," she said. "But that doesn't mean we're through here."

He picked up the puzzle box again, and focused on it again. "The police asked me lots of questions. My parents said I have to answer more questions."

"Yes."

"Why do people keep asking me the same questions? It's bullshit. I don't know anything." He ran a finger along the top edge of the puzzle, seeming to have no interest in solving it, but strangely comforted and grounded by its smooth surfaces and confounding geometric patterns.

"You're the only person who was there right around the time the man died. There might be something you saw or heard that might help the police figure out what happened." She didn't tell him the other suspicion the police had. That the boy might be

70

responsible for Karl's death. He needed to clear himself of blame, and she wondered if he knew this.

"So, you understand," she emphasized, "one of my roles is to make sure you're up to getting more questions from the police. A lot more."

"What if I just say no? That I don't want to answer any more questions."

She didn't want to have to tell him that one of the consequences might be that he could be charged, especially if he wasn't able to answer to any of the other evidence pointing at him.

"That's an option," she said, "but it might not be very fair."

"Fair?"

"To the victim's family. They want to know what happened, and why." She hesitated but went on anyway. "They want whoever might have caused their son's death to be brought to justice."

Nick drew back, setting the puzzle down. "I don't know anything. It's not my problem if that guy wound up dead and no one ever knows why." He folded his arms and looked away from her, but just for a few moments.

Christine knew that even if the boy hadn't intended to kill the bridge operator, but caused the man's death due to vandalism, he could be facing some prison time. There were consequences even to horseplay. She'd seen it before. Nick was exactly the kind of kid who would get himself into that kind of trouble. And she would be powerless to do anything at all to stop it.

Given more time, things might just get worse for him, particularly if he was not being honest about what he was doing that day. Arvo would spot immediately if the boy's story didn't add up, he was uncanny the way that he could keep track of all the conflicting details and later put it all together to create an airtight case. If the boy was guilty, he'd be sentenced in no time. There was also a possibility that the boy would slip up, and get himself in even deeper. He was also at an age where there was a remote possibility he'd be tried as an adult.

When he faced her again she was sure there were tears in his eyes. "I wish I'd never even gone there that morning. Now people are going to be on my case for who knows how long. As it is, I'm already grounded for life. I sure as hell don't feel like talking to anyone else."

Being grounded by your parents is the least of your concerns right now. Looking at him she didn't have a sense whether he'd done anything at all that day, and had just happened to cross the scene of someone else's crime. Just like he'd been saying. But she had nothing more to go on than the police did. Still her instinct to help him was at odds with her instinct to do her job. In other words, she needed him to admit his role in Karl's death, if he'd played one. If his guilt surfaced during her session, she would need to make him face it, not purely for legal reasons, but because the only way to move beyond it, to heal whatever needed healing within him, was to acknowledge it. Sometimes she felt like her role was to convince a lamb to walk to its slaughter.

"Here's the thing," she said, perching on the corner of her desk. "From experience I can tell you that it's probably best not to delay, too long, talking to the police." *The longer you wait, the worse it will be for you, especially if you're guilty.* "You're closer to the events, and your memory of the details is sharp." *You better have a good explanation of what you were doing out there on that day, and God help you if your story is the least bit inconsistent.* "If you were with friends that morning, before you headed out onto the bridge, they'll want to know because they might want to talk to your friends." *God help you if you provide an alibi that contradicts what your friends say.* "They'll take a look at all the information they have, follow up on any other tips that come in, and leave open the possibility of talking to you more later." *They'll take one look at your record of past vandalism, no matter how small the incidents were, and start there to build a murder case against you. So, you may as well come clean now if you're guilty, but again, god help you if you aren't and you play games instead of answering their questions.*

The longer she told him about what to expect, the more she realized why his mother hovered as much as she did, and why his father had all but washed his hands of the boy.

"So, what are you going to say to them?" Nick said, "when they ask whether I'm ready or not?" The reality of Christine's words was sinking in.

"That all depends upon the next half hour. Unfortunately that will have to wait until tomorrow. Can you handle another half hour with me? Tomorrow afternoon?"

Nick looked deflated. "You mean I have to come back?"

"I'm afraid so. You got here an hour late." *There are consequences to every action, even tardiness.* "I have someone else to meet, and I think it would be best if we talked a bit more."

"And we can't talk now?"

"It's not fair to keep someone else waiting." Christine really only hoped to fit in a last-minute hair appointment, though she hadn't actually scheduled anything yet. No clients were waiting. But the boy needed to understand that there were consequences to his actions. That there were others to answer to. That he needed to treat schedules with respect.

"So, we have to meet again, because you're not convinced I'm ready yet?"

"Do you think you're ready?" *To tell the truth? To face the consequences of your actions, even if you intended no harm?*

"Like I said, I don't know anything. I don't know why they even want to bother talking to me." He got up to leave.

She watched him walk out the door and wondered whether he would come to their next appointment. She glanced at the clock and calculated how much she'd have to hurry if she was going to follow through on this whim to make herself over, once again. Whether she'd ever land on a look she could live in for more than a few weeks, she didn't know. But perhaps this would be the time she nailed it. She dialed her stylist, and made an appointment, escaping her office almost as quickly as Nick had.

He wasn't the only one who felt out of place in her office that day. She was just as unsettled. Thing was, life's problems were not as simply addressed as a bad hair day. There was no new dye job for life, no stylist who would quickly get an unruly head under control. The troubles quickly resurfaced and oftentimes multiplied like stubborn gray hair, or a bad cowlick. You were stuck with them and either you had to learn how to live with the reality of your life, or condemn yourself to expensive, even more damaging fixes.

NINE

ARVO TOOK A DETOUR ON HIS RETURN to the county building. Not on purpose. He wasn't the best navigator under ideal circumstances, and when conditions were less than ideal—as they had been for most of the week—he wound up far from where he had intended to be, without noticing his mistakes until he was a long, long way down the wrong road.

He had been pondering the interview with the Lutzes that had gone south on him. He hadn't expected to get much information from them, but he knew better than to leave any stone unturned at this point in the investigation. It was early and, thus far, nothing solid was turning up.

With so many seemingly unrelated factors in the case, and no solid leads, he was thoroughly engaged in puzzling through it, his internal compass leading him in only one direction. He knew what he needed was substantial physical evidence, something that he could actually hold in his hands. So while he was driving in the wrong direction, after having made mistake after mistake in his personal life that day, he was feeling more in control of his destiny than ever.

There was nothing like an unsolved case to help him get his life back on course. Sheriff Ruud had pointed that out to him, time and again. The best thing for Arvo was to keep his mind busy with work, and Mendota County delivered, most of the time, but Ruud often suggested Arvo might be better off, mentally and physically, in a bigger city. Get away from the place responsible for all of his bad habits: the bad woman and the alcohol he consumed trying to get over her.

Arvo always turned him down flat, even when his boss reached out to his powerful friends in the city, who were eager to offer an investigator of Arvo's experience and distinction more power, more money, and more interesting work.

Unbeknownst to the sheriff, Arvo's best college friend, Jerrold Thomas (J.T.) Sanders, a cop in the city was not-so-quietly trying to recruit Arvo, with very little success as well. His former college roommate, J.T. made a comfortable living in the city as a corporate crime investigator.

When either man asked Arvo why he stayed, especially after the marriage finally ended and it seemed like the perfect time to move on, Arvo gave the same answer he always gave. "I'm not ready to start over. I don't think I will ever be ready."

Arvo always left the possibility of moving open, though he was fairly certain his answer wouldn't change. That part of him holding out hopes for Helen still ruled his decision-making, no matter the facts of their relationship. Even though they rarely, if ever, saw each other, she still lived in Somerset Hills. As long as she was there, Arvo stayed, clinging hopelessly to a beautiful vision of her that had nothing to do with the reality. He knew it was wrong, but his love persisted stubbornly, his substantial yearning surviving in the toxic atmosphere of Helen's behavior towards him.

Thankfully his work gave him relief from his worthless and obsessive thoughts of her. So he drove along, far off his intended course, and kept turning over the available facts he had at hand, which to be honest were as limited as they came. Lost in thought, he drove until he found himself at the scene of the crime, which was perhaps not too surprising considering the drift of his logic. He drove around the detour signs and parked at the entrance to the bridge.

He decided that his unplanned visit to the bridge turned out to be a great advantage. He had planned to talk to the boy sooner than Christine wanted him to. One more trip to the bridge before that chat offered him an opportunity to test some theories and better consider the areas of his discussion with the boy.

As he stood in front of the closed bridge, he heard pigeons cooing from beneath it. Other than a distant train, and the hushed sound of a breeze stirring the scrubby brush along the river, there were no other sounds and no one else around. He mentally reviewed what he had learned from the account the boy gave to the initial responders. The boy was said to have initially been on the bridge at the railroad level. He had made the dubious claim of having ridden along—in fact, on top of—the railroad tracks. On a unicycle.

Arvo laughed. He'd spent some time near the bridge as a kid. He had, in fact, been dared to push his bicycle across the train deck, though he never had ventured too far out, for various reasons. His friends had done that, and more. Some had hung from beneath the bridge and captured pigeon fledglings, carrying them home in birdcages fashioned from metal milk crates. That this boy had managed to balance his unicycle on the rail must have been something to see.

Arvo knew exactly where the kid would have gotten to the tracks. He hiked back into the woods off to the side of the bridge entrance, and ascended an embankment to get to the tracks. Thankfully, the hillside wasn't yet covered in the undergrowth and thick vines that would make it impassable in a few months. For now, a scattering of small blossoming plants and grasses, thick moss, and a couple of budding shrubs did little to get in his way.

Arvo, you are a fat idiot. He stopped to catch his breath after scaling the hill. *You really need to get some exercise and lose a few pounds.* Like everyone kept telling him.

He paused to take in the view, the excuse he gave for not immediately proceeding along the tracks. The real reason was that he was still panting. Nevertheless, it was the view that reminded him of the pleasures of that particular spot, the hours he had spent there as a boy. There was nothing quite like being a river town boy with perhaps too much time on your hands, exciting places to explore like an old double-decker bridge, and a gang of like-minded rowdy friends along for the ride. A mild breeze blew, helping him to cool down, and for the first time that day, he felt, if not at peace, maybe slightly relaxed. He'd figure out what happened to Lutz, eventually. Maybe Helen would finally lose all of her luster, for good, and he'd be set completely free of her. Christine? Well who knew? Maybe it was better to cut his losses and stop whatever it was they had going. She had, after all, made it plenty clear she was through with him.

He took a couple more deep breaths and began walking along the train tracks. When he came around the curve a short distance before the bridge began, he realized he was not the only person intending on walking across the bridge that afternoon. Just ahead, another figure walked along the last few feet of track, before the solid ground ended and there was nothing but the narrow, and in areas transparent, upper train deck of the swing bridge.

Jesus Christ. It was her.

"Christine Ivory."

Startled by his announcement, the woman stumbled, and then fell.

He hurried to help her up, more irritated that she might fall off the bridge than concerned she might have injured herself. "Damn it, Christine," he said offering her a hand. "Are you trying to get yourself killed down here?"

"Damn you, Thorson," she said, brushing him aside. "You startled me, but I don't need your help getting up, thank you very much. "

He stood back and folded his arms. "Little early in the investigation to start cussing me out."

She brushed off her skirt and examined the heel of her fashionable pumps. Arvo saw that the heel had held up, but looked scraped. "Not the best shoe choice for a hike along the train tracks. What brings you down here?"

She gave him a confrontational look.

"Ah, I see. Just out for a little stroll. Please," he said gallantly, "don't mind me, just out here on police business. I wouldn't want to prevent you from . . ." he thought for a moment ". . . a pleasurable walk along the riverfront. Considering how it's such a lovely spring day."

"Oh, for God's sake, Arvo, give it a rest. I'm out here probably for the same reason you are. Nick McQuillen was in my office this afternoon."

"So you've decided to turn investigator and see whether his story holds up?"

She frowned at him. "No, of course not. I'm not one to involve myself in your professional territory."

Arvo wanted to beg to differ, and remind her of the times she'd been both in his professional and personal territory, sometimes simultaneously. He thought in particular of one night a few months ago when he'd worked late and she'd arrived unannounced, closed his door, and spent a good long time exploring his personal territories to their mutual satisfaction.

"Go on," he said sighing, to her evident surprise. The mention of McQuillen engaged his receptive cop side, so he set aside the banter and the pleasant memories to hear what she had to say. "What did the boy say that got you out here—in heels no less—to an area usually only frequented by hobos looking for a free train ride and kids looking for some thrills?"

"He's being hostile and non-responsive," she went on, "and at the moment I'm not even remotely sure whether it's just fifteen-year-old boy arrogance, or whether he's deliberately covering up what happened here."

"So you are down here to—" he asked.

"I'm down here to . . . I don't know. I suppose I want to see whether the facts, as we know them so far, prove out one side or the other. Honestly I don't know whether I should strangle the kid or hug him. Not that I let my feelings rule me, ever," she emphasized, trying to make it clear she was ever the cool, detached professional.

He knew she'd made some missteps, in particular as relates to him. She'd let down more of her guard with him than she wanted to admit to, and that was what was really bugging her since the moment she figured out he'd been with Helen. He was almost bursting to point that out, pick at that scab of her vulnerability, just to irritate her. But like her, he was searching for something solid to grab hold of in the Lutz case. Something solid that might come out of the boy. He forced himself to shut up and let her vent. "Go on," he said in an interested manner.

"I can't figure out how to approach him. His parents are a piece of work. The father is frustrated enough with him to have him tossed in jail for life, and the mother has all the makings of a helicopter parent."

She went on. "I thought if I came down here, not so much to see if his story holds up, but to, I guess, maybe gain some understanding where he's coming from. As it is, I'm having a hard time feeling much sympathy for the kid."

She didn't have much sympathy for Arvo, either.

"These kinds of witnesses wear me down after a while." She gave him another appraising look. "They do nothing to help themselves, but only dig themselves in deeper. Sorry to say, but it's kind of typical for boys. Once they start down a particular road, they seemed determined to screw up their lives, and every life they touch."

He frowned at her, but said nothing. They both knew that she was no longer talking just about Nick McQuillen. Arvo and every other man she'd ever known had been swept into her assessment. There was nothing else to say to convince her otherwise.

"Ah, well," he said, "Nothing better than some time on a murder scene when the men in your life are driving you nuts."

They stood in silence, as close to each other as they could tolerate, and soaked in the environment the boy had encountered a few days earlier. Evening was about to arrive and the sun was behind them, but still a few hours away from setting. Spring in Minnesota was typically more apparent from lengthened days and late sunsets then it was from the weather. Snow was not out of the question as late as April, or even later, and July was the only month in Minnesota with no recorded snow.

Chilly air rose from the icy waters of the Mississippi. With the height of the snowpack this past winter, the river was rising at unprecedented levels. And heavy rains were predicted in spring as well, adding to the danger.

"It's a little dangerous out there, as you may have noticed. Have you seen enough yet?"

She answered by continuing her walk along the railroad tracks. He followed. Despite the uneven surface and her heels, she walked along steadily.

"You women and your heels," he said, "that you manage to stay upright in those things is one of life's unsolvable mysteries."

She didn't bother looking back and only paused when they came to where the bridge began. He wondered whether she was really going to step out onto the bridge.

"Don't look down," Arvo offered, thinking Christine might be getting dizzy.

"If you think I'm afraid of heights, you'd be wrong."

Arvo was the one afraid of heights, but nothing would convince him to admit it to her. He'd never admitted it to his friends when he was a boy, standing with his bicycle, in the very same spot where he stood now, watching as his friends headed onto the bridge. He had always stayed behind, telling his friends he'd keep a watch for trains.

This time he had no excuse. A mere girl was stepping onto the bridge ahead of him. For the first time in his life, he'd have to set aside his fears and go onto the train deck. So he proceeded, keeping his eyes focused on Christine's legs, which offered somewhat of a pleasant distraction from the dizzying view.

"I wonder when they'll get the bridge operating again." she said. She paused to let him catch up, and he almost stumbled when she turned around and he kept his eyes on her legs. "It's still early, shipping season-wise, but at some point you'd think they'll have to ready it to open up. Nothing can get through otherwise."

Arvo took a casual look downriver to see if any barge traffic was nearby, feeling himself sway just slightly from the motion of the water and Christine's sudden movements.

He answered in a calm, measured fashion. "Engineers are scheduled to be out here tomorrow to assess the damage, if there is any, and whether it can be feasibly reopened, safely."

She snorted. "Don't you sound like a know-it-all." She looked at him a little more closely. "You're looking a little pale. Are you okay?"

Arvo felt a little clammy, but ignored it. A drink or two might have helped calm his fears. It was a little late for that. "I try to avoid the sun," he said. "Bad for my complexion."

"Right," she said, clearly in disbelief. "The height isn't bothering you, is it? Of course not, fearless detective." Christine stopped walking, though Arvo really wished she had continued. Standing still only made him feel dizzier.

"So the boy claimed he'd been out, what was it, riding his unicycle? On the rail?" She squatted down to run a finger along the rail.

That seemed like a great idea to Arvo, too. He sat down on the rail, nonchalantly, gripping it lightly to steady himself. "That's what I'm told. It seems a little hard to believe."

"Oh, look," Christine said, picking up a handful of round, clay-covered pebbles. "These are . . . um . . . taconite. Does that bring back memories!"

Arvo picked out a handful. The iron-ore pellets were dusty red from the clay that was used in processing the pellets into the easily transportable form.

"So tell me how it is the well-dressed Ms. Ivory is familiar with taconite and how to cross the bridge in heels. I have to admit I'm impressed," Arvo said, feeling a little more at ease and less dizzy as long as he had a good grip on the steel rail.

"Oh, I made the occasional trip down here, just like everyone else back in the day." She smiled. "I saw you and your buddies down here, too, though, of course, you never saw me. Strange though. I remember seeing your pals out here, but you never seemed to make it all the way out. Now, why was that?"

She didn't wait for him to answer as she stood up, and continued along. Arvo slowly rose to his feet, and when he felt steady enough, he followed her. When he got to her side they were in the middle of the bridge, and Christine had located a one-wheeled vehicle that could belong to only one person.

"It seems there might be some merit to the boy's version of events." Arvo said.

"Perhaps I should try being a little more sympathetic when he comes in tomorrow," she said.

"Then he'll be ready for me, tomorrow?"

"If and when I say so."

"So I'm still waiting for you. And your precious professional judgment. Look, a kid who can ride that thing . . ." he said, steadying himself as he pointed at the unicycle, "all the way out here shouldn't have a problem answering a few questions."

"Don't raise your voice with me," Christine snapped.

"Don't throw a wrench in the investigation and bog it down," he snapped back her, his dizziness gone as soon as the anger fired up. "Again, do I have to explain to you that the more time that goes by, the less fresh the details will be? It seems like you'd know that by now."

Christine had no response.

"What, so you're speechless now?"

"Um. That's not it. Oh, this is unbelievable," Christine said, with an amazed laugh.

"What's so funny?" Arvo asked, only to have the rest of his snappy retort cut off by a sound approaching from behind him.

A train whistle blew, signaling a train was crossing the road that led to the bridge.

Arvo turned in time to see that a train was less than a half-mile away from entering the bridge deck.

"Come on," Christine said, grabbing Arvo's hand and leading him towards the Old Port side of the bridge.

"Christine, there is no way we can make it to the other side."

"Not where I'm headed Arvo."

She led him to a spot right above where the pilothouse was. Over the side of the bridge, a narrow ladder led down to the automobile deck. Christine stepped over the side of the bridge and began climbing down.

Arvo took one look and stepped back. "Oh, no. No, no, no." Climbing down the ladder on the *outside* of the bridge, with nothing but open air to the river below was simply impossible for a cop with a fear of heights.

Christine stopped and looked at him. "You have got to be kidding. Arvo, get back here."

She hurried back up.

"Um. I'll just stay here. There's enough space to stand here and let the train go by. Right?" The train was on the point of entering the bridge, its horns blaring. Clearly the engineer saw people on the bridge. Arvo felt dizzier than ever.

"No there isn't. Arvo Thorson, get over here. NOW!" Christine held out her hand. "Take it. Now!"

Arvo felt frozen in place. The train had entered the bridge, and though it was going slower than it had, there was no way it would be able to stop.

"Come on, Arvo," she coaxed. He edged his way over and took her hand.

"There you go," she said, pulling him towards her. "Now turn around and just don't look down. I'll stay right with you," she shouted.

Arvo held onto the top rung of the ladder for dear life and followed Christine's lead down a few rungs. She steadied herself and arched out on the ladder, straightening her arms as much as she could to form a tunnel between herself and the ladder. Arvo stepped down a few more rungs until he was standing on the same rung as she, her arms around him, embracing him.

Together they stepped down a few more rungs, then held tight just as the train closed in, rattling the bridge so fiercely that Arvo thought the vibration might either throw both of them into the river or rattle the ladder loose. "Put your head down," Christine urged.

The train roared past, sending pebbles and dirt flying. They held on as coal-filled boxcars, tankers, and flat cars bearing all manner of freight passed just a few feet from their heads, the long procession seeming endless. Christine urged Arvo to continue descending with her, the front of her body pressed against his back. When they finally reached the automobile deck, she stepped onto it first, and then a moment later he stepped onto it, collapsing onto the road in exhaustion.

He looked at her. "Go ahead," he panted. "Say it."

She shook her head. "I don't think either of us needs to say anything."

"You mean you don't want to make a case out of my fear of heights."

"No, but a thank you for saving your sorry ass might be in order." She held out a hand, one last time, and helped him to his feet. The noise of the train continued for another several minutes, giving Arvo the time he needed to calm down. Finally, the ruckus ended and the dust and silt descended around them in the contaminated air, souvenirs from the chaotic crossing train.

As his breathing returned to normal, Arvo recalled the feeling of Christine's arms around him. He knew she was observing him now, trying to ascertain what those death-defying moves meant for their broken relationship, when she coaxed him off the bridge and held him tight to keep the fear from bringing him down. Still, he was enough of a guy to feel embarrassed about his fears. He knew she would know that, and find a way of quickly moving on.

"So where did they find the guy?" Christine asked.

Arvo led the way to the small enclosure behind the operator's shed, but stopped. This time, he was the one holding out a protective arm, keeping Christine back. With the other, he reached inside his jacket for his gun. "Someone else is down here," he said in a low voice. "Wait here."

He peered through the opening of the enclosure.

"Hello," he called out, "Who's there? It's the police. Come on out."

In moments, they heard the sound of someone scrambling over the fence, and caught sight of a figure running in the direction of Old Port.

Arvo started to give chase, tearing around the enclosure to see a darkly clad, hoodie-wearing figure racing away from him. Already winded from climbing around on the bridge, Arvo was no match for what appeared to be someone in far better shape than he was; still, he was keeping up with the fleet stranger.

In a few hundred feet, the bridge ended on the Old Port side, and as soon as the roadway was on land, instead of over water, the figure took hold of the railing, and vaulted over the side onto a small path that lead up from the riverbank. Moments later, a motorcycle engine flared up, and when Arvo got to the railing where he'd last seen the intruder, the bike sped off with the unknown person aboard. Arvo caught glimpses of a shiny machine snaking through the undergrowth. It disappeared into the thick woods just above riverbank before Arvo could note the make of the motorcycle, or its license plate number.

He reached for his phone and called in a request to send the Old Port police searching for the rider. When he returned to where he'd left Christine, his heart rate was nowhere close to normal, yet, but at least he wasn't panting.

"More evidence that Nick is telling the truth?" Christine asked.

Arvo returned his gun to the holster. "I don't know. It could be a coincidence. Maybe just some crime-scene enthusiast, out scavenging. Or possibly one of his friends came down here, on his direction, to make adjustments to the scene."

"In other words, we don't know anything more," she said.

"That about sums it up. Unless the Old Port police chase this guy down and he turns up some evidence." He led her to the enclosure and asked, "Are you ready for a look?"

She nodded.

He wondered whether Christine had ever been to a murder scene. Judging from her fearlessness on the ladder, she might not react at all. Then again, fear had its quirks. He could handle almost anything except for heights. Maybe the neat freak would be taken aback by the unsightly scene of a death. Lose it without her trusty dust-buster and a spray bottle of cleansing solution.

Arvo showed Christine inside the enclosure where Karl had been found.

"So that's the spot," she said tenuously, looking at a large area that still showed signs of the huge pool of blood Karl's body created.

"Yep," Arvo said, keeping an eye on Christine as she took in stained, grim area. He saw her shudder.

More bloodstains were seen on a large area of the cable housing. "So he was caught in the cable reel somehow?"

"Yes." He watched her face closely, wondering whether the sight would impact her, if at all. "You all right?" He asked.

She nodded again, and he was relieved she didn't point out that he'd been not so all right, moments earlier. "I've seen murder scenes before, but only through witness accounts."

"It's interesting how both of us keep referring to this as a murder, though nothing conclusive supports more than an accident at this point," he pointed out.

"Gut instinct, I suppose, for both of us."

He nodded.

"This is the first time I've been on a murder scene. In person."

Arvo watched her even more closely. He knew that Christine had been present for many witness interviews, many conducted by him. She'd heard countless stories from witnesses, young and old, who'd seen complete strangers killed by others, or who'd come across the gruesome scene of the dead, mutilated bodies of their loved ones. She'd accompanied family members to the morgue. In short, she'd had every experience related to murder's aftermath that a person could have. Except for one. Being on the scene, with the victim in it.

"Even with nobody here, the place seems so real, on a visceral level, you know? Like I can see the body there," she said, pointing to the center of the bloodstain. "And yet it's so unreal. I'm so used to hearing the witnesses talk about their experience. It's like . . . I'm missing that voice to tell me about their experience. Without that voice, I don't know, I feel a bit lost."

Watching her talk about what she did for a living made the same impression on Arvo that it always did. Here was the real Christine, the one without the attitude. The one a person might actually be able to become close to. Not the sassy broad who gave him so much unrelenting grief. For a few moments, she was actually likable. For a few months, she'd become almost lovable to him. And he to her. It was hard to hold onto her esteem for long. In this place of death, he saw the Christine he missed. He felt sorry for himself, mournful for the loss of her belief in him, as momentary as that belief appeared to have been.

"Believe it or not, every new client telling their side of things brings me to the intimate, personal core of the experience in a way that literally being in the place they describe doesn't. Who would have known that was possible?"

"That says only one thing."

"What's that?"

"You're good at your job, because it never gets old for you."

She considered his statement with a tired smile. "No. It doesn't get old. But it wears on you. Some days I think I'm done. Despite the need . . . no, because of the unending need for my services, I wonder whether I can go on. Some days I'm sure that when I walk out of the office for the night, there's no way I'm coming back the next day."

Arvo knew exactly what she was talking about. Finishing up one case never meant the work was done. It only meant he was ready for the next one on the list. There didn't seem to be an end to the homicide caseload.

"Well that's interesting," she said, spotting objects on the far side of the enclosure.

Arvo followed the direction of her gaze and then approached an area under the cable reel. He stooped to get closer. "This, right?" He said, pointing to several dark mounds of material that had accumulated under the reel. Some pieces had become scattered in the area, a few close to Christine's feet.

"Piles of taconite pellets," he said, scooping up a few to bring to her.

"You wouldn't expect to find them down here, now would you? Piled up like that?"

They both looked up, and could see that directly above them where the railroad deck passed overhead, sunlight filtered through in places, the planking not tight.

"A few pellets might drop through, and if they fell onto the cable reel, they might wind up where those mounds are." Arvo whistled. "But that many?"

Arvo made another call, and soon after, several squads were on the bridge, setting up a perimeter around the operator shed. When Sam Banach arrived, Arvo directed him to extensively photograph the cable reel and the piles of pellets.

"Collect some. In fact, collect all of it."

"Not likely we'll be able to get anything off of it, if that's what you're thinking."

"You mean touch DNA?" The department had some success using the newer technique, which could evaluate skin cells left on an object after it had been touched or casually handled.

"Where would you suggest I swab for it?" Sam asked.

"Take your pick. Hit a couple of areas," Arvo said.

Sam frowned and gave an overwhelmed look.

"I know, kid, it's a needle in a rather large, grimy haystack. Welcome to the real world. Not so easy as it appears in the textbooks."

Sam pulled on a pair of gloves and took out a couple of swab kits.

"When's that engineer coming, by the way?" Arvo asked before departing with Christine.

"Tomorrow."

"Don't move that pile until the engineer has looked at it. I want to know all the scenarios that might cause those mounds to accumulate there, the way they did."

"Got it," Sam said, laying flat on his belly to swab pellets lying nearly out of reach.

"Need a lift to your car?" Arvo offered to Christine.

She accepted, and before he let her drive away he got her to agree to two dates. One with the boy for the next day. The other he only described as a dinner. To make up for his being such an asshole to her and to thank her for saving his life.

When she asked where he planned to take her, he demurred, only going so far as to say that the place offered a great view, and decent food. He hoped she wouldn't mind that he had a bit of professional business to attend to during their dinner.

The driven professional herself, Christine found nothing objectionable, and she accepted with no further questions, driving off.

Oh she'll get more of a view than she bargained for. He hoped she'd find some way of thanking him, later, for it. Arvo knew it might be unwise to bring Christine back to the strip club, but despite, or perhaps because of what they both just experienced on the bridge, he felt she needed more at risk than she was used to, a shock to bring her to her senses.

Danger, especially the peril of feeling out of control when carefully hidden, unwanted desires suddenly released, could be the perfect antidote to her cool indifference to him. It had worked before. It could again.

TEN

I TOLD YOU," CHRISTINE SAID INTO HER PHONE, briefly eyeing Nick McQuillen, who stood just inside her office door. She sat at her desk, her pencils, notepads, and case files neatly arranged on her desk. Close at hand, freshly poured coffee released its curl of steam in a vintage Limoges coffee cup hand-painted with violets. She'd snapped up the highly collectible cup and saucer for pennies at a consignment shop in her mother's neighborhood.

She motioned the boy inside, and mouthed to her assistant Sharon to close the door. Sharon acknowledged the request, but didn't act on it.

"Yes," she said into the phone, "I did." She reluctantly got up from her desk, and slammed the door shut, causing the valuable, fragile Limoges to shudder briefly in its saucer. To the cup—or possibly the boy, it wasn't clear exactly—she offered a quick "Sorry about that."

To her caller she said sharply, "I wasn't apologizing to you."

She threw herself into her chair.

"We've been over this at least twice." She glanced at the boy again, then turned away. "Client privilege. I don't owe you any info about who is in my office . . . oh, Sharon told you already."

The voice on the other end of the phone commanded the conversation for a few moments. Christine tried not to look defeated. "All right," she finally interrupted wearily, leaning her forehead on her hand. "Just wait for me there. I'll be by . . ." she eyed the boy, ". . . around four. But I'm warning you, if you so much as show up outside my office ahead of time, it's not happening. I don't care if Sharon ties me to my desk, I'm filing a complaint."

The voice on the other end spoke briefly.

"Not against her, you idiot. Against you."

Christine got up and walked to her window, listening. "Yes."
"Yes."

"Yes," she admitted, "We're still on." A hint of a smile crossed her lips, though had he been in the room, she would have done everything to suppress it.

"Yes, tomorrow night." She looked down at her nails, and thought whether she should schedule a manicure, or just clean off the bright aqua polish, and go with something more neutral. Or nothing at all.

"I don't know, with the way things have gone in this phone call, I might dress in armor."

"Ha ha. Only you with your perverse sense of . . ."she glance back at the boy, then made an adjustment to what she'd planned to say ". . . *style* would find that appealing. The most I can ever hope for you is that you'll put on a clean shirt."

"Oh, for God's sake, that's disgusting." She paced the length of the windows, then leaned against the wall. "I have to go. But please, remember what I said. Do NOT show up outside my door. I need a half-hour with him first. I'll do my best but I really can't promise anything. You know that."

She hung up at last, musing to herself briefly before turning her attention to the boy.

"Thanks for being on time today," she began. Seeing the boy was fidgeting uncomfortably in his chair reminded her. "Oh, I brought something in to show you." She opened her briefcase and removed a small cardboard box. "Go ahead, open it."

Nick opened the box and investigated the contents, pouring them out onto the side table and looking at Christine with questioning eyes.

"It's another Japanese puzzle box. Or, what the box looks like after a hyperactive, mute six-year-old finds it in his social worker's desk and takes it apart when she has her back turned."

The boy picked up a pieces and attempted to fit them together.

"As you can see, it could use some help. When I saw your interest in the other one over there, I immediately thought of this one."

"There must be twenty pieces here," he said. "It's broken. Isn't it?"

"Not really. It's only a matter of finding the right combination of moves that will make the pieces fit. And stay together."

He was already making an attempt to do just that.

"Don't you know how to get this one back together?" he asked.

"Here's the thing," she said, "I can barely get the simplest ones back together. I really just like how they look, the idea of the secret hidden in each one."

She watched him work. "Honestly, I count on people like you to figure it all out. I'm just here to watch. Ask a few questions, make a few suggestions. That's about it."

Christine sipped from her cup, noting nothing had spilled or broken when she'd slammed her door.

The boy looked at one piece after another, and as he did, Christine asked him a few simple questions. How school had gone that day. What he planned to do with his summer. The answers came easily from him, a relief, considering their last meeting. She had wondered which Nick McQuillen would be in her office today. The sullen teen or the obviously intelligent young man.

The fragments in his hands fascinated him, keeping the conversation on track. He easily multitasked: interlocking her barrage of questions with the complex task of solving a complicated puzzle box.

"That was that investigator on the phone. Wasn't it?" he said.

"Yes. It was."

"He wants to talk to me? Today?"

"Actually in fifteen minutes. As you probably understood."

He laid the pieces out on the side table, picking up each one and making a series of calculations, then laying the piece aside and moving to the next one.

The boy had the makings of genius, she thought. Or criminal mastermind. It was so hard to tell at this age. Or any age.

"Yeah," he said, "I pretty much figured that out the second I came into your office."

"Who dropped you off today?" Christine asked.

"My mom. As usual."

He came to the last piece and gave it the once over, then set that piece down and looked Christine straight in the eye. His enormous black pupils shrank in the bright sunlight, but he didn't flinch. "So do you think I'm ready to talk to him?"

"What do you think? Are you ready?"

He gathered the puzzle pieces and returned them to the box. "Can I bring the puzzle along?"

"Yes." Christine opened her office door and had a few words with Sharon, allowing her the time she needed to make the two phone calls Christine had requested she make. Sharon returned and tersely reported she'd accomplished what Christine asked. Dennis McQuillen had granted his permission for his son to be interviewed by Arvo, waiving his parental right to be present at the interview, and authorizing Christine to be present.

And Arvo learned that he should make his way immediately to the witness interview room used only for the fragile, and very often traumatized witnesses being seen in Christine's department.

"Okay. So let's go find the investigator and let him talk to you."

The boy got to his feet, closed the box of puzzle pieces, and followed her out with the box in his hands.

———

A FEW MINUTES LATER, CHRISTINE AND NICK were being escorted into county's crime witness interview room by the clerk who maintained it.

The brightly lit, calming room was unchanged from Christine's previous visits to it. Located in a spacious, airy wing of the courthouse, it contrasted completely from the Hollywood version often seen on televised crime dramas. Christine explained this fact as she schooled Nick in what to expect as they made their way to the room. He seemed relieved to find it exactly as she'd described it, which was better than being disappointed, in Christine's view. The longer she spent with the boy, the more she hoped he'd been the bystander he claimed to be. And not the perpetrator.

The room was furnished with overstuffed side chairs, a small table, a few lamps lit with soft bulbs. The wallpapered walls were a soft, baby blanket blue, with a border of friendly pastel-colored giraffes near the ceiling. A box of toys sat in one corner. Nick seemed not to be bothered that the room seemed designed for kids a lot younger than he was.

Christine showed him to the chair she knew Arvo would want him to sit in, the one that was positioned perfectly for the videotaping that would be done. The chair was in front of a small rectangular table that held a box of tissues, which Nick pushed aside to make room for the box of puzzle pieces. He immediately poured out the pieces and set to work on the puzzle box.

Christine had left some important features out of her description of the room, since they wouldn't be needed for the crime Nick was being questioned about. These features were actually important tools stored in a locked cabinet on one side of the room: anatomically correct dolls that young victims of sexual abuse used to reenact the bestial crimes committed against them. Christine was thankful they were not here today on a sex crime case as those interviews left her the most drained. She was sorry to admit that Karl Lutz's murder wasn't the most offensive crime she could imagine.

When Arvo entered the room, the boy barely looked up, and Christine stopped Arvo when she saw him noticing the boy was engaged in the puzzle. "A quick word with you?" she said.

She spoke to him in the anteroom. "Trust me. He'll be easier to talk to if you let him work the puzzle. It seems to calm him down, focus him, and he'll be able to hear everything you say."

"If you say so, Ms. Ivory."

They returned to the room after Arvo gave the okay for the clerk to begin taping.

Arvo had to gather his first impression of the boy without a clear look at his face. With the boy's full attention on the puzzle, he wondered how he was even going to proceed. The kid looked, at this stage of his life, like most boys of his age: something akin to a rangy, underfed, half-grown feral dog. The thatch of white blond hair was close to the same color Arvo's hair had been at that age. A comb was defenseless in such a thick mane. Without thinking, Arvo combed his fingers through his own thinning hair. It was still mangy, but only a sad remnant of what it had been in his youth.

The boy surprised him by looking up suddenly, without much surprise or interest, and Arvo noted the strangeness of the boy looking right at him, but taking no notice. He'd seen that kind of look before. Unfortunately, more often it came from a clearly guilty individual, from whom Arvo would shortly extract a confession, or gather enough incriminating evidence for a conviction.

But Nick's look was far from a blank stare, and seemed different, somehow, from the calculating but empty look of a criminal. The sight of the boy's piercing gray eyes, shot through with flecks of gold, suggested a wily, unschooled, but very capable intelligence. He was lost in the act of solving the puzzle, obviously, but one look was enough to convince Arvo of what Christine had independently concluded: this was not some wild dog of a boy seated in front of him, but a potentially vicious outsider. He wondered how long it would be before the kid would lash out with a sharp move. He knew enough to be wary of Christine's clients. He'd heard stories of disturbed boys tackling her to the floor without any sort of warning. She'd been bruised, pretty badly, and more than once. It was the ones who'd been victimized the worst that had to be watched the most. He hadn't heard whether this boy had been abused, but there was no way of knowing. Sometimes their troubled history didn't come out until long after the damage had been done. He knew he had to remain on his toes.

He could handle this kid if he had to. He was a good deal larger than Christine. But he wondered if one of them would really hurt her one day.

"So aren't you going to start asking me questions?" the boy suddenly piped up.

Yes. The boy was already proving himself capable of making a surprise move. Arvo's caution was warranted. He made note of Christine's position in the room, and knew that she was far enough out of reach. For the moment. But a rangy teen could move fast, faster than an aging wolf like him, a guy losing once-fast reflexes, whose eyesight was not so sharp as it used to be. The only difference lay in his years of experience, and battle with witnesses not willing, or able, to relate the horrors they'd seen. Or perps trying to hide the truth. Both could look the same to the untrained eye. Both could do a lot of damage.

Arvo would have to anticipate, stay on the offensive, and be ready to pounce on a moment's notice.

He allowed the boy a few more moments of concentrated effort, the only sounds in the room the slight, muted whir of fans, cooling the electronic recording equipment hidden in a side cabinet, and the hushed sliding of puzzle pieces, one against another, chaos seeking cohesion, pieces seeking a whole. Arvo began.

ELEVEN

L ET ME EXPLAIN THE WAY the interview works," Arvo began, knowing that Christine would have attempted an explanation. From the look of this kid, it wasn't clear how much he ever listened. Or would listen now. Any amount of concentration he might have was going into working the puzzle.

"Ms. Ivory already told me," he said without looking up.

Arvo noted the quality of the boy's voice. A few pitched vestiges of his child's voice remained, but he was really only a few months away from the man's voice that might convince a judge to try him as an adult. That was, if signs pointed that way. And the kid was doing nothing to dissuade Arvo from thinking the worst.

Arvo settled in. This was going to be more difficult than he expected. And he'd already expected tough going, given what he'd heard of the kid. He made another note of Christine's position in the room. Her usual demeanor, in this particular room, was calming, both to him and the person he was interviewing, though this time things felt off. He sensed a hint of ambivalence in her manner, unaccustomed as it was under these circumstances.

But maybe that was all directed to him. He'd smelled her perfume when he'd approached the room, signaling she was inside. Despite their playful banter on the phone not more than a half hour earlier, he wasn't sure she'd gotten over his escapade with his ex-wife. Not that he knew what to think of it himself. But there she was looking cool and distant in her usual place in the witness room, sexy as all hell.

He pushed the thoughts of her sexiness out of his mind. One moment of distraction could have severe consequences with this unknown quantity—boy of fifteen, either a witness or a person of interest—sitting across from him.

"I still need to explain, even though Ms. Ivory told you, so that I'm sure you're clear. I'll ask you a lot of questions, beginning with some very basic ones, like who you are, where you live, school. Then I'll ask you particular questions about what happened a few days ago. Answer as best as you can about what you know and what you remember."

Nick sat up suddenly, breaking away from the box. "I get it. Okay?" A couple of puzzle pieces fell to the floor.

"That's good. But I do have just a few more things to add." Arvo kept his voice steady, unchallenging but firm.

"Fine," he said, folding his arms, leaning back and looking away.

Arvo glanced past the boy to note a slight sense of alarm in Christine. He hesitated to make the next statement, because he didn't know how long he could hold the boy's attention. But he knew he had to offer it.

"We can take a break, at any time, if you need it. Ms. Ivory is here today for anything you need, too. She won't be asking any questions." He knew Christine would not interfere. "She's here on your parents' request."

"What, to report back? Of course they wouldn't bother to believe anything I'd tell them."

Christine stiffened. He knew she wanted to say something, but couldn't.

"Look. It's not like that at all." He could see the boy didn't exactly believe him. "It's just a requirement, given your age. Either a parent needs to be in attendance or someone they designate." *Moreover, your clear problem with your parents means it was out of the question that one of them attends. Obviously.*

The interview began. Arvo asked a series of simple questions, a laundry list of name, age, address questions that he already knew the answers to, but they established, for the purposes of the interview—and for the coming legal proceedings, countersuits, and appeals—that Nick's identity was the same as the boy found at the scene of the swing bridge when Karl Lutz was discovered dead.

Arvo's neutral tone and the mind-numbing drift of the questions sent the boy back to his puzzle, which allowed Christine to assume a more relaxed pose, and allowed him to move the interview along, at least the first ten minutes. He hoped that the calming monotony would put the boy in a good frame of mind for the more difficult probing that lay ahead. Too quickly that time arrived.

"So tell me about Tuesday morning. You got up . . . ?"

The boy froze, and he could see Christine instantly did the same. Since she wasn't giving off her usual calming vibe, Arvo had to think quickly. He crossed one leg, and nonchalantly brushed off a crumb stuck to his pants leg, noting it had left behind a greasy stain. He had Nichol's caramel roll to thank for that.

The boy had just managed to fit two pieces together on the box, and was examining another. Arvo knew the boy had heard him; he'd been answering, a little robotically, everything Arvo had asked him to that point. There was nothing anyone could do but wait and hope he would answer, without forcing Arvo to repeat the question. Or provoke him.

"I got up, as usual," Nick began. "Had my Wheaties, gathered my homework, and kissed mother and father goodbye."

"So you got out of bed. And we ignore the rest, right?"

The boy gave him a bored look. "Something like that."

"Then what."

"I grabbed my backpack and headed off to school. Well, no, actually. I got on my unicycle, and headed off to school. My mom came chasing after me with my backpack." A smile lit briefly. "*Mom* always makes sure I have what I need," he said dismissively by emphasizing the word 'Mom' in a dramatic fashion. He shook the hair out of his eyes with a quick move. "Father, on the other hand, was right behind her, ready to take my head off about something he wanted me to do that I hadn't finished to his satisfaction."

"Mom" and "Father," Arvo thought. Pretty much sums up most boys feelings for their parents at that age. Mother the good cop, father the bad cop.

He snapped two pieces of the box together. "Father can be a jerk, but God I love the old man." Another shake of his head to get the hair out of his eyes. "What was it . . . oh, yes. He wanted me to get the mower ready for the summer. We're frickin' weeks away from having to mow, the snow just melted what was it, last week? And he's harping at me to get the mower out.

"I don't know. I probably rode off without saying anything.

"My mom maybe shouted one last thing, maybe asked if I needed a jacket or something, and honestly it was still cold, but there was no way I was going back there with Father standing there waiting for me to throw myself down in front of him and beg forgiveness.

"Are you getting this all, Ms. Ivory," Nick commented, not even swinging around to look Christine in the face. "Boy with father issues. Check. Hovering mother. Check. Blah, blah, blah."

Arvo made note of Christine's expression. She seemed shocked by the amount of disclosure, given her gaping mouth and dumbstruck eyes. Perhaps he was getting more out of the kid than she had. Thorson, 1, Ivory, 0.

"Did you plan to go to school that day?" Arvo asked. "By the way, I don't mean to put you on the defensive, at all. Your parents are sounding familiar to me. Bringing back some memories, let's just say."

Christine was familiar with that boy, Arvo knew, another kid with a shock of thick hair and a bad attitude. One both of them had known years ago. "Nice morning like it was a few days ago, after the winter we've had, a person might just want to bag the whole day."

"You mean skip school?"

"Sure. Why not?"

"Will what I tell you get back to the school? To the principal?"

"No, indeed. I can guarantee that," Arvo said. The court was entirely another matter. *School is the least of his concerns*, Arvo thought, and *he doesn't even know the kind of trouble he's in*. Arvo knew he was trying to get the boy's sympathy, maybe convince him he had his back, so the kid would be willing to admit to something, anything about that morning. Even if it was incriminating.

"Okay. I was about ready to bag the day, like you said."

"Sure, why not? I've done it myself, many a time."

"When you were a kid?"

"Yep. And more recently than that." He winked in Christine's direction, and she mouthed "*asshole*" at him. "Everyone needs a break, every once in a while."

"I never thought of that, but it makes sense."

"So did you say you were by yourself? I can't remember," Arvo quietly asked.

The boy held a box piece up to the light, narrowing his gaze on one of the edges. "Um. Yeah. I'd gone by my friend Pelican's house, but he'd already left for school."

"Pelican?" Arvo asked. *A possible accomplice? Another witness?*

"That's just the guy's nickname. He can stuff food in his mouth like you wouldn't believe. Leo. Leo Frazier. You know him?"

Oh, yes. Arvo knew him. He'd heard about a boy with a big mouth who had another bad habit. Joyriding in cars that didn't belong to him. He wondered if Nick knew, or participated. The boy was a few years older than he was, so he wondered whether Nick's parents knew the unfortunate company he was keeping.

"Maybe," Arvo said, "I'm not sure." *Have to stay on the kid's good side.*

"I think he got picked up for stealing a car a few years back. Got off with a slap on the wrist. It belonged to one of our neighbors and she didn't want to cause problems for his family.

"Anyway, Leo wasn't around, so I kept going and rode down towards the school, but decided there was time for a quick detour down to the river. *Conditions being favorable*," he said in a mocking tone, "I decided on the railroad level for the first time this year."

"What are favorable conditions?"

"No trains, no barges."

Yes, he hadn't checked for favorable conditions the day before. Thinking of his close encounter with a locomotive made him break out in a sweat. The after-effects of vertigo gave him another sensation of dizziness, which strangely quelled with one glance at Christine.

"I picked up a handful or two of taconite, stuck it in my pockets, and headed across the rail."

Even Christine perked up when Nick mentioned taconite.

"Taconite?" Arvo repeated.

"You know what that is, don't you?"

Arvo said nothing, knowing exactly what taconite was and, even more, the impact the mere mention of Nick possessing any that day would have on the investigation. The pile of pellets under the machinery hadn't gotten there by itself after all. There was no clear connection between the taconite and Karl's death, but it was a strange coincidence that Nick mentioned grabbing some handfuls.

"You know. Iron ore pellets. Drops out of the train cars?"

"Oh, of course. Taconite. Used to use it in slingshots. As a kid. You ever done that?" Arvo's carefree tone seemed to convince the boy nothing had changed. "Who hasn't?"

"Exactly," Nick said. "But I didn't have my wrist rocket with me that day. In fact, my parents 'confiscated' it from me."

"So why grab the taconite then?" Arvo asked.

The boy suddenly grew quiet.

"I, uh—well, I ended up doing nothing with the taconite." He had set aside the puzzle and began fidgeting, jiggling both legs hard enough to cause a slight tremor in the table holding the box pieces. The pieces clattered around on the tabletop.

"Oh. Is that right?" Arvo wanted to ask what the boy had planned to do. He wasn't sure he should even believe the kid had done nothing.

"So, then, you brought it home?" Arvo said.

"Not exactly."

"Not exactly?"

"Look," Nick said. "I told you. Nothing happened with the taconite."

He seemed too defensive. Arvo knew he had to press for details, even if it shut the boy down. "If you didn't bring it home, and you did nothing with it, then what happened to it?"

"Why are you talking about this *stupid* taconite?" Nick looked wildly around, jiggling his knees even more.

"You're the one who brought it up. I was curious."

"So maybe I thought of doing something. But that was it. I only thought of it. Nothing more."

"Fine. We'll leave it there." There was nothing more to be gained. Arvo needed to know what the analysis uncovered before he could probe further. If taconite had played a role in causing some equipment failure, and Karl's death, there would be more questions.

"Have they found that motorcycle driver yet?" The boy asked.

"That's right. I heard you mentioned a motorcyclist."

"The guy did a hell of a jump across the bridge opening. While it was opening." The boy whistled.

"You saw this from where?"

"While I was on top of the bridge. The railroad part. I never did get my unicycle back."

Confirmed, Arvo thought. At least one fact lines up. "It'll be picked up," Arvo said. "Eventually."

"And I probably won't be seeing it again," Nick noted with a hint of disappointment.

"Well, not for a while."

The boy's shoulders slumped. "Well, I want a motorcycle anyway. That guy did a rad move. Let me think."

He began to speed up. "I got to about the middle of the bridge, when the bridge started to open, without warning. You know how the bridge has that warning horn that goes off before it opens?"

Arvo nodded. Everyone who lived in Somerset Hills knew the signals the bridge gave, the call and response between the bridge and the tugs. A few short honks from the tugs, the loud blare of the bridge horn. The sequence of sounds carried a long way, as intended. Its signals reached a crescendo as the shipping season kicked into high gear, and the river traffic increased with the addition of fishing and pleasure boats, including some enormous yachts that required an opening of the bridge.

"There was nothing. No warning at all. I've been up there when it's gone off before. Scared the crap out of me. It's deafening. But completely awesome." Nick had completely forgotten about working the puzzle, though he gestured with the pieces gripped in his hand.

"Then this guy blew out of there on his motorcycle and jumped the gap just in time. I couldn't believe it. I climbed down to the automobile level when the bridge didn't close, and that's when I spotted Karl."

Arvo patiently waited to watch the boy's reaction. The boy had quieted, in an almost solemn manner. Arvo wasn't sure that type of response could be faked, unless the kid was lying to himself.

"I didn't particularly care for the guy," Nick said. "Not that I really knew him. He didn't particularly care for me and my friends . . . he was always yelling at us when we were out there."

"But when I saw him . . ." The boy's hands were on his face, and Arvo could see him reliving his reaction to seeing Karl. The look of shock. "I puked. It was the worst thing I'd ever seen. I went to the side of the bridge and threw up into the water."

Arvo could believe that. He wished, for the kid's sake, that he'd vomited where someone could have collected it as evidence. Evidence was evidence. Even vomit had value.

"It was pretty clear that Karl wasn't going to be able to close the bridge. I don't know how long I was out there, just with him, but I could see that the cops and ambulances were all screaming down to the other side. Everyone was just standing over there, doing nothing."

"So I walked over to the pilot house, closed the bridge, and waited for the cops to come across." The boy had grown pale. "That's all I know."

Arvo saw Christine's eyes on the back of the boy. She seemed convinced. He was too. The kid had done nothing. Maybe. Unless there was something he wasn't admitting with the taconite. But Arvo was convinced whatever the boy had planned to do with it, he'd changed his mind.

"They need to find that motorcyclist," Nick offered. "He'll know what happened. He's probably the one who killed Karl."

"Can you describe him at all? The machine he was riding? His license plate?" Arvo waited.

"No, not really. I didn't see him clearly." The boy thought for a moment. "I can tell you he wasn't on a Harley. From the sound of it, it was a Japanese bike. It looked like a Honda, what I could see of it. Maybe an Interceptor. But not the touring kind you usually see around here. It was a sport bike, fast, I can tell you that, it looked like a rocket shooting across the open water."

Typical boy. He knew his street bikes.

"That helps," Arvo said. "We'll start looking for an Interceptor."

The boy had made little progress on the puzzle, and he began to gather the pieces together, sliding them back inside the cardboard box. He had apparently decided the interview was over, and Arvo signaled to ask for the tape to be marked.

Christine headed out with the boy, turning him over to his mother who had arrived and had been waiting in the reception area.

"May I have a word with you?" Arvo quietly asked Christine, as the boy and his mother left.

She answered quietly. "I'll give you one word."

"Just one?" He persisted, touching her lightly on the arm. She didn't flinch, but did brush him away.

"We'll see." She turned to leave him.

"You still willing to go out with me? Tomorrow night?"

She stopped, turning over his question with a quick look in his direction. "Yes. Tomorrow."

"I'll pick you up. Eight sharp."

She had given him enough words for the day, walking off with no further response, but also not rejecting him cold.

They had a date.

TWELVE

ARVO ARRIVED AT CHRISTINE'S high-rise condominium at 8:20 p.m., on time by his standards, not close by hers. He wasn't sure what she would think about the locale they were headed to, though as he recalled he hadn't told her yet where they were going. He'd be taking her to the King of Spades. The infamous strip joint that was the place to be if you liked a lot of female skin, in all colors, shapes, and sizes.

It was, of course, not Christine Ivory's type of hangout. An uptight, composed, finely tuned woman like Christine Ivory was the last person who anyone should invite to such a lewd venue. But she'd had one memorable visit there with Arvo that she seemed to enjoy, much to her surprise. Sure, Christine Ivory was a few echelons above the humanity that found its comforts in the King's dark basement of sex, but she could stand to be surrounded, at least occasionally, by people she didn't usually mingle with, people she knew existed given her line of work. Depravity paid her bills, though she would never admit it, and it was high time that she saw depravity in the spot light. The stage lights of a strip show certainly gave a different color to things, and had adjusted more than one person's perspective.

Christine had other compelling reasons for avoiding the place: she had spotted, during that past visit, a number of her former clients, and others who might have benefited from an earlier intervention from her. For Christine, the King of Spades catered to a "failure of the system."

Arvo disagreed—he saw the King of Spades as an escape valve, preventive medicine. A few strippers offering exotic and quasi-legal entertainment solved more problems than they caused.

Well, they hadn't exactly agreed to disagree on the King.

And she hadn't exactly agreed to another visit there. He expected that after a few relaxing drinks, she would probably be fine.

Probably.

He buzzed her, and she didn't answer, but he knew better than to worry whether that meant anything. She was good to her word, and he wasn't worried.

Much.

So he waited at the security door, checked his watch a few times, thought of buzzing her again, but didn't. He was relieved to see her exiting the elevators only a few moments later. Though she walked through the security doorway without a word, her face didn't look angry. If anything, she was stunning in her elegant way: she wore the lightest touch of makeup, and somehow that was enough to transform her from the no-nonsense professional Christine to the nighttime knockout Christine. With her fair and flawless complexion, she could have been a high-end model, even though she didn't have the classic beauty of a Grace Kelly.

Oh, there was a certain indefinable beauty to her face. It was and had always been an arresting, unusual face—her wide-set cheekbones and close-set eyes gave a sultry, ethnic look to her otherwise Northern European features. He wondered if he'd ever really feel as comfortable with her undefined, thrilling loveliness as he did with Helen, who was beautiful in a more familiar, visceral way.

Christine was wearing the most form-fitting dress he'd ever seen her in. Her hair was swept up, revealing the sensuous length of her neck, and when she passed by him, his eyes were free to take her in, sweeping down along the line of her spine. The cut of the dress was so low in the back that it exposed skin he'd seen and touched only in an intimate setting. His hand tingled with the memory of her smooth, warm skin under it, not so long ago, up in her condominium some twenty floors above where they were now standing.

He was aroused and he knew she was too, but not in the same way. Her arousal had everything to do with her anger. She had goods on display she had no intention of selling. It was going to be a long night.

He opened her car door and she got in, and as they drove away, she sat in silence, her eyes locked on the road. He wondered why she'd agreed to come with him.

"Nice night, wouldn't you say," he said, knowing she wouldn't answer, so he did for her. "I'd say so."

"Whew. We've had quite the week, haven't we?" He went on, playing a two-sided conversation to the best of his ability.

Still no response.

"Murder on Tuesday. Interviews with the only witness, or possible suspect, on Thursday," he said.

"You forgot something," she finally piped up.

"Oh yes, we both spoke with the kid's parents," he said. Maybe she was warming up.

"No," she said. "Not that. That other not so tiny little detail that started your week. Named Helen."

Just then, it dawned on him that it was a very bad idea to be taking her to the club. He might have to change his plans, fast.

"Say," he began, "I hope you don't mind, but I need to make a quick stop before we get to the place where I made our reservations."

He was thankful that she didn't ask where that was. It would give him enough time to sort out his plans, make a quick adjustment, and come up with some believable explanation. In the meantime, she might not strangle him when they "temporarily" stopped at the King of Spades.

"We're stopping here?" Christine asked when they drove into the King of Spades parking lot.

"Just briefly," Arvo said. "It's professional, meaning police-professional, business."

"Oh."

"You can wait here, if you like."

"Oh, no," she said, opening her door. "I'm coming in. I like to see how the other half lives, as you well know. On a purely professional basis, of course."

He wondered if she'd already figured him out. Or maybe she'd like to show off how she looked, how much better she was than the working girls inside. Who knew? Maybe she did want to go inside for the entertainment.

He held out an arm and she took it, and as soon as they were let in, a topless waitress escorted them to the private room Vern Eide had promised him. The girl let them inside, and Arvo could see her eyeing Christine in her dress. "She looks tasty."

"Hands off, Renae," Arvo said.

"She doesn't really look like your type, Arvo," Renae said.

"Hmm. And my type would be?"

"I thought you preferred blondes?" Renae was a redhead. "I know I do," she winked, "But for her," she gestured towards Christine, "I'd take on a brunette."

"Now, let's not fight over her, Renae. Why don't you go and get us a couple of drinks. Christine likes Manhattans. I'll take my usual."

"Coming right up."

"Well, now, aren't they trying to make us welcome here?" Arvo said. The room was softly lit with a few glowing candles. One side of it opened out to a view of the stage and the floor below, and a softly cushioned banquette ran the length of its back wall, offering privacy to anyone who might be seated there. There was plenty of room for company.

"Were they expecting us?" Christine finally asked. "Or are you such a regular that you have a box subscription. Maybe the sheriff's department has one, of course, for purely 'professional' matters."

Renae returned with the drinks, a couple of buxom doubles that were clearly not whiskey-based. Slices of lime floated in clear liquid.

"Tonight's special," she said. "On the house." She gave Arvo another wink and Christine another look. "If she gets tired of you—and who wouldn't—I'd be happy to keep her entertained," she offered.

"I think Christine can keep herself entertained," Arvo said.

"I'm sure she can," Renae said with an arched brow. "Women are quite adept." Renae gave Christine another once over, and then left.

"What on earth was that about?" Christine asked. "I'm not sure I like what she thinks of me."

"Oh, that's just a lot of bull," Arvo said, sipping from his drink. "Probably more directed at me than you."

"I'm not so sure I like her at all." Christine took a sip of hers. "What is this?"

"I don't know exactly," Arvo said, taking a long drink of the cool, lime-infused beverage. "Seems familiar, but I can't quite place it."

"It's delicious," she said, taking another sip. Her eyes began to sparkle in the glow of candles and the colored reflections of the stage lights.

The first show of the evening began on the stage below, and Christine was drawn to the balcony by the sounds of Latin-tinged music, part jazz, part samba, but slower; music that had coupled in the fragrant shadows of a tropical evening, a long, long way south of Somerset Hills.

"It's bossa nova," Arvo told her. "Vern's trying to be more eclectic."

Though the style had been around for more than half a century, the music seemed timeless in the way that desire was timeless. Bossa nova seemed to constantly yearn for release. The music, with its rolling sax, sounded unquenched desires, unrequited passion. It was the perfect music for a strip tease.

On stage, a beautiful Brazilian girl with a thick, gorgeous length of chestnut-colored hair swayed, her eyes closed, her body glowing in the heat of her dance. The air around the stage grew humid with mist that was so artfully staged it instantly transported all the patrons from a cold Minnesota adult club thousands of miles south to a sweltering evening in a Rio bar. The backdrop was painted with moody palms arched above a tropical horizon at twilight.

Arvo realized what it was they were drinking. It was Brazil's national cocktail, caipirinha, made with cachaça (sugar cane rum), sugar (preferably white powdered sugar), and lime. It was far sweeter than he usually liked his drinks. Christine, on the other hand, seemed to be gulping hers down, unaware of how much alcohol she was consuming. She began rocking to the music.

"It's really intoxicating."

"If you drink enough of *that*, it is," Arvo said, motioning to her nearly empty glass.

"I meant the music," she said.

"Enjoy it," he said. "I need to see to that bit of business I mentioned."

"Can't you attend to it here? I'm not sure I want Renae coming back and finding me here alone."

Arvo considered her request. Frankly he wasn't sure he wanted Renae lurking nearby either, without him around to police her. He was enjoying the attention Christine was drawing from her, but didn't care to have any gentleman honing in. Once again, Christine was making a splash at the club, and getting looks from customers and employees alike.

"Sure." Arvo looked out from the balcony and motioned the bartender, who sent Renae up with fresh drinks. Arvo spoke to her briefly and she nodded. He tipped her to her satisfaction, and moments later someone else was standing in the doorway.

"You have company," the man said in slightly accented speech. He was a young, Hispanic man. In the country awhile, judging by his speech.

"Please, come in," Christine said. "The more the merrier."

The man stepped inside and closed the door behind them. He was dressed in a kitchen uniform, and carrying a bus tray.

"I don't have more than a few moments," he said, his eyes darting around. Surprisingly he didn't linger on Christine, but joined her at the balcony.

"She's exquisite," Christine said, as the woman continued her slow-moving, dream-like act.

"Yes, of course. That's Astrid," the man said. "Almeida."

The man was far more taken with Astrid than with Christine. "Her fiancé, also my best friend, is in Afghanistan. No one touches her," he said. "Or else they hear from me."

"It's your friend I heard something about. Jose Rivera," Arvo said.

"Yes. He told me that I might be contacted."

They watched as Astrid completed her performance and left the stage.

"Cop friend of mine from the Cities is interested in whatever he might know about a trucking company that serves the refinery."

"Astrid's fiancé worked for them before he was shipped out," the busboy said. "They have been pushing to get a big refinery contract shipping gas to gas stations in the area. Jose heard about the tactics his employer was using to improve the firm's chances, and when they basically fired him when he was called up, he told me about what had been happening. Now that he has no job to come back to. While he's away, I've been keeping an eye out for who has been coming and going from the club, asking Astrid to pass along anything she hears."

"What kind of tactics are we talking about here? Bribes?" Arvo said.

The busboy glanced to the stage floor, then went on quietly. "You know that new river crossing that's been in the planning stages?"

"You mean upstream from here?" Arvo asked.

"Environmentalists have been blocking it. The refinery wants it. Astrid's fiancé thinks that his former employer has been applying less than legal pressure to get it done, since that will give them an upper hand in winning the business."

"Pressure? Meaning what exactly?" Arvo asked.

"That's all he's told her. Nothing specific."

"What's your interest in all of this? Friendship is one thing, and one look at Astrid has me thinking—the cat's away . . . Why are you involving yourself in this business issue? When she's looking like she could use some action."

"Don't confuse her professional ability with anything real. Jose's sister is my wife. We're family. Family is everything. Jose got screwed. He was supporting everyone in his family off the trucking company pay. Now he's got a soldier's salary and no job to come back to. Look at me. I'm bussing dishes at a strip club."

And probably not entirely legally doing that, Arvo thought, knowing that Vern's hiring practices were not up to INS standards.

"It's only one of my three jobs," the man went on. "I've got a family to support. Astrid's contributing, too, much more than I am, even though they aren't married yet."

"Got anything else for me?"

"That's all. When I know more, you'll hear. I need to get back to the kitchen," he said, gathering their empty glasses into his bus tray and leaving.

Arvo thought of something and went into the corridor to have a few more words with the man, who nodded and patted him on the back. "Of course," he said, "With pleasure. Right away."

"So you're involved in whistle-blowing corporate stuff now?" Christine asked. "Since when?"

"It's just some business a friend wanted me to look into," Arvo said. "That kind of stuff puts me to sleep."

Moments later the text Arvo expected came in. He glanced at it and smiled.

"Are you ready," he said to Christine, half-expecting she might ask to linger for Astrid's second act. "Our reservations are set for 9:15 at the Vista."

The informant had made contact with a friend in the swanky Vista's kitchen, and reservations were made in no time.

"The Vista?" Christine gushed. "Really? How on earth did you manage that? I heard that you need reservations months ahead?"

"Oh, I see you've heard of the place," Arvo said nonchalantly. "We can head on over now, that is, unless you'd prefer to catch another show, maybe get to know Renae better?"

"You don't have to ask me twice."

"Leaving so soon?" Renae pouted moments later. "Bring this one back again, Arvo. I'll personally entertain her, my compliments."

"Um, no thanks," Christine said as soon as they were out of earshot. "I didn't think that much silicone was medically safe."

They exited the lot and turned north. Not long after, Arvo noticed another vehicle following them some distance behind, far enough away that it might have been a coincidence. He might have let it go, and done nothing more than to proceed to the Vista, happy to put business aside for the rest of the night. Already the thought of their famous lamb chops was making him drool.

Had it been any kind of vehicle other than the one following them, he could have let it go. But it was a motorcycle.

He opened the window to let in some of the fresh evening air, in time to catch the sound of the cycle accelerating, closing the distance between them in seconds.

Arvo had been a typical boy, just like Nick. He knew his motorcycles. And this one sounded like a Honda street cycle, bearing down on them fast and threatening to derail his evening plans.

Damn, he thought. And just when Christine seemed to be warming up to him again. "Hang on, sweetheart," he said. "The ride to the Vista may be a bit bumpy."

Thirteen

O NCE AGAIN, HERE WE ARE, ARVO," Christine muttered through clenched teeth. "How do you manage to always have someone on your tail when I'm with you."

"Who's to say they aren't after you, this time?"

"For all we know it's Helen trying to chase you down for your overdue alimony check," she said without any sarcasm.

"Will you just quit it with Helen? Look—" Arvo said, taking a hard left to head up the river bluff just north of town. "You knew my history." He briefly eyed his rearview mirror, and saw that the motorcycle driver had turned in the same spot. "You knew my hang-ups. You knew them from the start."

Christine glanced in the side mirror, squinting to see who might be following.

"Think it's the same person who was on the bridge?" she asked.

"No way of telling until he, *or she*, gets closer. And I'm not so sure that's a good idea to let whomever that is close in. If it's the motorcyclist Nick said he saw, potentially a murderer, then we definitely want to keep our distance."

"So why aren't you calling this in?" Christine said, sounding more pissed off than nervous.

"What, now you're on me about my police techniques?" Arvo sped up slightly, following the road that curved along the edge of a runoff-carved ravine. Arvo called in to report a high-speed chase along the northern border of Somerset Hills.

"Satisfied? With my luck, I'll be pulled over for speeding while this suspect gets away." Arvo took another hard turn.

"Okay. Now I'm ready. Lay the rest on me, Ivory. Get it all out. The ex-wife, the excuse I am for the detective. And by the way, keep your eye on that bike behind us and see if you can get a lock on anything: license plate, helmet style, whatever."

Christine swiveled around in her seat. "Arvo, here's my only request. You know that I never wanted a thing to do with you."

"That's not a request. Sounds more like an excuse. For what? Your mistake?" Arvo said, taking another look in his rearview mirror.

"Don't interrupt, she said.

"I won't," he interrupted. "Except to say your backside, as charming as it is, is blocking my view."

"Well pardon me," Christine said, sliding away from him. "By the way, I think the guy's gaining on us, so you might want to speed up."

"Thank you for letting me know. Hang on." He pressed the gas pedal to the floor, and swerved around the next curve, nearly sliding off the road into the ravine. They skidded away, but not before Arvo heard what he thought was a gunshot whizzing by.

"Get down," Arvo said, pressing Christine's head down on the seat. "But please go on with your analysis. Sorry you were interrupted by my lousy driving trying to get away from, oh, a murder suspect who maybe has more murder on his mind."

"You don't need to be so sarcastic." Christine shouted, her head nearly bumping the dashboard as they sped over a bump, "All I want to say is that I'm sure it's hard getting over someone as significant as Helen. Though honestly, I can't see what her good points are, except—Ouch!" Christine cried as she was thrown against the door.

Arvo yanked her back into position. "Sorry, I told you it was going to be rough."

"I don't care about the ride. The relationship has been far rougher. I feel like the third wheel. Helen's there in the driver's seat, taking both of us along for her not so merry little ride. That she was physically there with you in the wee hours Tuesday morning hardly matters. She's been pretty much present the whole time we've been together, these past months. You're not one hundred percent there for me, Arvo. Not yet. Which brings me to my request," she said. "You're going to have to speed up," she said, peering over the seat.

"That's your request? Speed up how? To get over Helen?"

"Oh, don't be such an idiot. You know what I'm talking about. The guy's gaining again."

"I'm going as fast as I can," Arvo said as they neared the summit.

"Here's my request. I need you to be there one-hundred percent for me. I'm not sure you'll ever be one-hundred percent for me, because even if Helen is taking up just one-percent of you, it's one-percent too much."

They had reached the summit and Arvo took a sharp turn onto a hidden driveway that led off the road, immediately cutting the engine and the lights.

He pushed Christine down flat onto the front seat and covered her protectively with most of his body, lying there with her in silence, their hearts pounding. They could hear the motorcycle arriving at the summit and passing by where they had turned off.

Longer than it was necessary he lay hard against her body, wishing harder that she was wrong. But it was just as she'd said. Helen was still there, a presence between them even when they were so close it was almost impossible for one to inhale without the other exhaling.

The one-percent of Helen suffocated any chance they had.

Arvo looked down at Christine, taking in her beauty, her intelligence, her self-possessed and realistic view of the world, and knew that he loved her, and that possibly she loved him.

"So you're through with me? Is that it? Because of the one-percent of Helen, who won't let go of me?"

"The one percent of Helen that you won't let go of." she said, struggling beneath him. "You're suffocating me."

He got off her, allowing her to sit up now that the danger had passed. Squads flew by in pursuit of the motorcyclist, now long gone. The drive to Christine's condo was silent, though not awkward. Arvo was not searching for a way to keep the conversation going. He just felt raw from what Christine had exposed in him, and was thankful for the weariness that hit after the adrenalin rush of the dangerous pursuit. It was the reason he welcomed intoxication, the deadening elixir that cancelled out the excited jumble of pain and superfluous passion his ex-wife left in her wake.

Christine left the car without a word. A different Arvo, a better man than he was capable of being, would have considered how his actions had hurt her, caused a larger ripple in her life than she was used to, and would have understood that he'd been a huge asshole, that the frustrated tears Christine shed, that he caused, could and should have been prevented.

An even better man would not have become involved with her to begin with.

But he was not that man, and might never be, even though he knew that what he felt for Christine had the potential to make him into that man.

The real truth—the one Christine didn't necessarily know— was that he couldn't come to terms with what she lacked. Christine didn't excite in him the wild, uncontrollable feelings that he associated with true love. Only one person in his life had ever elicited such a response.

Moments later, he was in front of Helen's house, staring at her front door. A few lights were on, her car nowhere in sight, her garage door closed. Only four days earlier he'd been inside her house, with her, knowing he had wished he would never have to leave it. Now that he was in front of her house again, with the possibility of her only a few feet away from him, he wished the opposite. That he could drive away and never come back.

He'd switched his lights off, but left his car gently idling. In the back seat he had a bottle of wine he'd purchased earlier that night, intending to drink it with Christine. He licked his lips, thinking of drinking it, with Helen. How he would welcome the deadening sense of alcohol, wiping away all of the pressure from Christine's unmet expectations—hell, his own unmet expectations for himself—all forgiven and forgotten in the easy temporary escape of booze.

He turned to grab the paper sack out of the back seat, rested the bottle between his legs and toyed with the keys, still hanging from the ignition. There it was—the key to his ex-wife's house, the one she'd slipped in his pocket a few days earlier. He should have given it back to her then, immediately. Instead, he hung it on his key chain, even though he knew her invitation to use it meant nothing to her, and everything to him.

He felt the pressure of the bottle in his lap. He shut off his engine, grasped the bottle, and still he couldn't move. The burden of his disorderly, unwanted feelings straight jacketed him. He badly wanted a drink, and the wine bottle between his legs wasn't offering any resistance—he kept a corkscrew in his glove compartment. He remembered the long, dark months of turning to the bottle to fight off a return to Helen. Now both were so tantalizingly in reach.

He killed the engine, opened his door, and walked to Helen's door, the wine bottle in his hand, and her key between his fingers.

A SHARP RAP ON HIS CAR WINDOW made Arvo jump, waking him from a deep, almost dead-drunk sleep. He shielded his eyes from the bright morning sunlight, and cranked open his window.

"I know that you like the caramel rolls, but you're making me nervous being here so early." Nichol said to him. "So you have two choices. Come inside and I'll get you some coffee and the first roll that comes out of the oven, or sleep it off here," she said, her eye on the empty wine bottle on the passenger side.

Arvo cleared his voice. "I'm as sober as you are."

"That right? What's that on your floor? Recycling? Or are you accusing me of falling off the wagon?"

"Oh, that," Arvo commented. "I dumped it out on my ex-wife's door."

"On her door? What, trying to remove her curse or something? What like a reverse Passover? I thought you smeared blood on a doorway so the hand of death would pass you by."

"I was thinking that I'd fight my demon with another demon, and maybe both would pass me by. I don't know. It was late," he said, winking in the bright light. "Believe it or not, I had her key in my hands at the time."

"Were you planning on using it? Going in there? Taking her back?"

"I don't know. I really don't know. I just stood there, and before I knew it, the bottle was open and I was pouring it all over her door frame."

"Love makes you do crazy things. Crazy makes you do crazy things. This sounds like crazy to me."

"I hope when I grow up, I'm as smart as you are," he said, smiling.

"I'm not really that smart, "she said, raising her fist to him. "Just getting through, one day at a time."

He bumped it. "One day at a time."

He followed her inside the restaurant, lit the GOOD FOOD sign, and got the coffee started while she put the first dozen caramel rolls into the café oven.

FOURTEEN

DEAR SOMERSET HILLS EDITOR,

You frequently publish my extensive commentaries about important development issues in Mendota County. As a concerned citizen, I feel it's my duty to bring light to the closed-door decision-making process that too often results in bad planning, over-development, and losses to our precious landmarks and history. Among the past losses are the streetcars: the vibrant and efficient mass transportation system that the bus system never effectively replaced. The poorly planned highway system has only exacerbated the problems of urban sprawl, not to mention the fact that the gridlocked traffic contributes more pollution.

Most recently I've written extensively about the county's latest wasteful idea: that of to replacing the Stone Island Swing Bridge with a multi-lane freeway crossing. For more than a century, the bridge has functioned as an efficient river crossing for not only automobiles, but trains as well. The environmental impact of the new bridge's location—in a sensitive, protected area—is enormous, but worse than that is the size and cost of the structure. I've already pointed out the many flaws in the plan on numerous occasions.

Now I have a more personal reason for writing. As your newspaper reported, my son was killed two weeks ago on the swing bridge. We were finally allowed to bury him this past week, after an autopsy was conducted as part of the ongoing investigation into his death. That is what brings me to the topic of this letter.

The Mendota County Sheriff's office is a disgrace to our community. I know from personal experience, having been interviewed by Investigator Arvo Thorson.

My son Karl Lutz was slaughtered in an unspeakable manner, and the department's immediate assumption is that my son invited his own death. Why? I can barely bring myself to mention the unsavory activities Investigator Arvo Thorson suggested my son engaged in, but I will here. I myself find it irresponsible and pathetic of the investigator to suggest that my son indulged in gambling and whoring and this is what led to his death. My wife won't even speak of the cruel and insensitive manner in which Mr. Thorson and the rest of his department seek justice. Meanwhile, the scofflaws responsible run free, including the juvenile who professes to have come across the scene innocently. Hogwash. Why is no one looking into what that boy was doing on the bridge on a school day?

Mr. Thorson made the excuse that he needed to know the intimate and personal details of my son's life as part of the investigation. He called his line of questioning routine. How can accusing my son of unsavory crimes—before he was even laid to rest—be considered routine? Is this how the department conducts all of their investigations? I can't even begin to imagine the horror of other crime victim families, dealing with the loss of a loved one, whose first encounter with the people we trust to bring justice is one such as what my family encountered. I am outraged to think of all crime victim families, knowing what I know about how the department operates.

Mr. Thorson and the rest of the department should be ashamed. I have already taken my complaint to the appropriate authorities, both within and outside of Mendota County, and recommended that Mr. Thorson be disciplined.

Further, I would remind Mendota County citizens that the sheriff is up for re-election this fall. Time and time again, he has run unopposed, and we've returned him to his office without so much as a second thought.

It's time for the citizens of Mendota County to unite and rid our community of such disgraceful leadership. A new leader needs to step forward to be elected and clean house, from top to bottom, so that never again will crime victim families endure what my family has endured.

Sincerely,
John Lutz
Somerset Hills, Minnesota

FIFTEEN

"CHRISTINE, IT'S THE FIFTH TIME I'VE seen you in the past few weeks," Dorla Ivory said peevishly, setting aside her Word Search puzzle to meet her daughter at her door. "What on earth brings you here today? Again?"

Christine stood in the doorway, struggling with two overflowing grocery bags filled with food and cleaning supplies. She knew her mother would use neither, but she always tried.

"Mother you don't need to get up. You know perfectly well I have a key and can let myself in." Christine herself wondered why she kept turning up at her mother's. It was never pleasant. But she knew her mother needed her in the way her patients needed her. She had long accepted the fact that she would encounter much resistance and never be thanked.

"What on earth have you done to your hair now? I don't believe I've ever seen it that short."

Indeed she hadn't. Christine knew it was her most daring look, and she'd done almost everything to her hair over the years: she'd dyed it many shades, including platinum white with touches of electric blue at the nape, the deepest hennas, all the shades between blond and black. Most people weren't sure what her natural color was. She'd had it many lengths and styles—bobs, crops, layered, long and flowing. She drew the line at dreadlocks, her compulsive, orderly self not being able to stand the thought of such a disordered hairstyle.

This latest style was a radical change from almost an entire year of doing nothing but let it grow, in its natural color. She had buzzed it off herself the night before, shaving it down to not more than a half inch or so on top, and slightly longer on the sides. She'd colored it a vibrant, angry shade of purple. She knew it would be shocking, and the look on her mother's face told her it delivered exactly what she hoped it would.

"It looked so nice when you let it go back to your normal shade. For once you were starting to look like a normal person. What on earth possessed you to shave it off? And put that color in it?"

"I'm coming off an intense time at work." She was gleefully thinking of what her assistant Sharon might think of her new look. She knew she'd likely hate it, too, exactly as Christine hoped. Her mother's reaction was a preview of what to expect from Sharon. "Thought I needed something to better match my mood and the summer wardrobe I'm planning."

After she finished at her mother's, she was heading to her favorite consignment shop to see if there was anything to fill in her remaining spring needs, and looking ahead to summer.

"Summer is more than a month away. It's still freezing outside."

"No, it's not that bad and you know it. The doctor told you to get out and walk, that would help improve your circulation and probably you wouldn't feel so cold all the time," Christine said, walking to her mother's kitchen. She began to restock her refrigerator for her, tossing out the soured heavy cream and the moldy leftovers. She always wondered why she bothered. She knew her mother took almost every meal at the Tin Cup, the restaurant located just below her apartment. She met her friend Margie there and together the two of them smoked and gossiped. The Tin Cup owner sent her the monthly tab, and Christine paid for both her mother's and Margie's meals, never saying a word about it.

Dorla bustled into her kitchen. "I suppose I should get some coffee started for you.

"Mother, you don't need to. I don't want any coffee."

"Sure you do," she said. "Now where did you put those coffee filters? I swear I can never find where you put things away."

Christine opened a cabinet right above the coffee maker to show her mother where the filters were. Which is right where they always were, though she didn't point that out.

Dorla moaned when she stretched to get the filters out of the cabinet. "They're too high. I can barely reach them without straining myself. I get such a pain in my shoulders all the time."

Christine took them out of the cupboard without a word, knowing that even though she really didn't want any coffee, her mother did.

Her mother took a seat at the kitchen counter and primped her tightly permed gray hair. Christine started the coffee, washed the few dishes that had accumulated in the past few days, and by the time the coffee finished perking, she was finished with the dishes.

Dorla took a sip and puckered. "You make it so strong, Christine." That didn't stop her from taking a few more sips and leaning back with a pleased look on her face. She almost looked content.

"Did you get me those magazines I asked you about? You know how I hate the weekends. My soaps aren't on and I've got nothing to do."

Christine dug into the grocery bag and handed her mother the glossy gossip weeklies she loved: *People*, *Soap Opera Digest*, and the *National Enquirer*. She didn't wait to hear her mother mutter her thanks. Her mother settled into her easy chair, and Christine headed off to clean her bathroom, but not before answering to another request.

"Oh, Christine. I left my coffee on the counter. Would you heat it up and bring it to me? My knees are killing me."

Christine refilled her mother's cup and brought it to her.

"So what do you have planned for your evening, Christine? I haven't heard you mention Arvo lately? Aren't you seeing him anymore?"

Christine blanched. She instantly regretted having ever mentioned Arvo to her mother. For a long while after she started seeing him, she said nothing, knowing that once she brought him up, her mother would instantly be on her expecting constant updates.

"As a matter of fact, no we are not seeing each other at the moment."

"I can't say I'm surprised. I never expected it to last," Dorla sniffed dismissively, flipping through her magazine.

"Oh, really," Christine said, taking a seat on her mother's couch. For a moment, she ignored the stains and dust on the coffee table.

"You're impossible to get along with, Christine."

"Me? Impossible? You have to be joking."

"Isn't it obvious?"

"What's so obvious?"

"Look at you, Christine. With all of your accomplishments, that's a lot for a man to deal with. Then, your personality is a bit on the domineering side. I'm not sure where that came from, probably your father," Dorla said.

If anything it came straight from you, Christine thought.

"You could try being, oh I don't know, a little more submissive." Her mother barely looked up from the magazine. "Have you thought of that? Of course you haven't. And now, with that hair. Well it just says back off."

"Good. That's exactly what I want it to say. And by the way, and I'm sure I'm going to regret telling you this. I broke it off with Arvo. Not the other way around."

"What? Well that was a bad idea, your worst ever, though it's debatable whether it's a tie with the decision you made about your hair. Honest to Pete, Christine," she said, tossing one magazine aside and digging into the next, "At your age, you aren't going to have a lot more time. You need to accept that Christine and try to settle."

"You have no idea what you are talking about, Mother."

"What was wrong with him?"

Christine said nothing. She didn't want to say Helen's name, or go into the sordid mess.

"Exactly what I thought. Nothing." Dorla Ivory put up her footrest and leaned back.

Christine went into her mother's bathroom and began to clean, ripping open the shower curtain and spraying the harsh chemical cleaners onto it. On purpose she'd gotten the heavy stuff, knowing that the less harmful and environmentally friendly stuff would never work on the accumulated scum and mold she'd spotted on her previous visit.

She cleaned, hell-bent on removing every bit of dust and grime, not letting the acrid smells get to her. She was a girl from Somerset Hills after all, she was used to the toxic fumes of the refinery and the stockyards the next town over. Still, the cloud of chemical spray was suffocating, and she cracked open the bathroom window to let some of it out.

She scrubbed the toilet and the floor, wiping up what looked like years of scum, though she knew it was only a few weeks worth, as she regularly cleaned her mother's apartment.

She tackled the mirror and when she got every spot of spattered toothpaste crust off of it, she paused to look at her reflection. Yes, her new look was shocking. She had hoped she would look as ugly as she felt, and her red, sweaty face and nearly hairless head was satisfying. She had long hated her wide-set bone structure, recalling photos of her dumpy-looking, sturdy ancestors. Her eyes were too close together. Good. No one would ever notice her again, of that she could be glad. She was the ugliest, most undesirable woman on the planet.

She certainly couldn't hold a candle to Helen, as slutty and ordinary and, what was it her mother said? As submissive as she was. To hell with being submissive.

Christine finished with the bathroom and put all of the cleaning supplies under the kitchen sink. Her mother was snoring in her chair, and Christine watched as her glasses slipped down her nose. She gently removed them and grabbed the coverlet from the sofa to tuck around her. Before leaving, she turned off the coffee pot and poured what was left of the coffee into a thermos. She made one last pass to wipe up the dust and stains from the coffee table before heading out to her favorite consignment shop, just a few miles from her mother's apartment. She drove south on the main thoroughfare passing through the working-class neighborhood where her mother lived. Her destination was a better-maintained, safer neighborhood on the other side of the interstate that cut through the city.

Her mother had lived at the northern edge of the city, some forty minutes from Somerset Hills, for a few decades now, moving there in the years after her marriage to Christine's father ended, once Christine had graduated from high school and moved out.

The neighborhood where Dorla lived was the one she'd had grown up in, she felt comfortable living near her friends. Christine never cared for the grittiness of the City North neighborhood, with drunks stumbling around on almost every street corner and street crime rampant. Many shops along the main drag were boarded up, and the remaining ones were secured with iron grates and heavily fortified doors. Shop owners were known to keep rifles under their counters, particularly after a heinous murder of a flower shop owner.

Christine feared her mother would be mugged. But Dorla wouldn't hear of moving any place better. She was done with Somerset Hills. It only reminded her of her failed marriage. She claimed she felt perfectly safe in her little urban neighborhood.

In some ways, Christine knew her mother's attitude was healthier than most. Dorla had countered a bad phase of her life by starting over. And while she was the most negative person Christine knew, always complaining of various ailments, she was healthier than she'd ever been.

Christine remembered her mother's shock when, after college out of state and a few years in working on the East Coast, Christine accepted a job and moved back to Somerset Hills. Christine knew her mother had been making the most out of her pride in having a daughter working in a prestigious, Eastern city. To come home seemed like a failure. Christine never saw it that way, but given the last few weeks, she really had to wonder if her mother was right. And maybe she should follow her example to make a fresh start. Get away from an environment that had become toxic.

At minimum, it was time for the next phase of her makeover and the thought of what lay ahead was wearying, even though she loved consignment shopping and the idea of organizing and planning an entirely new wardrobe. Her back seat was piled high with the neutral, form-fitting outfits she'd been wearing the past months, looks that drew men's stares and women's envious comments. Now she couldn't wait to sell off that version of herself.

She crossed over the interstate, and drove through a neighborhood lined with stately homes, enormous nineteenth-century churches and long, wide boulevards. Christine saw that the crab apple trees were blooming and the grape hyacinths and bright yellow jonquils were flowering. Many aspired to live in the prosperous neighborhood, but even this area had not been spared in the latest economic crisis. She saw more than the usual numbers of "FOR SALE" signs on the lawns of the mansions, the best of which were being kept in perfect condition by the banks that now owned them.

"Christine!" Bobby Wick called out the moment Christine entered Do-Over. "Oh, what have you brought us today? Goodness." Bobby Wick was still slender and strong, somewhere in his mid-seventies. Somehow he'd managed to survive even though he was HIV-positive, and had run Do-Over for decades. His natty bowtie was perfectly tied, a wavy blond wig sat only slightly askew on his bony skull.

Bobby ran his fingers over the stunning, well-maintained collection of consignment designer dresses, blouses, and slacks Christine laid out on the counter. "Oh, I recognize these ones—you got them here?"

Christine nodded.

"Well, we'll have no problem selling them again. You really take good care of them. Are you staying to shop, dear?"

"Yes, of course. Take your time. I'm here for a major overhaul."

"We got some great new things in. The economy has been wonderful for consignment, you should see the stunning Lilly Pulitzer frocks that came in last week—an auction of another bankrupt millionaire. I can't remember which one this time. From the look of your fabulous new do, I'd say maybe you should check that rack, a couple Stella McCartney dresses that I think would really work with that amazing hair." Bobby examined her face and after saying, "May I?" fingered the wispy, chin locks that Christine had left untouched from her razor. "Impressive, though to be honest, dear, I'm not sure what I think of it yet."

The fact of the matter was that Christine didn't really know what to think of it either. She was still playing dress-up, just as she had as a girl. Her mother had saved some beautiful silky dresses she'd worn in her teens, and one of Christine's earliest memories was trying them on. They were so many sizes larger than she that they became ballroom gowns on her, with their wide, puffy skirts. She'd slid into her mother's oversized pumps, and paraded around the house like a runway model. She remembered her dad, who was then still living with the family, applauding and whistling.

"Dear, are you sure you want to sell this one? It really might work with your new look?" Bobby held up the backless dress Christine had worn on her last night out with Arvo, a few weeks earlier.

She touched it briefly, remembering the way he looked at her that night and, later, the protective, crushing weight of his body on her in the car. She wasn't sure which felt more smothering: his weight or memories of that train wreck of an evening. Would some other woman sense that if she allowed the dress to be sold at Do-Over? But not everyone had the sixth sense in clothing that she did.

She had often sensed someone else's tragedies in a beautiful, used designer item, and even when the price and the look were right, somehow she couldn't bring herself to buy it.

She took it out of her sell pile. "So you're keeping it?" Bobby asked. "I think you'll be glad you didn't sell it."

Yes. She was keeping it. But not for the reason Bobby suspected. She never intended to wear the dress again. She simply didn't want to foist her drama on some unsuspecting bargain hunter.

Christine strolled through the store, browsing through the racks for a different identity, someone no one would recognize. Someone no one would want. She needed a uniform for her new life, one that would work for the career search she was planning to start in the coming week. She was looking for the job that would take her away from Somerset Hills for good. She should never have returned to begin with, and the move she was planning was one she should have made years earlier. Screw Sharon. Screw Arvo. She was done with Somerset Hills and Mendota County.

Sixteen

Nick's spirits were high as May began, and the weather couldn't be better. Now that a few weeks had past since his witness interview, things were getting back to normal, for the most part. People were more concerned about the rising river, so the attention was off him, and he didn't miss it. He'd finished the Monday morning chore (roll the trash barrel out to the curb) and was ready to head off to school, the prospect of riding his skateboard there a pleasant anticipation. In fact, he'd probably arrive at school early for once.

Things changed the moment he stepped inside the house to grab his backpack. His father stood in the entryway, clutching a rolled wad of newspaper as if it were a bat. Was the guy going to hit him with it, he wondered? Nick's father had never lifted a hand against him, but that didn't mean he never would.

And as close as Nick had come to fighting with other boys, he never had either. One thing he had in common with the old man. They might both have tempers, but both knew how to keep it under control.

However, there was a first time for everything, and maybe this was it, or both of them would crack.

Nick mentally reviewed the list of grievances his father might have with him. Was he leaving for school too late? As long as he wasn't tardy too often, he was never questioned, and he knew he'd be early. Had he missed an important chore? He was on top of things, at least for that day.

"So what's the problem now?" Nick asked, knowing it was best to spit it out.

"Judging from *this* story, I'm having my doubts as to how honest you've been with the police," his father finally said. "Or with any of us." He held the newspaper out to Nick.

"Sit down and read it. Then we're going to talk."

Nick drew a chair up to the kitchen table and sprawled in it. "So what's the problem? Worried about the spring flooding? Maybe that will ruin the golf course? You know they are asking for sandbagging volunteers. Oh, yes. I'm supposed to stay away from the river."

"Stop the sarcasm." His father jabbed a finger on the page. "Read this." He pointed out a letter to the editor.

The Mendota County Sheriff's office is a disgrace to our community. I know from personal experience, having been interviewed by Investigator Arvo Thorson.

"This is what has you riled up? A letter to the editor?"

"Keep reading," his father told him.

Nick kept reading, though it was somewhat difficult to pay attention with his father watching him so closely. The man seriously looked like he was going to explode. His face was red and puffy, sweat stained his collar.

Near the end of the letter, he saw what had caught his father's eye.

Meanwhile, the scofflaws responsible run free, including the juvenile who professes to have come across the scene innocently. Hogwash! Why is no one looking into what that boy was doing on the bridge on a school day?

The letter was signed by John Lutz, Karl's father.

"So I'm guilty? Is that it?" Nick couldn't believe his father would go so far as to believe anything that was printed in the paper. Nick had witnessed him daily, ranting about how the journalists were all biased. He very often threw the newspaper away before anyone else could read it, and threatened to cancel it at least once a week.

His father gave him a grim, tight look. "Let's be honest here and face the facts."

"What facts, exactly?" Nick mirrored the face his father was making. If that was the way it was going to be, he'd fight fire with fire.

"The facts as they exist," his father said, taking the newspaper back and once again rolling it tightly, then slapping it on his hand. "For all anyone knows, you killed the guy."

"What?"

"There's nothing anyone has to go on. And now, this?" His father began to pace the kitchen floor.

"So you believe this . . . this garbage?" Nick almost spat. "That's what you've always called almost everything you've read on the opinion pages. Garbage. Why do you believe it now?"

Nick's father's cell phone buzzed on the countertop.

"Damn," he said, scrolling through a long list of messages. "I don't need this." He typed in an answer to one, and then looked at the clock. "I'm already running late. What if people at the office have read this letter? They will think the worst. Of me! They'll wonder what kind of man has so little control over his children."

Nick's father laid the paper aside at last, dumped the rest of the coffee in the sink, his half-eaten breakfast in the trash. "I'll probably be replaced as division head. They'll think I can't handle any more pressure."

He stuffed his phone in his pocket. "Did I even take my blood pressure pill today? My doctor's going to give me hell when he sees me."

His father headed out the door. "We'll talk about this more. Tonight. I mean your mother and I will. What a mess," his father said. "Tell your mother I won't be home for dinner. I have a department meeting that goes late. It's budgeting time. God. Probably I'll be the one cut."

So how was he going to talk with Nick's mother about this "mess" if he was working late, Nick wondered. But that was it. It was clear his father's reaction to the letter had nothing to do with Nick and everything to do with Dennis McQuillen's reputation. He'd visited his father's office, not lately, but in years past, as part of "Take Your Child to Work Day." Everyone had cooed at the cute blond boy, but now that Nick was no longer the tow-headed toddler that his father could crow about, he hadn't been invited back. Instead, he was the father of a boy connected with a gruesome murder.

Nick wondered whether his father would defend him. Wouldn't it be simple to dismiss the allegations quickly, since they weren't true to begin with? Of course, that would require a cooler, calmer frame of mind. Apparently something his father was incapable of. Nick heard the car door slam and his father making a speedy exit out of the neighborhood.

He reread the letter and felt his face burning. What the hell was wrong with everyone? They seemed to be looking for the easy solutions, maybe hoping that Nick would just go away. That would solve everything.

Even the cops hadn't figured it out yet. That detective had seemed to have things on the ball, but it turned out he was just like everyone else. It was obvious that Karl Lutz was not responsible for his own death, contrary to what John Lutz accused the detective of insinuating. Clearly, if anyone had been listening to Nick— and they clearly had not— they'd have located the motorcyclist already and the case would be solved.

What was he supposed to do? Go and set everyone straight about who they should be looking for? He already told them everything. Nick grabbed his backpack and headed out, but before doing that, he did what his father should have done. He tossed the newspaper into the trash, where it belonged. He locked up and jumped onto his skateboard, his thoughts spinning hard and fast like the wheels under his feet. Instead of enjoying the fresh spring air and the warming sun, he felt nothing but dread. Everyone was going to be stirred up again today. It was never going to be over.

SEVENTEEN

"D
ID YOU SEE THIS LETTER IN THE PAPER? From Lutz?" The sheriff tossed the newspaper opinion page to Arvo.

Bill Ruud had requested Arvo come to his office, first thing Monday morning, and the only way to get Arvo's attention that early was to sic Juney on him. He could tell from the sarcastic tone of her texts, at 9:00 a.m. She disliked being forced to police Arvo's behavior.

The overuse of emoticons said it all. A long string of frowning faces told him the level of Ruud's discontent, and her unhappiness with being his messenger.

He tried to answer with smileys, not sure whether he was supposed to put a space between the colon and the bracket. Before he knew it, he'd hit send, not knowing what exactly the confused jumble of symbols translated to.

"The hell was that?" Juney texted back.

He shot back a feeble question mark.

"Just get here. Ruud wants your @ss. Again!"

He called her back when he got frustrated with his fat fingering of texts. "I'll be there. But first I have to drop off your May basket," he said joking lightly in hopes of calming her down.

"Yeah, right," she said. "You come near me with flowers, I'll kill you. My allergies are worse than ever."

"Who said I had flowers in your May basket?"

"Shut up and get moving," she said.

Now he had another irritated member of the Mendota County Sheriff's Department facing him. Waiting, and not very patiently, for an explanation.

"You know I don't read the papers, Bill. They never get the details straight, and the mis-reporting wastes our time. All the kooks start calling in worthless tips."

"Well you'll need to pay attention this time," Ruud said.

Arvo read quickly. *The Mendota County Sheriff's office is a disgrace to our community. I know from personal experience, having been interviewed by Investigator Arvo Thorson.*

"Just what exactly does this guy mean by—" the sheriff ripped the newspaper out of Arvo's hands, "'*it's time for the citizens of Mendota County to unite and rid our community of such disgraceful leadership.*' Me? Providing 'disgraceful leadership'? What on earth did you do when you talked those people?" He spat out his accusation, his spittle landing on Arvo's face.

Arvo wiped the sheriff's DNA off his cheek nonchalantly. "Bill, you know it was nothing out of the ordinary."

Bill stared at him, demanding more of an explanation.

"You know the drill," Arvo said calmly and simply. "We have to look into everything. How else are we going to even hope we might find out what happened, stop the murderer from striking again?"

"You're sure you didn't make some unnecessary inquiries? Maybe some unwarranted judgments?"

"Absolutely not. Look at the facts here. You have the victim, Karl Lutz, still living with his parents. The guy's in his forties. Never married. From the sounds of things he probably never would have married or moved out. How's a guy like that keep himself entertained?"

"And this is what you told John Lutz?" the sheriff said.

"Of course not. You know better than that. But if we don't look at this from all possible angles, including not taking as bible everything the guy's parents *say* they know about their son, then I'm not doing my job. I can give you fifty examples of when someone (not me) screwed up because assumptions were made about a fine upstanding citizen of the community who could not have possibly hacked, beaten, raped, or murdered, etc. And the criminal got away, some even to kill again. Finally when someone had the guts to follow up, Arthur Upstanding Citizen was the guy. I won't let that happen here."

Arvo grabbed the paper again, "Look—this accusation—*the department's immediate assumption is that my son invited his own death.* It's bull and you know it. The last thing I would do is 'blame the victim.' Are you losing your nerve, Bill?"

The sheriff sighed and leaned back in his chair. "I've already got the state making inquiries."

"The state? Well, don't worry. It will blow over," Arvo said.

"That's cavalier, as usual, on your part. Just brushing off any criticism," the sheriff said.

Arvo wanted to remind the sheriff that as many times as the sheriff complained about his tactics, he routinely praised Arvo later, apologizing for his doubts in his best investigator. Instead, he knew it was not the time to point that out. He would unite with his boss against their common enemy. The state.

"Trust me," Arvo said. "They'll find nothing. And by the time they conclude their supposed investigation, the whole thing will have been forgotten. It's just some bureaucrat trying to look like they're earning the taxpayer's money."

"I'm not so sure," the sheriff said. "I don't like this coming up when it's an election year. This is the perfect time for someone else to jump into the race."

"So? Do you want to get out?" Arvo couldn't believe what the sheriff was saying. "After all of this time?"

The sheriff got up from his desk and walked to the window. "I don't know. Sometimes I think I should just retire."

"Are you kidding me? You'd walk away? Because of this?" Arvo shook the paper at his boss. "Bill, you'd never forgive yourself."

Bill returned to his chair and sighed, straightening his tie. "You're right. I wouldn't."

"I give you my word," Arvo said with conviction. "No one will find anything when they look into the investigation. You know me. You know Juney. The paperwork is—" he thought to himself, *will be*—"spotless." *Thanks to Juney's meticulousness.*

"So, how is the investigation going?" the sheriff asked. "I haven't heard a thing from downstairs."

"Autopsy's due today."

"I can't see how that's going to tell us much. Didn't the guy basically fall into the machinery? Maybe while trying to unjam it?" the sheriff asked.

"I don't buy it was an accident. Not at all." Arvo was convinced but had nothing solid to prove it.

"But what about that kid? I read the interview transcript. Sounds like he could have, maybe not on purpose, jammed the equipment with taconite pellets?"

"The engineer's preliminary report is coming in this week, too, if it hasn't arrived already," Arvo quickly pointed out. "I hope for the kid's sake taconite had nothing to do with it."

"Kids can get in a lot of trouble without intending to," Bill said.

"Somehow with this kid, I'm not sure *what* he might have intended. But he better hope that luck is on his side," Arvo said. "Or we find the mysterious motorcyclist who miraculously leapt across the open water."

Bill huffed in disbelief.

"I had a run-in with a cyclist that might match up with the bike he described."

"When was that?" Bill asked.

"A couple of weeks ago," Arvo explained. "The guy seemed hell bent on tailing me, almost ran me off the road. We've been looking for a street bike matching the description the kid gave and the one we, I meant I, heard."

Arvo realized he hadn't used the word 'we' in a few weeks.

"What the H are you talking about?" Ruud's face reddened and he reached for a bottle of something in his drawer, shaking out a handful of antacids. "I read about the call-in down on the bridge, when you'd gone back to investigate. No one found the cyclist. Who is this 'we' you're talking about?"

"No, not that time." Arvo realized he'd have to bring up Christine. There was no point in evading Ruud, and it bothered him to say her name. "I was out with Christine."

Ruud frowned, still chewing on his mouthful of antacids.

"We're in different departments, there's no law or policy that says we can't spend time together," Arvo said. "But don't worry. It's over."

Ruud gave him that searching look, the one he made when he was looking for signs that might reveal whether Arvo had been drinking again. Arvo hated when people looked at him that way.

"I'm fine," Arvo said. *And I don't want to talk about it. Let's move on.*

Ruud held out the antacid bottle and Arvo waved him off. "I never touch the stuff before six at night."

"Women," Ruud said, tossing the bottle back in his desk.

"So the bike that was tailing us fit the description this kid gave. It was fast. I've never seen a bike like that around here."

"So that's it?" the sheriff said, a bit incredulous.

"It was dark, the guy got away, and no one tracked him down."

"I don't know, Arvo. That's pretty slim pickings to hang an investigation on."

"I've got Kieran tracking down every make and model of street bike registered within a hundred miles of here. I have the word out to every bike shop within five hundred miles of here. We'll find him."

"*If*, he's out there, Arvo."

"We have to make the effort." Arvo said. *You know that even better than I do.*

"You better make progress. Fast. Now that I've got the state breathing on me."

Arvo ripped the newspaper away from Ruud and held it up. "You know this is bull. What's your gut telling you?"

Ruud sighed and opened his desk drawer. He held up the antacid bottle once more. "My gut's telling me that there's trouble. And it's not going to be over until we have a break in this case."

A knock sounded on the sheriff's door and Arvo opened it to find Juney standing outside, breathless.

"Coroner's report's coming in," she chirped. "Freakin' unbelievable from the sounds of it."

"Well, Bill?" Arvo smiled. "Looks like a break may have arrived."

Arvo followed Juney and turned to see if Ruud was joining in.

"You two go ahead. I'm expecting a friendly visit from the state." Ruud sighed, the bottle of antacids in his hand. "Just find something, a bone, to toss at this animal. Anything. Please?"

EIGHTEEN

AN UNEXPECTED VISITOR WAS WAITING outside Arvo's office when he and Juney arrived in the county building basement suite. Investigation department intern Sam Banach was standing with the strange fellow, a guy with iron-red skin and wavy, chestnut hair that matched the ruddy complexion. He looked permanently sunburnt, but he didn't appear to be the type who'd spend a lot of hours in a tanning booth.

Later Sam explained what he'd learned about the man's appearance from chatting with the guy while they waited for Arvo.

"It's hereditary hemochromatosis." Sam told Arvo.

"Hered—what?"

"Hereditary hemochromatosis." Sam grinned. "Say it three times fast. 'Hereditary hemochromatosis, hereditary hemochromatosis, hereditary hemochromatosis.'"

"Stop goofing off and just explain." Arvo enjoyed the young man, but his impish sense of humor could put the morose detective off his game.

"Iron overload. It's a genetic condition that's actually somewhat common, as far as genetic conditions go. Did you know they actually have to bleed these people, literally siphon off some of their blood so this thing doesn't kill them? Kind of amazing."

At the moment, the only amazing thing about the guy was that he had come forward, voluntarily, with engineering information about the bridge. Arvo was eager to read the coroner's report, but he knew he'd have to entertain whatever this engineer, if he was one, had to say.

"Matthew Arndt," the man said, introducing himself. "I have important information for you related to the bridge case." He held out a hand to shake Arvo's and when Arvo shook it he had the same sensation he'd gotten from holding taconite. He looked into his palm as the gentleman withdrew his, expecting to see it covered with a dusky red substance. It wasn't. Still Arvo's hand felt dry and dusty, almost grimy from the man's touch.

Arvo ushered him inside his office. Arvo set his recorder on his desk and noticed the guy briefly hesitate, then eye the door.

Arvo grew irritated, wondering how much of his time the guy was going to waste. He'd have to be blunt. "If you have something to say about this crime, I need it on tape." A less experienced detective might have let the guy's discomfort rule, and put the recorder away. Arvo preferred the man leave, and leave now, if he had any hesitation at all. Arvo had better things to do.

"Oh, of course, no problem at all."

"Now, please tell me again. You said you were an engineer?"

Arndt cleared his throat, eyeing the recorder again. "Sorry, it's just stage fright."

Arvo could swear the guy's face grew several shades redder, which seemed impossible since it was in permanent blush mode already.

"There are a number of defects on the bridge that have been documented over time," he began. "I want to call your attention, oh, wait a moment." He reached into a battered leather briefcase he'd brought along and extracted a pile of papers. "Can we shut off the recorder for a moment? I don't want to waste your time," he said, his bloodshot eyes darting around. "I apologize for my disorganization."

Arvo left the tape running. He checked his watch. A few of Arndt's papers slid off Arvo's desk.

"I really do apologize. I know you're very busy."

Arvo held his frustration in check, but found himself tapping his fingers anyway. Everything told him this guy was probably a crank, but he knew better than to dismiss him out of hand.

"Take your time," Arvo said, wishing he didn't have to give the guy another moment. He caught another glimpse of the guy's strangely wrinkled, red hands. He could swear those things were leaving red marks on his desktop. Arndt still didn't say whether he was an engineer. Just that he had engineering information. He was exactly the kind of person he'd warned Ruud about. Cranks that turn up when stories get into the press.

"So you're an engineer then? Who do you work for?"

The man either didn't hear him or ignored his question.

"There we go," Arndt said, putting a few documents in front of Arvo. They appeared to have been printed from a website, judging by the footer on each page which showed an URL and a date.

"These are two key inspections of the swing bridge. One dates from five years ago and another, completed in the past year. I specifically wanted to call your attention to this one."

Arvo interrupted. "A moment. I'm sorry. I'm a little slow. I don't have your engineering background." Arvo wondered if the guy even had an engineering background. At the moment he was bleeding nothing but papers all over Arvo's desk and there was no evidence the man had any professional credentials of any kind. "Who did you say you work for?"

A text buzzed on Arvo's phone. It was Kieran. "Don't worry, we're checking him out."

"You see, right here," Arndt said pointing out a paragraph. "Based on this report, and corroborated, right here," he motioned to another page, "by the other. The bridge is due for replacement."

Arvo broke in. "Can you specifically explain how these . . ." Arvo swept his hands over the reports "say anything of the kind?" Arvo had spotted a few lines on the pages Arndt was waving around. "Over there I read 'eventual' replacement."

Arndt snatched up the paper. "Oh. That was the wrong report. One more moment. I apologize."

Arndt came up with another document. "This was the one I was looking for."

"This? Let me see. It's a newspaper piece." There seemed to be no official reports of any kind in the man's possession.

Arvo read the story briefly. It called for immediate replacement of the bridge with an interstate crossing. It referenced other editorials, written apparently by parties opposed to replacing the bridge, and pointed out all the errors of the opposition's 'supposed' engineering reports, which stated there was nothing wrong with the bridge.

"It's from the editorial page," Arvo said. "It doesn't even say who wrote the piece, that part is cut off. I can't see what you are doing here, other than wasting my time."

Arvo had had it with newspapers. Was his job being ruled by the opinion pages of the local rags?

"You have exactly one minute to provide me with credible evidence. A real engineering report, not some claptrap printed off a website or some blowhard's letter to the editor."

The man's taconite-red, wrinkled hands began to shake. "I can honestly say," the man began, "that I know that bridge is doomed. Anyone can see from what happened to that poor man. It was an accident waiting to happen. There's no murderer, other than the bridge itself. The evidence is all here in front of you, but like everyone else you don't want to believe it. It has taken nothing less than the death of this man to bring the bridge's true condition to light."

"That's it?" Arvo said. "That's all you have to say?"

"Yes." The man began to gather up his papers. "It's obvious you aren't interested in the facts, which are plain for anyone to see."

"One last question." Arvo hesitated to ask, but he knew he had to. "Where can we reach you if we need to follow up?"

"I don't know why you'd even bother," the man said. He shoved the papers back in his brief case, his shaking hands making an even bigger mess.

"I'm not sure why you bothered to come down here in the first place," Arvo said, shutting off his recorder.

The man left without further comment and the next person he saw at the door was Sam. Arvo asked him what Kieran had learned about the guy.

"He's still looking. I'm guessing you want us to continue, right?"

Arvo wished he could tell them not to bother, but he didn't. His hands still felt strange from the guy's touch. "Yes. Damn it."

Arvo went in search of Juney. "I thought you said that coroner's report was coming in."

"It is. Arvo, we'll have it in the next few hours. Why are you so jittery? Go, get out of here for a while. I'll let you know the moment it arrives. You mentioned a May basket?"

He shrugged.

"So where are my goddamned flowers?" Juney sniffed.

He'd meant it as a joke, but then he realized she was right. A break from the office, especially after what he'd been through for the past few hours, would probably help.

"Just promise me you'll let me know," he said.

"You got it. I want my flowers when you get back."

He pointed to his derriere.

"Yeah? Kiss mine too." She walked away from him. "Asshole."

Nineteen

ARVO DROVE AROUND AIMLESSLY. He had no idea where he might find a florist, even if he wanted to bring back a May basket for Juney. It had been some time since he bought a woman flowers, and his past efforts in the floral area had mixed results. Either his timing or his taste was off, sometimes both, and it was possible Juney was joking and really didn't expect anything.

Her husband was long dead, her dating days were far behind her, but that didn't necessarily mean that she never wanted a bouquet the rest of her life. She was a woman, after all.

Instead of resolving his May basket dilemma, he took care of other pressing business. He realized he hadn't eaten anything yet, so he thought the best spot to kill time might be one that offered some food. So he headed to the Good Food cafe and Nichol stuffed him with more caramel rolls than he should have. An hour or two passed during which no call came in alerting Arvo that the impending coroner's report had finally been issued.

"Well, it's past noon. I may as well get your lunch for you," Nichol said. "The roast beef sandwich is today's special." She filled his coffee cup again.

"That the one with Wonder bread? Real mashed potatoes?" He was drooling and he knew he shouldn't be hungry at all. He felt for his paunch.

"It's still there," Nichol nodded. "Same as yesterday. You should come running with me."

"You?" he said. "Run? You have time to run?"

"My mom always said—well, when she was sober enough to make sense—'if you want something done, give it to a busy person.'"

"Let me guess . . ." Arvo said, "you were the one she turned to when she need something done."

"Yep. Though in those days, it was mostly half-assed. But my little brothers got square meals, at least once a day," she said winking. "So what do you say?"

"Serve it up. Put extra gravy on it too."

She sauntered off.

While he waited he checked his phone, but nothing came in. *What the hell is taking so long?*

He licked his plate clean and there was still no word, even after he'd paid his bill. Since there was really nothing left to do, he asked Nichol for a florist recommendation. He'd be forced to buy flowers after all. It was the only way Juney might allow his early return to the office. They both knew that while there were many other cases demanding attention, this high priority bridge death needed to get pushed along before anything else.

"Oh. Who's the lucky girl?"

"Juney."

She laughed. "How is the old gal? She's beyond cougar material isn't she?"

"Cougar? Hell is that code for 'hot fifty-year-old'? Well, Juney and I are strictly professional. I was told to return with a May basket. Or else. I know enough not to mess with her orders. And even an old broad like Juney deserves flowers once in a while. Cougar." He shook his head at the term. In his day, one might call a sexy older woman *foxy*. As in cunning and mysterious. Cougar suggested a sort of predatory woman of a certain age, but not yet past her prime. He knew the type. He'd been married to one.

"The mini-market next door might have something," Nichol said.

"Oh, I don't know, Nichol. Sounds a little trashy."

"Then go to Brach's. The little nursery in town. It's not too far from the county building. But next May I'll be expecting flowers, too."

"I know. I'm setting a precedent I'll wish I hadn't."

Cranky old Gladys Brach ran her little garden store like a tyrant. She was an offshoot of a gardening family dynasty, but she was the lesser-known, weird, runty aunt who'd been plucked out and discarded like a noxious weed. The healthier and more prosperous part of the family had a huge mega-nursery a few suburbs away. Well they could toss her out, but she wouldn't be kept down. She sprouted her own little place, and lived in a back room like a hermit. The old-timers in Somerset Hills preferred her no-nonsense approach to the big-box nursery of the overgrown scions across town.

Gladys spotted indecision from a mile away, and had no tolerance for browsers or amateurs. "May basket? Bah! You don't want that," she said, quickly dismissing whoever had put that idea into Arvo's head. "May baskets are for kids."

She let herself down from the shaky three-legged stool behind the cash register and bustled away to the back of her dirty shop, which frankly stunk of cigarette smoke, ruining any floral bouquet that might have sweetly scented the air.

Arvo understood too well her mindset—the uncomfortable visit of Matthew Arndt quickly coming to mind. She hated it when amateurs wasted her time. So he gratefully accepted her not-too-subtle upsell and left with an expensive spring flower arrangement in a crystal bowl.

To his eyes, it was a fine collection of pastel-colored blooms he couldn't name. They had the appearance of wildflowers gathered from a Somerset Hills' meadow, though meadows had not existed in Somerset Hills for quite some time, given all the suburban growth of the past decades. Yet the bouquet convinced him that there must be a few quiet meadows to be found. A charming aroma began to fill his nose, and once he was outside the shop, all he smelled was the cool, delicious fragrance of spring.

The full stomach, the pleasant hours with Nichol, and the spring bouquet gave him a sense of calm purposefulness that often evaded him. *Well-being*, he thought. This was what well-being felt like. He'd rarely experienced it, he knew. He tried to remember when he'd last had a whiff of it, the scent of the flowers filling his car interior now. Not during his marriage with Helen, that was for sure. The excitement she caused was the opposite of well-being. In fact, in those early years he would have found well-being, well, a little dull. It was thrilling to the very core to be with Helen. Arvo hadn't realized how rare it was to have, as his first love, the kind of passion that only seemed possible in Hollywood movies and storybooks.

From the very beginning of their relationship—when both were popular high school kids in that first flush of lust—Helen had gripped his heart and body with a mad, overpowering magnetism that left him incapable of keeping his mind and hands off of her. Except for when he had been in the middle of quarterbacking a football game, he was unable to get Helen out of his thoughts. He'd barely made passing grades, and did the worst when Helen was in the same class as he was. He flunked literature and history, but managed to score A's in math and science classes. Helen never signed up for those. It was only because he'd aced those classes, and managed to deliver a solid result on his pre-college tests, that despite his mind-emptying lust for Helen he got accepted. How he made it through college he didn't know. The haze of parties, particularly the swirl and deception of Helen, made everything from those years blur.

Helen knew that the best way to keep Arvo's interest was to withhold her charms, and there was no one better at holding back than Helen. But those moments when she gave in to him were the highest of highs. She seemed to give off a chemical that, had it been bottled, might have helped scientists discover the perfect cure for erectile dysfunction, years before Viagra. There was no erectile dysfunction around Helen. So when she did begin to push him away, then eventually hurt him by cheating on him with other men, Arvo only blamed himself.

He'd loved her and wanted her too much.

He actually felt sorrier for her than he did for himself in those sad, final years of their marriage. He knew that it was his overwhelming passion that caused her to look outside their marriage for solace and comfort in other men's arms. When he thought about his logic with regard to her cheating, he knew it seemed more twisted than logical. The times he'd thought of explaining why his marriage fell apart he knew he could never explain it to others the way he perfectly understood it, though few asked anyway. Guys didn't talk to guys about relationships, and he wasn't interested in women who wanted to talk about relationships. Any suggestion that therapy might help him he scoffed at. The way to overcome a weakness was to avoid thinking about it. That philosophy had served his stoic Scandinavian ancestors. It would work for him.

But given the right circumstance, he could easily fall under her sway once again with little trouble. He craved her kind of love the way addicts craved a fix. It was that desperation for the unrequited fix that always led directly to the first drink. The drinks that followed were a foregone conclusion of that first one. The cycle of his attraction to Helen, her reaction to him, and his subsequent response were all linked in a death spiral, he knew all too well, and sometimes that knowledge kept him from the first drink.

For a moment he'd considered driving by her place and dropping the bouquet off. The cycle always started with some attempt to win her approval. Helen would have hated the flowers he was bringing to Juney. She wanted flowers that made a statement, not small tasteful, pastel arrangements. He recalled her roughly shoving a vase off their dining room table in a snit once, claiming they were fit only for a funeral or an elderly grandmother and who did he think she was.

So, no, these were not her type of flowers. She would not have approved, and that recognition prevented him from one cycle of the pattern. Anxiety quivered at the edge of his sense of well-being. One thought of Helen could change the course of his whole day, and many, many other days after. Really, all he wanted was to link a few moments of peace together, and feel normal.

So he took another deep breath, bathing his lungs with the delicate scents around him and found a way to relax once more. When he turned off his engine in the Mendota County Building parking lot, he felt calmer again.

He stepped through the doors of the building and was ribbed by the cops minding the scanner. Once he passed through he saw Christine, struggling with a box she was carrying off the elevator.

She set it down on a lobby table, and opened the box to adjust whatever was causing the contents to shift around, and then she saw him, flowers in hand. He'd have to talk to her, whether he wanted to or not, but her startling new look left him dumbfounded.

"Those are nice," she said neutrally, glancing at the flowers. "Freesia, lavender, lily of the valley." She rattled off the names of the flowers in an almost robotic manner.

"You wouldn't know this," she pointed out, "but people associate the lily of the valley with a 'return to happiness.'"

For a moment he wondered if she thought he was bringing them to her. For a moment he thought of giving them to her. A *return to happiness*, was that what she said? That thought passed quickly, too. The look she gave him suggested that she wanted flowers from him about as much as she wanted him to throw acid on her.

"Well, you're going to make some girl's day, I can see that." She had a haughty, cold look to her expression, which seemed to complement the new hairdo and unsexy wardrobe of her most recent personal makeover. He'd noticed her new look a week earlier, spotting her from the distance, and wasn't terribly surprised by it, even though it was the most shocking of her changes over the years. Up close, she looked positively scary.

He stammered. "They're for Juney. Kind of started as a joke."

"Oh. Well, that's thoughtful of you," she said sarcastically. "So you only give women flowers as a joke? Not much for sentimental moments, are you?"

The tone suggested he'd never been terribly thoughtful in her regard. He was ready to beg to differ, but then he noticed what was in her box. Her framed diplomas and commendations. Recognitions of her years of service to the county. Photos of her at award ceremonies. Knick-knacks, the ornate wooden boxes, and other desktop items he remembered from her office.

His puzzled expression presented the questions he didn't want to ask, but couldn't ignore.

"I'm leaving," she answered to his unspoken question.

He stood in front of her, not trying to bar her way but unable to move. The well-being he had experienced just minutes earlier evaporated. Good feelings were apparently like true love: a pretty arrangement of cut flowers, immediately doomed to die. That was why he rarely bothered with the flowers—you killed them, and used the fragrance of their dying beauty to express your undying love. Not only did it seem ironic, but it was somehow just completely sick in a way, when you thought about it. No wonder it had never worked out for him to give a woman flowers.

"Where?" was all he could manage to say.

"I've got a couple of solid prospects in the city. But with so much vacation time, I thought I'd just request a leave of absence for now."

"So you're not coming back here at all?"

"Today's my official last day."

He wanted to ask why, but he knew she didn't want to answer that question. And maybe he didn't really want to know how much he figured into her decision. He still cared enough for her that he didn't want to force her to lie and say something about it not being him. They both knew their soured relationship had played a role in her decision. And the crappy mood he'd been in for the past weeks.

"Look. It's not really you. It's me." She said it anyway, and with her new look—the buzzed-off hair colored an outraged, bruised purple had "back off, Arvo," written all over it. "I've needed a change for sometime."

She picked up the box again and left him standing there, speechless, passing by security and exiting to the parking lot without another word.

There was no point in following her, but for a few moments Arvo thought of waiting long enough to be sure she was gone, then calling it a day. They still had one thing in common: both looked for some outside stimulus, whether that was the passion of a love affair, or the excitement of a new wardrobe, or a fresh bottle of booze—something, anything, to dress up or cover up or just basically ignore what was really wrong. But sooner or later the new look got old, passion died, or you woke up the next day with a headache and a hangover and the same old problems were still there.

Maybe she was right.

The only way out of the mess was a fresh start. Well, she'd have hers sooner than he'd have his. Good luck to her.

The bitch.

Arvo finally responded to the insistent buzzing of his phone. It was Juney. No, the coroner's report wasn't yet in, but the engineer's report was. It was waiting for him in the basement. He'd better have a hell of a good excuse, or flowers, to explain why he'd been ignoring her messages.

Her text wasn't quite that detailed, but Arvo could read between the lines of the expletive-laden messages. If there was one woman he understood, it was beyond-Cougar-age Juney Janette.

He didn't have a good excuse for her, but thank god for Gladys Brach's good sense to upsell him a decent floral arrangement.

Return to happiness? He was just hoping to survive another day mostly unscathed. He was relieved to hear there was work waiting for him in the basement. To hell with Christine Ivory and her messed up "it's not you, it's me," speech. For once it could be all her.

TWENTY

T HE SIGHT OF ARVO CARRYING A DELICATE arrangement of flowers might ordinarily cause a lot of laughter in the cramped, dank, subterranean investigation department of Mendota County. On a typical day, it might have invited an afternoon of expletive-laden ribbing, lots of guffaws. In particular, Juney Janette would ordinarily have made a number of juicy, arch comments in her baby-doll voice, which strangers quickly learned was *not* an affectation but in fact her actual range, though if they messed with her about it she'd soon make it clear in no uncertain terms that she wasn't to be trifled with.

Under normal circumstances, there would have been an extended repartee amongst the staff about Arvo's bedroom skills, who he might be trying to woo with the flowers. Some might have even hinted Christine, even though it had been common office knowledge that the two were on the skids. Office humor in a homicide wing could inflict wounds, but they were typically flesh wounds, and the instigator expected a parry in return, nothing serious. The highlight of such antics, on a more normal day, would have been Arvo's presentation of the flowers to Juney Janette, executed with an exaggerated bow. Raucous laughter would have ensued, highlighted with a shouted remark by someone (and emphasized with a few graphic gestures) insinuating perhaps that Arvo had more to gain from a liaison with Juney than the opposite. Days later, laughter would still erupt at the sight of the flowers on the evidence clerk's desk.

But nothing like that happened. Arvo set the flowers on her desk, and everyone saw the bitter look on his face, including Juney. She issued an out-of-character and simple "thanks" and he slammed his office door behind him.

Arvo bellowed for Sam and Kieran. They arrived outside his door moments later, knocking gently to alert him they'd arrived.

"For chrissake, just come in." Arvo presented them with a wounded face, and he saw them register some shock. He moved on.

Arvo held up a document. "I need an interpretation of this gobblety gook." He took in the contrasting pair of unlikely friends—the almost willowy Kieran and the sprite-like Sam—as an unintelligible series of unspoken communication was transmitted between them. He thought space aliens were visiting him. An agreement was apparently quickly reached and it was the computer geek Kieran who spoke.

"It's the official report of the most recent bridge inspection."

"Haven't we already looked at this? You showed me a report a few weeks ago. Right after the accident. The thing had been classified as . . . a . . . death trap."

"Structurally deficient." Sam offered.

"Yes. Structurally deficient. Like I said. A death trap. So why do I receive an urgent page for old information?"

"Uhhh. That's not what's in your hands." Kieran said. He glanced at Sam, seeing if he could explain better.

Sam took the next tenuous step, and quietly spoke up. "Look at the date on the top. Two months ago."

"The hell. Where?" Arvo demanded.

"Eighth of March of this year," the youthful intern said, with an uncertain look on his face.

"Why do they put the day before the month? Damn it. That's what confused me." Arvo searched the young men's stricken faces, and he was about to scream at them when he realized that it was his grouchy outbursts that makes them uncomfortable. He needed the information locked inside their geeky brains and his bad mood was getting in the way.

Give it a rest, he thought to himself, his mouth feeling parched, the familiar thirst insinuating itself at the back of his throat, screaming at the base of his skull. He excused himself and stalked out of his office, telling them he'd be back in a moment. Arvo walked down the corridor to the break room, remembering that he used to stash booze in his locker, but knowing nothing was in there and those days needed to remain behind him, at least for the day.

He entered the break room and opened the spigot on the kitchen sink.

Get a grip, he told himself, staring at his reflection in a paper towel dispenser. He could swear he saw a weary old man's face staring back at him, not too far from the look he remembered from his father waking up from yet another hangover. *Just focus on the next hour.*

He stuck his face under the running water and let its cool river restore him, greedily slurping from the tap like a dehydrated dog. He followed up by splashing handfuls of water on his face, rubbing it over his face with vigor, and splashing some on the back of his neck to help loosen the tense muscles that had been aching since the moment he spied Christine.

He would not let her, or any other woman, get in the way of his job for the rest of the day.

A damp, calmer Arvo returned to the office, noting that Juney had removed the flowers to a less noticeable area inside the evidence room. Everyone was walking on eggshells around him, trying to avoid irritating his obvious wound.

"So this report is from two months ago?" he said.

"It didn't turn up earlier," Kiernan offered.

"Why was that? I thought you could find anything in thirty seconds, Kieran.

"Hadn't been finalized," he said. "If it's not on the web, it's hard to find. It was Sam who located it."

"Sam?" Arvo looked at the intern.

"I made a few phone calls," Sam said.

Arvo smiled for the first time in an hour, and he saw the young men relax. "Old school. Phone calls. I like it."

Arvo pored over the report, flipping through a few pages, and then looking up with a perplexed look.

"Is there, a problem?" Kieran asked. "Something that doesn't make sense?"

"I didn't see that phrase. What was it? Structurally deficient? Is there something wrong with the report? This is for the Stone Island Swing Bridge. Right?

Sam came around to Arvo's side of the desk and ran a finger over the report. "Yep. That's it. Says right here. You had me going for a minute. Not sure how they would have given me the wrong one."

"May I?" Kieran asked.

"What does that mean, anyway? Structurally deficient? That was what the other report said. Right?"

Kieran spoke, still perusing the current report. "The term 'structurally deficient' was created by bridge engineers to classify a bridge is in need of maintenance, rehabilitation, or sometimes replacement."

"But doesn't that mean it just gets shut down? End of story?" Arvo said.

"Nope," Kieran said.

"Really?" Arvo said. "I thought that meant exactly that."

"It just gets posted for restricted loads until the necessary repair is done. Sometimes it means the bridge needs to be replaced," Kieran stated.

"And what did that earlier report say?" Arvo asked.

"Just said that loads were restricted," Sam recalled.

"So does this report say the bridge needs repair or replacement. Or is still deficient?" Arvo wanted to be perfectly clear on the bridge's status.

Kieran continued reading through the report, Sam now at his side. Sam pointed to a phrase or two and read "scheduled maintenance work was completed in the past year . . ."

"While he reads this thing, can you explain the process more? Did you ask the person you spoke to," Arvo emphasized the word spoke, "What they look at?"

"Yes," Sam began. "Mainly it's five areas. Deck, superstructure, substructure, structural evaluation, and waterway adequacy. Each item is rated on a scale of zero to nine, where zero means bridge closed and nine means excellent condition."

"What's a failing grade?" Arvo asked.

"A bridge with a condition rating of four or less for the deck, superstructure, or substructure or an appraisal rating of two or less for structural evaluation or waterway adequacy is classified as structurally deficient. But remember," Sam said, clearly in his element, "This still doesn't need they mean to close the bridge. They just need to post load limits."

And this report here," Arvo said pointing at the report, "Is from a full month before the accident. Right?"

"Right."

"So, Kieran, what's the report card read?" Arvo asked.

"Sixes and sevens." Kieran smiled.

"The earlier one had a three on the deck," Sam added. "That's what made it structurally deficient back then."

"So a month before the accident it had passing grades. Right?"

Kieran looked at him. "Right."

Sam nodded.

Arvo went on. "And the bridge engineers that wrote this report . . . It's official right?"

"Swear it is," Sam said. "I picked it up from the Highway Department myself."

Arvo patted him on the shoulder. "That's my boy."

Arvo pushed back from his desk. "Son of a bitch," he said shaking his head. "Son . . . of . . . a . . . bitch. There was nothing wrong with the bridge. Nothing at all."

"That's what we understand from the report." Kieran said.

Arvo turned his attention to Sam. "Did you confirm that? Did you speak to the guy who wrote this up?"

A grin grew and widened on Sam's face. "Of course!" he said proudly. "That's what you've been telling me to do. Go to the source."

"And what, pray tell," Arvo said, "did they say about this bridge's capacity for carrying a fully loaded freight train and full load of cars at the same time?"

"They said it was fine. No problem."

"Son . . . of . . . a . . . bitch."

"I've scheduled some face time for you with this engineer," Sam announced. "Unless you just want to talk to him on the phone, in which case he's available later this afternoon."

"Let's call him," Arvo said eagerly. "I want to hear the guy tell me there was nothing wrong with this bridge. Did he look at the crime scene photos? The taconite?"

"Yes, he did," Sam reported. "There hasn't been time to get an official report through their system yet, but he has some preliminary results he'd feel comfortable sharing."

Arvo's day began to look up. "Well then, I'd like them shared. Today."

"Three o'clock soon enough for you?" Sam said.

"That would be soon enough. Oh, one more thing. Have you tracked down that character that came in here, Arndt was it?" Arvo asked. "The guy full of info but no apparent credentials."

"Yes, we have," Kieran said.

"Schedule some more face-time with him. But not here. I want to see where this guy with the hereditary . . . what was it?"

"Hereditary hemochromatosis," Sam piped up.

"Yes. I want to see him in his lair, or near it." Arvo got up from his chair and got ready to head out. "And by the way, try and be available, Sam, to come along. You seem to have a knack for real detective work."

"You," Arvo said pointing to Kieran. "I want research, lots of it, on motorcycle experts. Where's the best place near here to find people who might sell, or know a lot, about street bikes. Find out if we can get that kid, Nick McQuillen, to join us for an outing to a bike shop. We need to ID whatever motorcycle it was he heard or saw. This case has been dragging its sorry ass for long enough."

Arvo knew he'd been dragging his own sorry ass long enough too.

There was no more time for that. Apparently there was a murderer still on the loose, one who would go to extreme lengths not only to kill a bridge operator, but also to endanger the lives of countless citizens of Somerset Hills, regular folk who crossed the bridge everyday, the many regularly loaded freight trains that supplied the North Country with food and fuel, and were refilled with valuable exports from the region—grain from the plains and iron ore from the range—bread and metal for a hungry world.

A bridge breakdown could put the busy river shipping season on standstill as well. The effect of someone tampering with a bridge that commerce depended on was bad enough, but the fact that many more lives could have been lost that day had an even more disastrous result occurred was horrible to consider. There was no telling if the perpetrator would make another attempt to keep the bridge out of commission, permanently.

"But isn't the kid still under suspicion?" Kieran asked. "Now that it's looking clearer the bridge may have been tampered with?"

"How's that saying go? Keep your friends close, your enemies closer? In either case he needs to be somewhere nearby we can keep an eye on him. While we're figuring out whether he belongs behind bars or free and clear to unicycle wherever he likes."

Arvo was halfway across the office when he stopped and issued one last order.

"Changed my mind about the meeting with the engineer. See if he can meet us at the bridge. He may be able to give us a better idea whether this boy is a friend or enemy. I want to know, from a *real* bridge engineer, what it takes to break that bridge down. If a mere kid can do it, then maybe they should condemn the goddamned thing. Aren't we in the age of child-proofing everything? Chrissakes you can't even get on a plane without passing through multiple layers of security."

Arvo had one thing to do before he moved on. There was one woman he knew he'd been unfair with. He made his way to the evidence room and casually enquired of its occupant what she thought of her May basket.

"You're such a jackass, Arvo. I don't need second-hand flowers, by the way."

"What do you mean by that?"

"You know what I mean. I saw the two of you," she looked up, "in the lobby this morning. I don't want Christine Ivory's rejects."

"Those flowers were never intended for her. Trust me on this one. The look on her face when she saw me coming . . ." He remembered. What had happened to last year's Christine Ivory? The one who'd respected, and yes, almost loved him. Until a few days ago.

She was partly wrong. The blame wasn't all on her shoulders. And it wasn't all on his either. The two of them had no business being in a relationship, and certainly not with each other. If anything was structurally deficient, it was the combination of Arvo and Christine.

"You're still a jackass in my book," she squeaked.

"That's just what I wanted to hear, precious. Wait till next year, Juney. It'll be like a funeral parlor inside here. Speaking of that, where is that autopsy report? I don't have until next May to get this thing figured out."

"I'm on it," she said. She even almost smiled at him. Nothing cheered Arvo up more than an investigation that had just been cracked wide open.

TWENTY-ONE

THE "ROAD CLOSED" SIGNS WERE STILL in place at the swing bridge later that first day of May—a full three weeks since Karl Lutz's death—when Arvo arrived there for his and Sam's meeting with the Minnesota Department of Transportation bridge inspector. The investigator and the intern had driven separately as Arvo had another meeting planned afterwards, and he wasn't ready to involve his intern in the seedier location where Arvo's interview was being conducted.

The town was unified in their disgust with the slow pace of repair. In fact, repair work was not at all evident as none was being done. Which led to even more disgust. Detours took everyone miles out of their way and were fraying tempers across town.

The engineer had a few choice words to explain why repair work was not being completed. "There's not a damn thing wrong with it."

"Say that again?" Arvo asked.

"There's nothing wrong with this bridge." Jim Schneider, the crotchety sixty-year-old bridge inspector seemed annoyed that the bridge was still closed down. He lived in Somerset Hills and always took the swing bridge to his job in the city.

"Look. I'm a head bridge inspector, the top inspector in the state, which means not only do I have a structural and civil engineering background, but people count on me to determine whether a bridge is safe or not. And believe me, if I make a mistake, and some bridge goes down, there's hell to pay in my department and jobs are on the line. Beyond that, I worry every day about the conditions of some of the bridges in the state. There's no one more concerned than me about how bridges are holding up, and the consequences to everyone when they don't.

"I've been in this business for forty years and I've looked at every bridge in this goddamned state, more than once. I'm telling you, I drive across this goddamned bridge everyday. Every day. Well, a' course *now* I can't exactly do that, but I would be, if it were open. If I had my way, the signs you see out there would be down in a flash."

The man chomped on his cigar and took another look over the side of the bridge near the pilothouse control room, then adjusted his trousers, which were sagging under his enormous belly, but secured with a heavy-duty pair of gray suspenders.

"I've had my team look over every inch of this thing, top to bottom, just a few months back. We had to since it was a follow up from the inspection a few years earlier."

The inspection report Arvo had seen just after the accident. "Was that when it was deemed 'structurally deficient'?"

"That was the one. It was really a modest problem with the decking, because even then the bridge was still as solid as a rock. The county resurfaced the bridge, as we'd suggested, and the thing was closed a few days at most during that process. Even then, closure wasn't necessary."

Sam asked a question. "Why is it that this bridge has such a bad reputation? If it's so safe."

"Let me ask you a question," the engineer said. "If it's so unsafe, why are most people on my case to get the thing reopened? Except for a small, very vocal minority who want the thing condemned and taken down."

Arvo's ears perked up. "Let's come back to that vocal minority. First I want to ask you a few questions, if you don't mind."

Schneider sighed. "Sure." He shifted around his unlit stogie and walked with Arvo and Sam to the pilothouse.

"We've sent the crime scene pictures down to the Department of Transportation, and asked that a complete inspection be done, since, as you know, the operator died out here and we're investigating what caused his death." Arvo paused, seeing that he was getting on the guy's nerves.

Schneider said. "What do you think, I didn't know that? That my department is slacking?"

"All I know is that my department hasn't gotten a response," Arvo said, without apologizing. Schneider seemed like a solid guy, but he needed a leash, not a reward.

Schneider huffed on his unlit cigar with irritation. "I'm the guy who looked at the pictures and came out here a few days after the accident to conduct the investigation."

"I'm sorry for imposing on you, asking you questions you've already answered. But has that report been finalized?"

"I don't have to tell you twice that bureaucracy slows things down."

"No kidding." Arvo nodded. "I practically have to give birth to triplets while doing a handstand to order a stapler. I won't tell you what they make me do to actually get one."

"I think we understand each other perfectly, detective."

"So what happened to the report?"

"I wrapped it up weeks ago and sent it on. It hasn't made it back to your department yet?"

"No."

"Well the thing made lightning speed in my group. Why? I'll tell you it isn't because law enforcement or the media is breathing down my neck. My people are focused only on safety. That's it. We don't answer to law enforcement and we don't answer to the media."

Schneider was so whipped up he was pacing, still furiously chomping on the unlit cigar. "There are two factors that impact safety: design and maintenance. Good design and solid maintenance mean a safe structure. Miss one or the other, and you're screwed. But here's the kicker on this bridge. It may not be pretty, but because it's been designed well, that's why it's been in operation so long. Maintenance has been an issue over time, but we've kept a close watch on it. The review in my department went quickly because basically nothing had changed since we were out here in

March. Not one thing. Well, of course there was that big bloodstain. What a mess that was, but it didn't contribute to any safety problem with the bridge."

"So you finished your review, completed the report and sent it on."

"Yes. Apparently whatever is delaying it happened when the report left my department."

"Ask him about the taconite," Sam whispered.

"Taconite?" the engineer asked.

"Yes," Arvo said. "We noticed a pile of taconite that seemed out of place under the cable housing. We wondered if the machinery had been jammed? Maybe on purpose?"

"Yes. Let's go take a look at that taconite, shall we?" The engineer again adjusted his trousers under his belly, an unnecessary flourish as the suspenders seemed to be doing their job and the belly wasn't going anywhere, even though it looked precariously perched above such skinny legs. The man seemed to have no problem getting around, and Arvo and Sam hurried to keep up with him.

He took the two men to the area they'd just mentioned, and there lay the pile of taconite under the cables, still undisturbed.

Schneider gathered handfuls of the material and stuffed as many as he could into the cable housing, where Arvo and Sam could clearly see the thick cable would be wrapping the next time the bridge was operated.

"Who'd like to play swing bridge operator?" the engineer asked with a hint of glee. "How about the bright-eyed young man, there. Sam? Like to take it for a spin?"

"Are you sure this is a good idea?" Sam asked, quickly seeing that he'd insulted the state's bridge expert.

"If you don't want to, I'd love to take a shot at it." Arvo said quickly, before his intern got an earful from Schneider. He was actually surprised to find himself looking forward to playing with the big toy. Though the day had nose-dived on him midday, things were really looking up.

"Age before beauty," Schneider said, extracting a large set of keys from his pocket. He unlocked the control booth quickly.

"Young man," he said, turning to Sam once more. "Do you mind watching the cable roll? Keep your eye on the taconite and let us know what happens."

"Won't it jam up? Like it did during the accident?" Sam had a stricken look on his face.

"Oh, is that what you think happened? The taconite jammed up the machinery and somehow poor Karl Lutz got killed?" Schneider mocked the intern's hypothesis with a dismissive chomp of his cigar. "If that's what you really think, then please, you had better keep a close watch on that reel. You'll get all the evidence you need that will tell you what this magnificent piece of machinery is capable of."

He removed a pencil from his pocket and set it right where the next portion of cable would wrap the reel. Sam gave him a quizzical look

"Keep an eye on that pencil, too. Detective Thorson, right this way." Schneider pointed in the direction of the control panel. "You're in for a real treat. Not everyone gets to command a magnificent old man like this one. I hope you have a steady pair of hands."

Arvo hoped he did, too.

TWENTY-TWO

Arvo stood in front of the swing bridge control panel, almost giddy. "Do I need a license to operate this thing?"

"Not with me standing next to you," Schneider said. "Didn't that boy manage to operate the bridge by himself? With absolutely no instruction?"

"That's the story." Arvo said. "Lutz was certainly in no condition to operate the thing."

"A little secret: although operating the bridge isn't quite as simple as throwing a switch, it's not exactly brain surgery." He handed a key to Arvo and pointed to the ignition. Arvo fired up the equipment, and the engine rumbled to life from some depth underneath the operator's shed. The thick vibrations could be felt through the instrument panel, reverberating into his forearms. He'd never felt such power, and the idea that he could operate the bridge he'd known all his life energized him.

"First of course you should check for river traffic."

It was a little early in the boating season for river traffic, but they were close to a busy marina and the shipping season, which should have started weeks earlier, had been delayed by the bridge closure.

"How is that accomplished exactly?" he asked.

"Well they actually need to look out for us more than we need to look out for them. Just give this button three solid pushes."

The bridge horn sounded a deafening burst. When Arvo heard it, he knew exactly how long to wait before hitting it a second, then a third time. Every child who grew up in Somerset Hills knew the pattern it made in its call and response to river traffic. As the river was empty, there was no response.

"First of course we need to shut the traffic gates. Even though the signs say "closed" on the roadway, and trains have been rerouted, the step is necessary."

"So there is a separate step you take to close the warning fence for the traffic."

"That's right."

Arvo was thinking about the motorcyclist the boy mentioned. The gates must have been left open when the bridge opened during the accident.

Schneider began Arvo's bridge operation education. "Now, there are two ways to operate the bridge. Most operators prefer to use the manual controls—and typically the operators open and close the swing through these levers." The engineer explained to Arvo how the mechanism worked, and it seemed not much more complicated than operating a lawn mower. "Just start out slow. You'll get into the swing of it."

Arvo gave the man a look.

"Just a little bridge engineer humor," Schneider said, his ire apparently in check.

"What's the other way the bridge is operated?" Arvo asked.

"Well of course there is an automatic switch, right here. You have to fiddle with some of the settings you see on this side of the panel to use the automatic control, depending upon weather conditions, but it's really not that difficult. You just hit the switch and off it goes. It's kind of like setting auto-pilot on an airplane."

So if a perpetrator had hit the switch to automatically operate the bridge, they knew enough to leave the security fence open to enable the getaway. Or perhaps dumb luck kept them from setting it correctly in the first place.

To tell you the honest truth," Schneider said, "I think most of the old-timers like the levers because it's more fun to open and close the bridge that way. Boys will always be boys"

"I'll use the fun method then."

Arvo slid the levers just as the engineer had demonstrated, and the bridge began to pivot on its axis. A few loud clanks sounded, just as the engineer had told him would happen when the bridge initially separated from the stable spans. There were various metallic groans as the materials flexed to muscle the swing arm, and the large structure spun on its axis, but other than that, the only sound that told anyone the bridge was operating came from the throbbing motors that rolled the cables through reels and made the bridge move.

Once the bridge had completely opened, the engineer cut the engine.

"Let's go see what happened to the taconite. Shall we?"

Sam was standing still near the cable reel. When he heard Arvo and Schneider approaching, he stepped aside. The taconite had fallen from the cable reel back into the same pile it had been in when they first arrived.

"So did any cataclysm occur? Did the taconite jam up the cables and cause the bridge to malfunction?"

Sam shook his head sheepishly.

"But what happened to the pencil?"

Sam held up the broken pieces he'd retrieved once the bridge stopped moving.

"Imagine, now, if that had been your finger?" The engineer said.

"Or a body?" Sam added.

Bloodstains were still clearly visible on the cable.

"From what we can understand so far, Karl Lutz got pulled into the cable reel, and was snapped in two when the bridge opened." Arvo said. "And that's all we know. Initially it looks like a freak accident, but the more you look into it, the more you question whether it was an accident at all."

"Exactly. How on earth did he get in there? Did he fall into it somehow?" Schneider cocked his head trying to make sense of it. "I mean, come on: how does an experienced swing bridge operator manage to get killed in equipment he's been operating and maintaining for years?"

"We don't have a coroner's report. We don't have toxicology back. We don't have anything yet that might tell us how that happened. Only a kid who arrived at the scene, apparently after it happened." Arvo kicked at a taconite pellet.

"So things are clogged up on your end, too?"

"Yep."

"Could there have been an altercation with the boy?" the engineer asked. "Maybe he got into a fight with Karl and pushed the guy into the cable reel?"

"Then the kid runs into the pilothouse and figures out how to start up the bridge, yet somehow keeps Karl from extracting himself from the reel in time? Seems pretty unlikely." Arvo thought more about Nick. He was a smart kid, who could focus if set to a task. He just needs to be kept busy, Christine had spotted that in a moment. An engaging puzzle kept him out of trouble. Much like Nick, Arvo needed the full engagement of challenging work to keep the rest of his life on track.

"I can't imagine any possible motivation for that kid that would cause him to get into a fight with Karl. He's just a kid, high-strung, bored, maybe a little on the hyperactive side, but a kid. He's got no other criminal history other than skipping out of school."

Now the bridge engineer took on the role of detective. "When you look at how angled the cable is as it wraps onto that reel, and you try do the calculation that results in a man basically being snapped in two—right there" the engineer said pointing to the blood-stained area of impact, "you can immediately also eliminate the possibility that the guy was wasted—on drugs or alcohol—and somehow climbed up there to take a nap. These guys get both regular and random drug and alcohol screening. Even if that did happen, let's say he blacks out due to a medical condition—then how did the bridge start moving? As I said, we looked at everything, top to bottom. There was no malfunction. Or, maybe Karl has become suicidal and decides to kill himself by having the bridge cut him in two. Somehow he has to lay down up there and start the bridge up. Not entirely possible. There isn't a timer on the switch. So the only circumstance that makes suicide by bridge possible is that the thing is already moving, and he comes back and jumps into the equipment. I just don't buy that."

"It's a remote possibility. The other one is that someone sticks him up there, and he can't escape, and the perpetrator hits the on switch," Arvo said. Either scenario seemed almost impossible, but there was no way to be sure.

"I can only hope the poor guy was unconscious, and didn't have time to know what hit him." Schneider said.

"I think he knew," Sam said.

"He's right." Arvo remembered the frozen look of horror on Lutz's dead face.

"Then the only person who knew the identity of the killer was Lutz. And he's not too much help to you at the moment."

"No he's not." Arvo said.

"It's a shame the whole thing has people convinced that this bridge should be condemned. As I told you, we've inspected it thoroughly. There's absolutely no reason to keep it closed." The engineer stuck his slimy, chomped-on cigar into his chest pocket.

"That reminds me of something else I want to know. If you have just a few more minutes," Arvo said.

"Well first we should close the swing. Maybe we let the rookie have a turn this time."

Sam gleefully accepted the challenge. Like Arvo, when instructed in both options for operating the bridge, Sam chose the levers over the switch.

Arvo watched as the young man operated the bridge, and felt it shudder in his inexperienced hands. Soon enough, Schneider took the controls and gently brought the swing span back in contact with the fixed ones. Karl had a good run out here on the river. Arvo wondered if the old bridge noticed his absence. The bridge was a fine instrument—like one of those expensive and sought-after Stradivarius violins—that Karl had all to himself all these years. He'd played it over the river for decades, answering the call for a duet from tugboats, stretching and relaxing its long cables to perform its melody of creaks and clanks, accompanied by its signature swing dance, a one-man/one-bridge concert for the audience of barges, tugs, and pleasure yachts.

"Sam," Arvo asked his intern when he had finished closing the bridge and had his performance thoroughly reviewed by the engineer. "What was the name of that guy who came forward with the bridge information?"

"That other engineer guy? Arndt. Matthew Arndt. "

"He never actually came right out and said he was an engineer, as I recall. And I asked him more than once," Thorson said to his intern. He was still pretty green.

"That's right. He didn't," Sam said, concurring.

"Do you know a guy named Matthew Arndt? He voluntarily came down to our office with a lot of documentation, none of it that appeared official."

"Arndt's the name?" The engineer thought briefly. "Never heard of him."

"I'm guessing you know every bridge engineer in this state," Arvo asked.

"That's right. I have all the sharp ones working for me and we evaluate all the bridge construction underway, so that brings my department into contact with everyone not working for me. And I never heard of this guy."

"He flashed a bunch of materials in front of us, most of it printed from the web. He didn't let us look at anything too long. Mostly he wanted us to look at newspaper editorials."

Schneider immediately spat. "I am constantly being asked to comment on these things. I hate it."

Sam spoke. "There has been a lot in the press from groups calling for the immediate replacement of this bridge with a brand new, multi-lane interstate crossing."

"The story he showed us referenced other editorials," Arvo said, "written apparently by parties opposed to replacing the bridge, and all of the reasons why those groups' opinions didn't count. In fact if I'm remembering, the article specifically called into question the 'official' engineering reports stating there is nothing wrong with the bridge."

"I'm far too familiar with the debate," the engineer said. "It's ridiculous. I spend too much time having to respond to these things when I should be out with my people in the field."

"Well the buck stops with you," Arvo said.

"Unfortunately. And I wouldn't want to waste any of my staff's time dealing with the media. I've got the best group of engineers and inspectors anywhere, and they need to be out, doing their jobs, unencumbered by political nonsense. So, yes, the buck stops with me. Gladly."

Schneider locked up the control room and said he was available for anything else Arvo needed, the sooner this case got wrapped up, the sooner the bridge could be reopened. Schneider said there were rumblings at the state that hearings were pending on the bridge, and he was afraid even with his expertise, the structure might be doomed if no other cause could be found for Lutz's death.

Arvo assured Schneider that he was as interested as Schneider was in getting the case solved. He thanked the man for his time, and had Sam accompany him back to his car. Arvo remained behind, alone on the bridge with his thoughts. He peered inside the control booth and remembered the feeling of the bridge under his control. He thought how simplified his own life might be if he had a job like this one, grimly reflecting that there was an opening available.

To have as one's only coworker an elderly but well-engineered piece of equipment, to spend long quiet hours in the operation booth, to have the occasional company of all types of birds, and to be suspended over the powerful and elemental Mississippi seemed like a dream job.

The river that expected nothing and gave its all, never complained of its burdens, the length of its workday, the demands it was expected to meet. Environmental regulation had helped return the river to a more pristine condition after many decades of abuse, and in spring it was in its glory. The cool air above the high, fast moving water was refreshing in its singular and muscular way. It recharged him. Arvo didn't consider himself a religious man—or one subject to new-age whims, but the river made him feel as if he was in the presence of a divine, otherworldly being.

Still, he knew himself well enough that the quiet, repetitive pace of a job like Karl's really wasn't for him, no matter how much he wished he could be a person who'd be satisfied with that type of job. Standing in a place that spun in circles around you, but never moved you forward, had already proven disastrous to him. The worst part of his life had that kind of motion. Helen had danced around him with her swirl of dizzying deceptions, and even when he knew she'd cheated on him, he'd stayed right there in the marriage, the world around him spinning out of control like a sickening carnival ride that wouldn't stop. He reacted by not reacting.

He knew he needed a focal point, not an axis. An actual destination, not a beautiful fantasy. The futile immobility had almost brought him down, and he reflected that Christine may have had the same motivation in leaving Mendota County. She'd tested his ability to focus, taken him outside of his comfort zone—which to be honest was actually quite a painful place—but the only man he knew how to be was the one Helen had trashed. He did not yet know how to be the man who could have made a decent companion to Christine, a woman who was not a beautiful fantasy but one who came with a dizzying universe of her own, one she attempted to control with color-coded labels, rigid schedules, the latest electronic devices, and, when none of that worked, a new wardrobe.

He realized how much he had in common with the irritable, stressed-out Schneider, much more than he did with a deceased bridge operator. Their demanding jobs helped keep the public safe. There really was no down time. Too many innocent lives were at stake if either of them missed a beat. Though Arvo didn't have people reporting to him like Schneider did, he was still responsible for bringing the next generation of capable investigators up.

The sun dropped below the western river bluffs and the western sky turned crimson while the refinery, just down river, glowed, not from the setting sun, but from long sequences of flashing warning lights on the pipes and towers that lit up as the sun went down. After dark, the refinery was a dazzling silver-white city, the bright lights both beacon and warning to the distant planes making their descent to the nearby airport.

Arvo checked his watch. He was due for a late meeting with his cop friend in the city in an hour, and he had to make a quick stop to collect some information from the informant his friend had asked him to check on. The next day would be packed, too. He'd arranged a meeting with Matthew Arndt and he'd heard, finally, that the coroner's report was ready to be released. For real this time, Juney promised.

Then, he knew, he needed to have another discussion with the boy. The visit to the bridge had surfaced as many questions as it answered. There was, however, an obstacle or two blocking his access to Nick McQuillen, and this being Mendota County, the detour was not clearly marked. Christine Ivory was gone, but her permission, and possibly presence, was needed in order for Arvo to interview the boy.

He left a message for Sam, directing him to contact Christine's office for another discussion with Nick. After hanging up, he thought there was no particular inflection to his voice when he said Christine's name. Maybe this one last interaction with her would be fine, and they could work together one last time, with no problem. They'd have to. He owed it to Karl Lutz, he owed it Schneider, who needed his goddamned bridge operating again and the press and the protest groups off his back. Most of all he needed to prove to himself that there was a least a possibility that he could be another man, maybe not the asshole Christine thought he was, and certainly not the one Helen had deceived, but a better man than he'd been to either of them. An asshole with integrity—like the state's chief bridge inspector. Jim Schneider was the type of man he aimed to be.

TWENTY-THREE

JERROLD THOMAS (J.T.) SANDERS was everything Arvo Thorson wasn't. Arvo's former college roommate had come to the U from a small town in Tennessee with a full-ride football scholarship. He'd played all four years, including a bowl appearance, kept up a full course load, and graduated on time. He married and stayed married to his high school sweetheart who became a highly sought interior decorator, had two beautiful daughters, a gorgeous city home, and entertained lavishly. A few years with the local professional football team contributed to his star power, and after his early retirement due to an injury, he was now a solid, if adopted, member of the community. He never thought of moving back to his backwater hometown. Instead, he was quickly hired on at the Nokomis County Sheriff's Department and made a comfortable living investigating corporate crime.

While Arvo managed to finish college, it took him an extra year to finish all the coursework satisfactorily, given all the partying he'd done in his first few years at the U. An early injury and lackluster effort meant he'd been benched for much of his college football career, which really pretty much ended halfway through the first season. His numerous curfew violations saw to that. After graduation, he moved home to Somerset Hills, got hired on as a Mendota County investigator, and unhappily married his high school sweetheart. The eventual divorce was made simpler by the lack of children, and he presently lived in a small, undecorated studio apartment too close to the interstate, and would never think of having people over to his place.

Still, the two friends, who couldn't have had more different lives, always reconnected quickly when they got together, picking up as if they'd never left off. When the evening ended, Arvo always wondered why he didn't reach out to Jerrold more often. It was good to talk with his buddy. Jerrold's positive attitude and enthusiasm were infectious, and Arvo thought if Jerrold had gone into therapy instead of police work, Arvo's personal problems might all have been solved.

It was an investigation of Jerrold's that brought Arvo to town, and J.T. was paying far too lavishly for Arvo's work on the case with dinner at an exclusive nightclub. The Foshay was open to members and the select few who were allowed past the bouncers. Though both were approaching fifty, J.T. drew stares when the two friends made their way past the long line of party girls. A handsome, fit black man, his straight arrow habits (he was sipping mineral water while Arvo tossed back a few more scotch and sodas than he realized, but less than usual) were helping him retain his youth as well as his youthful outlook on life. J.T. politely smiled and offered up a few rounds of banter with the young ladies who passed by the table, but Arvo knew all the flirtation meant nothing. There were three beautiful, smart women waiting for him at home, and J.T. would never have thought to accept any of the invitations being flirted his way. Roberta, his wife, also told him he'd be dead if she ever so much as sniffed the hint of another woman's perfume on him. Arvo knew that was no joke.

After they'd dined on the best steaks in town, Arvo began to fill J.T. in. "I looked into the trucking company situation you're investigating. The one where the whistle blower was shipped out for duty in Afghanistan and fired by his employer?"

"There have been a few more developments on this end, too," J.T. told his old buddy. "What have your contacts told you?"

"The guy's fiancée passed along some information directly from your informant, who is still on active duty. But it's confusing me, or maybe it's just the scotch." The drinks, as usual, had gone down too quickly, too easily.

J.T. smiled. "Well, Arvo, I've been telling you for years you gotta lay off the booze, brother."

"I know. I have been." Arvo pushed his empty glass aside, and made a show of waving off the waitress when she offered a refill. J.T. ordered him a Perrier with a twist of lime. "After one sip, you'll be convinced it's a gin and tonic. You won't even notice the difference."

Arvo felt embarrassed that his friend felt the need to look out for him. But he needed looking after.

"So tell me more," J.T. said. "What's confusing you?"

"Well I thought you had asked me to look into the trucking company. Get more information, anything solid the informant might have learned? So this Astrid, the guy's fiancée, told me the other day she had more info to share. I stopped by tonight at her place of employment expecting to hear more about whatever pressure the trucking company has been applying to win the refinery contract and what I get back is this." Arvo pushed a printout of an email across the table.

J.T. read it. "This looks like an internal email from RoadCon."

"The big construction company," Arvo said.

"Right. They mostly do freeway work, right? Interstate roads and so on?"

"Yes. And bridges. Big ones," Arvo pointed out. "So I get handed this email that isn't about a trucking company. It's about a construction company. You know that new river crossing that's been in the planning stages? The one that would replace the bridge that had the accident?"

"Down in your neck of the woods?" J.T. asked

"That's the one. Environmentalists have been blocking it. The new bridge would be a boon for the big trucking companies, too, since there are so many load restrictions on that little bridge from Somerset Hills to the refinery that things get really jammed up, and the only legal way to the refinery is to go the long way, and the long way means wasted time and fuel. " Arvo had been filling in the gaps not supplied by the email with what the informant and his friends had passed along. He told J.T. that none of them was willing to come forward, given what had happened to Astrid's fiancé.

J.T. considered what Arvo had told him, and began to build on it. "I think I see what's going on. It's what I've been starting to hear from other sources, but so far there hasn't been enough to pull together a solid case. From what you're telling me, a big new bridge means the trucking companies' problems are solved. Still, this email, which mentions a new, unannounced contract between the refinery and RoadCon, may seem like it's connected, but from what you're telling me, I can't see it."

"Here's the thing Astrid told me," Arvo said. "This RoadCon, the highway construction firm that won the new contract to do some roadwork inside the refinery? That's not their usual business. They do highways. Not little service roads. I ask you, J.T., what business do they have inside a refinery?"

"Arvo, for a guy who doesn't ordinarily involve himself in the corporate stuff, you seem to know a lot. And you got all this information from a stripper?"

"She's got relatives who work at the losing road construction company. A small outfit in Somerset Hills."

J.T. sat back and stroked his chin and reread the email. "Still, all it says here was RoadCon won the roadwork bid for the refinery. Nothing more."

"Yes. Beating out another firm that put in a better bid," Arvo said. "A firm that had been doing their roadwork for years."

Arvo went on. "Astrid's relative told her the big company had put in the lowest cost bid, but something was fishy in how the bids were scored. A number of costs were left out of the equation that should have been in there. The small company's protests were ignored, according to what Astrid's people tell her."

"Arvo. That's a lot of hearsay. And all coming from a stripper. If people directly connected to any of these other companies won't come forward with solid information, I can't do anything with it. Plus, all of the legit information I do have is about the trucking company. This is the first I've heard of a RoadCon's involvement. They've got a longstanding reputation for fair dealings."

"Hear me out, J.T. I know I'm way outside of my territory, but the more I heard about this tonight, the more I wondered about the connection. Not only to your corporate investigation but the murder on the swing bridge." Arvo said out loud what he'd been pondering since he spoke with Astrid.

"Murder?" J.T. said. "I thought that it was an accident. Poorly maintained bridge falling apart, that sort of thing."

"Tell that to the head of the State Bridge Investigation Department. Biggest asshole I ever met," Arvo said with a grin. "After spending so much time with him today, I can tell you I aspire to be the kind of asshole he is. An asshole with integrity."

"Sounds like the two of you hit it off," J.T. laughed.

Arvo continued, the effects of the alcohol wearing off. He hardly noticed that he'd sucked down the Perrier J.T. ordered him. "Let's discuss the background going on with all the players and see if we can connect the dots a little more. As we all know, the economy is in the crapper."

"There's no question there," J.T. said, flagging the waitress down for another round of Perrier. "MinnFreightways, the trucking company, is close to bankruptcy, and some other funny bookkeeping is what alerted my office to the need to dig deeper."

The waitress returned with two ice-cold Perriers, winking at Arvo as she handed him his. "You two seem to be having an animated conversation."

The waitress was a pretty, thirty-something black woman.

"Interesting name," J.T. said, reading the waitresses nametag. "Jade. Matches your eyes?"

The waitress ignored the comment. "You're both cops, right? You," she said with her eyes on J.T., "you've been in here before, I know, but I haven't seen your friend around."

"Yep. Jerrold Thomas Sanders. J.T. is what my friends call me. Arvo Thorson, my buddy, he's with Mendota County. I'm with Nokomis."

"J.T. was with the Vikings, but you're probably too young to remember that," Arvo pointed out.

"Oh, I'm not that young. And even if I was, I've seen all those girls out front drooling when he walked by, I know exactly who you are." Her dismissive look said "player," and not in a complimentary way.

To Arvo, however, she smiled brightly. "It looks like conversation is good for you. Let me stay out of your way, and be sure to let me know if you need anything. I'll be right over there," she said, pointing to the bar.

"Oh," J.T. said when Jade left. "She likes you."

Arvo waved him off. "Nah." Despite his professed disregard, he did look in Jade's direction, and saw her eyes on him, finding himself unexpectedly pleased by her interest.

"So where were we before that hot waitress made her interest in you known?" J.T. said.

"I was saying that even a homicide cop like me can figure out the basics. I can put two and two together to see that a bad economy means there's less freight for trucks to haul. MinnFreightways fired Astrid's fiancé when he started to question what they were expecting of the drivers, extra shifts without extra pay. He found out about a MinnFreightways' bid for refinery business where they also had low-balled a few costs and won the deal."

The light started to go on in J.T.'s eyes. "I'm starting to see the connection. So now there's this other firm, RoadCon. They also have a lot less business than they used to since the economy, as you said, is in the crapper. Less state money flowing to big projects means less work for them. They're starting to dig deep, and lowball a bid for work they never do. They get some work, not a lot, and now they are suddenly the preferred service road vendor for the refinery. MinnFreightways has also had to drastically cut prices to get the refinery's business, and the only way they can do that is cook up a deal for the refinery that looks good to them, but isn't necessarily going to cover their costs. So how else are they going to remain profitable?"

"So how else is the trucking company going to remain profitable, and out of bankruptcy court? How is RoadCon going to get the big contract it needs to stay afloat during hard times?" Arvo asked as if he'd been studying big business all his life. "Meanwhile, MinnFreightways needs cheaper access to the refinery. It's expensive, and slow, to get gasoline trucks to the refinery, given the load limits on the swing bridge. The legal alternative takes them miles out of their way."

"So what's the solution to both MinnFreightways' and RoadCon's problems? How about a big fat interstate crossing construction project for RoadCon with some nice juicy kickbacks for MinnFreightways, to tide them over until the improved access is in place?" Arvo said.

"But there isn't any money," Arvo continued, "due to the bad economy, and the interstate project is bogged down in environmental issues. And there's this little old bridge passing inspection that can handle some trucks, but not too many at a time. See what I'm saying?"

"So this is where the guess work comes in," Arvo said.

"Meaning the information trail goes cold, so you're improvising." J.T. said.

"Hypothesizing," he said. "Hear me out. So how is RoadCon going to get this project fast-tracked? Well it would help them if the little bridge was out of the game."

"So you're suggesting that either RoadCon or MinnFreightways—" J.T. began.

"Or both," Arvo inserted.

"Or both had something to do with the death of the swing bridge operator? The supposed 'failure' of the swing bridge that's been splashed all over the news? You gotta be kidding me, Arvo."

"I know. It seems a little far-fetched," Arvo said. "But not impossible."

"Well, here's your problem with this whole scenario, Arvo. It's all conjecture and gossip at this point. This email announcing the agreement between the refinery and RoadCon doesn't tell us anything. Maybe it's just a lot of sour grapes from Astrid's friends and family, who work for companies that lost out on a bid."

"Why do you think I got so invested in your corporate business, J.T.? I need you to look into RoadCon, now that they might be involved. I'm guessing you might find what you've been finding with MinnFreightways. I'm betting the big construction company is having financial problems and they're running out of legal ways to cut costs and survive. I have another little nugget to toss at you. And his name is Matthew Arndt."

"Never heard of him."

"Well, you're going to need to get more knowledgeable on the guy because guess what? He came to my office with a lot of crap, web printouts and newspaper editorials in favor of replacing the swing bridge with a fancy new river crossing. He had my guys convinced he was an engineer, which he wasn't. He was waving papers in front of our faces, claiming that the old bridge should be condemned. But when we looked into what he gave us, there was absolutely nothing substantial he was providing, and my meeting with the state bridge inspector today corroborated that everything the guy told us was a lie."

"So what? He's just another guy with an agenda, crawled out of the woodwork the moment the swing bridge death hit the papers. Happens all the time. We both know it," J.T. said.

"Well here's the interesting thing about this Matthew Arndt guy. My intern just tracked this down," Arvo said, knocking over his empty Perrier bottle when he leaned in to tell J.T. what Sam had learned.

"Guess where he works?" Arvo said. "RoadCon."

J.T. whipped open his Smartphone and sent an email to his team.

"My 'hypothesis' is making more sense?" Arvo said. He smiled as Jade turned up quickly to remove the downed Perrier bottle and provide a new one.

"Meaning . . . why is it in this Matthew Arndt's interest to bring information forward, trying to convince you that a bridge is unsafe—" J.T. began.

"When it's actually safe. When, in the state bridge inspector's words, 'there's not a goddamned thing wrong with it'?" Arvo said, his eyes fiery with rage.

"I'll tell you why Arndt wants you to believe it's unsafe," Arvo said, his words speeding up. "He's taking advantage of the death of the swing bridge operator to get the bridge out of the way so that his company can profit."

J.T. quickly typed up another email, this one asking his team to begin the process to look into RoadCon's accounting and bid history.

"I think that's only the tip of the iceberg," Arvo said. "I think one, or both, of these companies is directly involved in Karl's death."

"Arvo, Arvo. You got to slow down, man. Are you asking me to charge two corporations with murder? Whoa." J.T. held up his hands.

"Oh, not at all. Just keep your eyes open as you look at what you can look at. And keep me informed. I'll handle the murder investigation side of this."

J.T. nodded. Jade dropped off the check and her phone number. "Sorry, miss. I'm not available. But my friend is."

"This was for him," Jade said, sliding her phone number in Arvo's direction. "I like a man with his kind of quiet fire," she said making it clearer. "And I saw your wedding ring flashing at me."

J.T. laughed.

"You," she said to Arvo, "are more my type. You can call that number if you decide I'm yours."

She left the two men to settle up.

"Arvo, you dog. I'm a little disappointed that dark beauty dismissed me so quickly."

"You're an old married man. J.T., she's just hoping for a big tip. The girl's been playing flirty waitress all night long."

"Well one things for sure," J.T. said, tossing a credit card on the check tray. "I'll be expensing this bill after all." He tossed a handful of bills on the table. "The size of that tip, however, is all for you. Might help ink the deal for the waitress?"

Arvo considered the waitress' offer, and a few more drinks in him, he might have taken her up. Instead, he pushed half of the tip back into his friend's hands. "I don't want to encourage her, not that much anyway. Like I said, I may be an asshole, but I'm an asshole with integrity. Anyone who wants me needs to get me the old fashioned way, not because my bank account is adequate to whatever lifestyle they aspire to."

J.T. gave his old buddy an appraising look. "Still hung up on that ex-wife of yours?"

Arvo didn't answer. His old friend knew him better than anyone, and any other time they'd met, the look on Arvo's face and the amount of liquor he'd consumed provided the answer. This time, J.T. had asked the question in a way that made it sound he wasn't too sure about his old friend. That after all this time, maybe there'd been a change.

"Old habits die hard, brother," J.T. said.

"I can agree with you on that one," Arvo said. "But some new habits," he said, polishing off the last of the Perrier. "Are long overdue for the firing squad."

"Amen." J.T. said. "Amen. I'd encourage you to pick up that pretty habit over there. Looks like she's more than willing to take you on."

The waitress gave Arvo a hot smile.

"See? You still got it, brother."

Arvo decided to linger at Foshay's after his friend headed out. Jade's cool energy contrasted delightfully with the smartass commentary she directed at the bartender, and a select customer who'd been invited to take a ringside seat at the bar. There, Arvo kept his thirst quenched with Perrier, wondering if J.T. had left behind instructions that were intended to help manage his alcohol intake.

Elisa Smyth did get her nickname—Jade—for the unusual set of green eyes that sparkled in the ebony setting of her perfect complexion. When her shift ended, she said that Arvo had been sufficiently prepared to drive her home to her apartment on the northeastern side of the city, an area of artists' lofts and industrial warehouses. What the hell, he thought, taking her up on the invitation that J.T. had encouraged him to accept. He'd been right about the Perrier. He was probably right about the waitress. When they arrived at her apartment, she invited him in to see her etchings.

"That's the oldest line in the book," Arvo said.

"You used most of them by now, I bet," she snapped back.

She did indeed have etchings to show him. "Why do you think I live in this part of town? My studio is across the street."

He was mesmerized by the woodcut prints she showed him, the best of which hung on her walls. Many of the designs were expressive—suggesting flowing water, wind, and natural settings—without being true to life. Vibrant patterns combined to form a primitive, but no less authentic, picture of the world as Jade saw it.

"See. It's the idea of the thing. That's what I'm shooting for. The feeling you get from being in nature without all that soft-focus crap. Some people respond to the natural world with fear. Some with joy. Sometimes both are there."

She suggested a nightcap, but before the drinks were even poured, Arvo took J.T.'s full advice. He had Jade in his arms, eager to sample the artist's form, one just as vibrant and expressive as the wood cuts on her wall. Her smooth, supple skin yielded to his touch and for once his mind wasn't elsewhere, comparing her to ex-loves. He gave in to the sensation, the sensual experience, unimpeded by memory, guided only by instinct.

TWENTY-FOUR

ARVO THORSON WOKE IN AN UNFAMILIAR bed, the familiar buzzing of his Smartphone sounding from somewhere nearby. When he reached for it on his nightstand, the Smartphone was not there. Nor was the vaguely familiar, glass-topped nightstand, the one that felt cool to the touch, under his fingertips. He remembered that his ex-wife had taken the glass-topped nightstand with her, along with everything else, when she'd left him. Fuzzy memories of waking up in Helen's house came back to him, and he was relieved that he was not waking up in his ex-wife's bed.

But he was not in his own apartment either. Linear shapes came into focus, assembling themselves into a peaceful forest of pine trees, and he thought he remembered dreaming of sunlight filtering through a vast forest of cedar trees, a forest so huge that it might have felt quite lonely to be alone in such a place. Instead, he felt alert, and rested, and not alone considering the many tall trees all around, and the many birds flickering in the tree tops and searching for seeds on the spongy forest floor. His eyes adjusted to the room, and he realized that he was looking at an original woodcut print hanging on a nearby wall, and that the lines that had been so carefully arranged were indeed intended to represent an endless, serene forest complete with scattered jagged lines suggesting birds.

Nearby, he saw an interesting handmade lamp crafted from driftwood, and a collection of hand-carved toy animals arranged around the lamp. These objects sat on top of a pile of art books that had been stacked up to nightstand height.

He'd slept peacefully in the small bed, which was made even smaller by the woodcut artist who was curled up next to him, her arm draped over him. He remembered how comfortable a bed could be. His own cardboard thin sofa-bed mattress back at his apartment was worthless, and it pained his back to sleep on it. He was convinced it was high time for the forty-something Mendota County investigator to grow up and get his own bed. Something more like the comfortable bed he'd awoke in that morning.

"Morning," a sleepy voice mumbled next to him.

He kissed Jade lightly on her deliciously smooth cheek and whispered good morning, but told her to go back to sleep, he needed to head out to work, but would call her later.

"Promise?" she said sleepily.

"Promise."

"Promise you'll wear a uniform when I see you next? I told you, I love a man in uniform."

Arvo smiled. "We'll see. Now sleep."

He quietly got dressed in his street clothes and retrieved his messages when he got to his car.

Autopsy's in. From Juney

Matthew Arndt aren't talkin'. From Kieran

Arvo replied to Kieran. *Says who? Get him in.*

Can't get through to social services. They say Christine's out of office, no info as to when she's due back. From Sam

Screw that, Arvo thought, thinking better of replying to Sam the same way. He'd get to her later. He wanted to see that autopsy before the ink dried on it. It had been long enough.

Juney handed him the reports the moment he stepped inside his office.

"Coroner apologizes for the delay. There was a lot to piece together."

"No kidding. Wait," he reconsidered. "Were you joking with me?"

"What? Oh, piece together. For cripes sake, Arvo, that's not my style. That's what the coroner said."

"Well, I'm glad our coroner has a sense of humor. Tough audience, though, down there at the morgue, wouldn't you say?"

"Oh, now, look who's joking." Juney jabbed her finger at one of the documents. "First things first. Toxicology."

Arvo flipped through the report. "Nothing. Expected that, but I'm glad to hear it's been confirmed."

"Okay, here's the *piece-de-resistance*."

"Victim had extensive trauma to the torso . . . yeah I'd say . . . blah blah blah . . . wait a minute," Arvo said, whistling.

"Bingo," Juney said. "You saw it?"

"Entrance wound at the base of the skull?" Arvo pointed out.

Juney held out a small evidence bag, which held one bullet.

"Well," Arvo said with wonder. "What do we have here?"

"That, my dear, is called a bullet."

"You don't say. A bullet? Sam!" Arvo shouted. His intern came running. When he saw the bullet, his jaw dropped. "That from Lutz?"

He smiled at Juney. "Thank you for saving this news for me, first."

"You're the boss. You shouldn't be the last to know."

Arvo read further in the autopsy. "They determined that he'd died from massive head injury, caused by an execution style shooting. Entrance at the top of the guy's head, although if you ask me, that's an unusual place to execute someone, but maybe this guy's signature? Though there was tremendous blood loss, most appeared to come from the head wound. Traumatic injury to the torso came later, but the guy was already dead."

"That's what I read. But then that was the mess the coroner tried to piece back together."

Arvo handed off the toxicology and coroner report to Sam. "See if I missed anything. Maybe there's something new they are training the kids at the U these days."

"Ballistics?" Arvo said, turning back to Juney.

Juney handed him yet another report.

"When it rains it pours," Arvo said whistling.

"Kind of a downpour today," Juney said.

"I'd say. We didn't locate any shell-casings at the scene, did we, Sam?" Arvo said as he flipped through the ballistics report.

"No."

"Killer might have been smart enough to locate the shell before he left," Arvo surmised. "Kind of hard to extract a bullet from deep inside a dead man's skull. Sam, did you see any report of an exit wound?"

"No. Due to the condition of the body after the traumatic torso injury, coroner could not determine location of exit wound, if there was any. The bullet was found imbedded in victim's lung, but the coroner could not determine if that's where the bullet stopped, or if the traumatic torso injury resulted in movement of the bullet."

"That guy burst apart like an overripe tomato when the cables hit him," Arvo concluded.

"I'll never enjoy ketchup again," Juney said. "Not after that description."

"So, the guy couldn't have been leaning into the cable to maybe clear out some taconite pellets that might have been keeping the bridge from properly opening and closing," Arvo said sarcastically.

"Well, not with a bullet lodged in his head. Probably not," Juney cracked.

"Especially one that killed him," Arvo said.

"Oh, most certainly not." Juney fired back.

"The ballistics report says the bullet appears to have come from a gun with a silencer . . . blah blah blah . . . there's a potential gun description here, are we looking into it?" Arvo asked.

"We will," Sam answered.

"Kieran," Arvo shouted, so far out of earshot of the code-geek that no one was sure why he bothered. "Sam, come on." Arvo raced down the hall to the computer lab.

"What's the latest on this Arndt guy?"

"Plenty," the lanky geek told him. "Too much, in fact. For starters? All of those print-outs and newspaper articles he was flashing at us? They come from the River Valley Business

Coalition, a group that includes a number of large, local transportation- and construction-related businesses."

"These businesses wouldn't happen to be MinnFreightways and RoadCon, would they?

"How did you know that?" the geek asked him.

"I've heard of Google. Is there a contact name listed on these materials?" Arvo asked.

"A guy with the name Matthew Arndt. Ring a bell? He also authored all the letters to the editor about the swing bridge's poor condition. Almost every source he mentions in each letter comes from the Business Coalition. Any 'official' report they cite is, you guessed it, their own material. Nothing they claim as fact comes from real engineering studies."

"In other words, it's all made up."

"That's right."

"So not only does Mathew Arndt work for RoadCon, but he also heads up this quasi-lobbying group, the River Valley Business Coalition?"

"That's right," Kieran confirmed.

"Have you gotten through to him, telling him we want to talk to him again?" Arvo asked.

Sam told him that the guy wasn't returning their calls.

"Keep trying," Arvo said. "Find out where his office is. Where he works. If he won't come to us, we'll go to him."

Arvo was halfway out the door before Sam could call after him.

"Where are you going?" Sam said.

"To see a certain, stubborn case worker and get her sanctified approval to have that kid talk to us again. Jesus, it's like pulling teeth to get anything done around here. I'll be back later. Maybe. Depending upon what I can get out of Christine Ivory."

TWENTY-FIVE

"WHAT ARE YOU DOING HERE," Christine asked Arvo. "And how did you even get up here? Past the security door?"

"In case you don't remember, I have a badge. It tends to open security doors," Arvo said, walking inside even though he hadn't been invited in. "So why'd you open your door to me so easily? You didn't even ask who was outside standing in your hallway. You didn't see me through your peephole?"

"I wasn't expecting anyone, and I thought you might be the cleaning woman," she said.

Arvo laughed. "You? With a cleaning woman?"

"So what's your problem with that?" Christine said.

"Look at this place," he said gesturing. "Why would you need to hire someone, you already keep it spotless."

Christine looked flustered. "She isn't actually due until tomorrow."

"So you were giving yourself extra time to dirty things up for her so she has something to do. Brilliant!" Arvo guffawed.

"Arvo!" Christine roared. "No. You don't even get it. I let you in because I thought it was someone I knew. She never remembers the right day. She can get past security because she has the code for the security door, though, with a woman that disorganized, I'm surprised she remembers."

"I still don't get it Christine. Why do you need a cleaning lady?" He ran a finger along a ledge, and held it out to her. It was dust-free.

"I know that tidiness is certainly not a virtue to you." She batted his hand away."Now. What are you doing here besides dropping by to criticize how clean I keep my place?"

"I'm here on official business."

"I don't work for the county anymore, Arvo. Take it up with my department."

"I have. Your assistant."

"Former assistant," Christine reiterates.

"Oh, who the hell cares," he said dismissively. "Your former assistant said you could be reached at home in an emergency."

"That was not the direction I left. But I'm not surprised she told you to do that. One reason I left was that annoying woman."

"So why didn't you fire her?" Arvo stood. "By the way, aren't you going to offer me a drink?"

"Arvo, it's not even 10:00 a.m. yet.

"A cup of coffee, Christine? What do you take me for? A drunk?"

"If the shoe fits. Whatever." Christine sighed, signaling her defeat in the face of the insistent detective. "Sure. I'll get you a cup of coffee."

She carried the carafe and an extra cup to her patio, where Arvo could see she'd been sitting with the newspaper, opened to the help-wanted ads. He grabbed the chair that was the farthest from the edge.

"That's right," Christine said, noticing him shoving a chair as far away from the edge of the balcony as he could. "You don't really like it out here."

"So, now you're going to be sadistic and force me to sit over there? I wouldn't be surprised," he said, sipping from the cup she'd set down in front of him. "The incident you're referring to was a bit extreme, if you recall."

"Yes, it was. And I saved your life, if you recall."

He recalled. "Yes. You did."

"I don't remember much gratitude for that."

"Well, you know me. I'm not the kind of guy who stops to say thank you. I'm not sure why you bothered to save my sorry ass, given the amount of disappointment you've so abundantly expressed with me over the past several weeks."

"And we know you didn't barge in here to apologize." She looked away, gazing at something in the distance, her expression still hard.

Still he was sure he saw a few tears welling in her determined eyes. For a woman was so unyielding in her expectations of others, she was obviously even more demanding and unforgiving with herself. With such an obviously exquisitely spotless apartment, she still felt she needed a cleaning woman. She'd set impossibly high standards for herself. The tears in her eyes acknowledged her defeat. The exhaustion on her face told him how difficult that acknowledgement had been. Given the quirky personal economy of Christine's life, a breakdown was bound to happen.

"Look," he began. "I apologize for barging in on you like this. It's clear you're going through hell. You don't need to put on a show for me that you aren't." He leaned towards her, speaking quietly. "And I know the last thing you want is to have me dragging all of the stuff you want to be away from right into this place of sanctuary for you."

A tear dropped down each side of Christine's face, and even though she'd caused him a lot of grief, it was obviously nowhere near the amount of the pain she was now experiencing. Arvo could sympathize with that kind of woe. He made his way to her bathroom and located a box of tissues.

"I've been where you are. Hell, in lots of ways, I'm still there." He handed her one of the tissues. "But you're a smart, talented woman, Christine. You'll figure this out. You're going to make it. Whatever you decide to do, if you need something from me, a job recommendation—"

He saw her smile.

"I know, probably a recommendation from me wouldn't be the best thing, but, hey, at least I got you smiling. Anyway, just say the word. I'll come running or stay away, whichever you decide you need."

"Thank you," she said, blotting her tears. "I must look terrible."

"You look fine," he said, glancing at the purple hair. "That look is growing on me. It's kind of hot."

"Oh, shut up." Christine blew her nose.

Arvo refilled her coffee cup.

"So, why did you come all the way over here, anyway?" she said. "The house is a mess, as you can plainly see."

Now he smiled. At least she was able to joke about her compulsiveness.

"That bridge murder case has cracked wide open, but there's still a big gap, and for that, I need your help," he said.

She took a deep breath and sat up straight.

"It's the kid. I need to involve him in the investigation again." Christine stiffened.

"Don't worry," he said. "He's not in trouble. Actually it's pretty evident that he's completely in the clear."

Christine took a few moments to decide. "Okay. I'll help you. But I need to be there, with the boy."

"Oh, so you're going to go back to the county, after all?"

"Temporarily. For one case only."

"Good. Glad to you have you on board," Arvo said, relieved. "When do you need him?"

Arvo glanced at his watch. "This Sunday."

"This Sunday? That's kind of unusual. Why not during normal office hours? You just need to talk to him, right?" Christine looked confused, her eyes still glistening.

"Well, it goes beyond that. There's an event going on that will provide an opportunity for us to get up close and personal with the biker crowd. It's a big annual event that takes place all along the stretch of highway that runs from Somerset Hills and down along the river. Probably you haven't heard of it, given your tastes," Arvo said.

"You mean the River Run?" Christine said.

"So you have heard of it?"

"Every river town kid has heard of it. It started during the historic flood years back in the sixties when the bikers banded together to help with sandbagging?"

"You got it. This year is looking to be a grand daddy for floods, too, so you can bet that every motorcyclist from miles around will be converging here," Arvo said. "It's our best chance of being able to ID the motorcyclist the kid saw. Practically a line-up."

"They do some good, just so you know. The River Run raises a lot of money for charity," Christine pointed out.

"I know. We're only looking for a rotten apple in a bunch of upstanding citizens." He paused, trying not too sound too sarcastic. Yes. Many bikers were absolutely no problem. But it was hard to keep perspective with the whole lot when you knew there was a murderer in that crowd. "So you'll help?"

"It might be a little hard to arrange something that quickly, and it sounds like you want Nick for an entire day, right?"

Arvo nodded. "Looks like you aren't really doing anything. Don't worry, I'll have you back in plenty of time to meet your cleaning lady the next time around. If it helps, I'll track some dirt on your carpeting so you can be sure that the place is ready for her."

"Oh, shut up." Christine began to tidy the patio, reflexively making a grab for Arvo's coffee cup.

"Hey, hey, I wasn't done with that," Arvo said.

"Oh, sorry. See, I'm already in action mode," Christine said.

"I'm glad to see it," he smiled. "You'll probably need to do a little shopping, by the way, so we fit in with the biker crowd. If you're coming along for this next part of the ride, I need the appropriately attired Christine at my side," Arvo said. He didn't want to specifically point out that she typically drew attention to herself whenever they'd gone out on professional, or other, business.

"What type of dress is required for whatever you're planning?"

"Blue jeans. And if you have some Harley boots, strap those on, too. The hair is perfect for the place we'll be checking out, by the way. You'll fit right in."

She gave him a brief, inquisitive look before hurrying off. "Give me a couple of days and I'll be ready to go. A girl always likes an excuse to play dress up."

"This is more of a dress down occasion."

"Just a figure of speech, Arvo. I need to make a few arrangements, too, as you know," she stood next to him, tapping her foot. "Look, I know you enjoy the view, but if you want me to have the boy ready in time, we better get going," she said, giving him a sharp look.

"The old Christine, roaring back."

"I can see you approve."

"Not that it would matter. My standards are pretty low, as you know," Arvo said, moving into the chair Christine had vacated, one that was closer to her sliding balcony door, and farther away from the balcony edge.

"Oh, it matters. It matters more than you know."

TWENTY-SIX

JUST A FEW MILES SOUTH OF SOMERSET HILLS, the river widened
into a glistening expanse of water that covered forty square
miles, roughly the same area as the town. This was not too unusual
for Minnesota. There were many bodies of water as large as towns,
and a few that were quite a bit larger than the state's major cities.

Given the vast acreage of water in this part of the river, it was
named Lake Frontenac, the largest such lake in the entire
Mississippi. Along with its other attractions, it had acquired its own
lake monster, an American relative of the "Nessie" of Loch Ness,
Scotland.

There'd been no sightings of the Mississippi River lake
monster in over a century, but legend had it that the shy creature
only felt safe enough to emerge during the most vicious storms,
such as the one responsible for capsizing a ferry and causing the
deaths of nearly one hundred passengers. There was another story
passed down through the centuries, though there was even more
dispute as to its veracity. It was said that the creature was driven
from its underwater cavern during peak flood years, when it had to
go far outside of its murky territory in search of food, as floods
tended to stir the dense particles at the river bottom, making it
difficult for the creature to feed as usual.

Most people dismissed the entire tale as a PR spin intended to
give the area an interesting allure for tourists. And allure it had.
Generous breezes flowing down into the river valley made the lake
a destination for sailors, and the natural beauty of the area was a
magnet for hikers, campers, and tourists. Small creeks flowing
through the narrow coulees that cut through the river bluff were
perfect for trout fishing. In addition to all of these recreational

possibilities, the hilly country near the lake had a number of scenic winding roads, which made the area perfect for motoring enthusiasts, particularly the biker crowd.

And so it was that a trio of Somerset Hills' residents found themselves headed south on Highway 61 the first Sunday of May, not for the scenery, the beauty, to search for the lake monster, or any other recreational possibilities. Their destination was Roadsters, a biker bar tucked away in the tiny river town of Battle Landing, located at the southernmost edge of Mendota County. There, they hoped to locate a modified import motorcycle, a machine capable of unthinkable speeds, and in particular, confirm that it was the same motorcycle seen racing away from the swing bridge the morning Karl Lutz was murdered.

In the back seat of Arvo Thorson's car, a sullen, tow-headed, but mercifully occupied Nick McQuillen worked the most complicated puzzle box Christine had in her collection. He'd already solved the broken one she'd given him in record time. Judging by the speed at which he was working through the biggest brainteaser she could locate, she wondered what she would do next to keep him occupied.

His unicycle was jammed next to him in the back seat.

The currently unemployed and always properly attired Christine Ivory wore a subdued pair of blue-jeans and a tight black leather biker jacket, and had covered her purple hair with a bandana, tied biker style. She looked as if she'd been riding Harleys all her life.

The detective also looked biker-bar appropriate in a little get-up the social worker had snapped up for him at a bargain price, a few days earlier.

"How on earth did you manage to convince the parents to let him come with?" Arvo had asked Christine out of earshot of the boy, as he loaded his unicycle into the car. He'd ridden it to the county building, meeting Arvo and Christine there at the designated time.

She told him what the boy had told her. "He says he got permission from his parents."

"You believe him?"

"I didn't ask. I thought the better of it."

"Will there be trouble for you if he turns out to not have asked?"

"I turned in my notice at the county. They can hardly fire me. Honestly, I really don't care what they do. I've moved on. Time to break out of a rut."

"Sounds like a good move for you," he said.

"It is," she said smiling.

Before they left, Christine ran back to her car, and brought back a grocery sack, which she handed to Arvo.

"I thought you should look the part."

Arvo removed a black leather biker's jacket from the bag. "Nice. This must have cost you."

"A friend located it for me, a guy who runs a consignment store near my mother's place."

"I like it. How much do I owe you?" Arvo said.

"Keep it."

Now he was riding next to her in his Taurus, the earthy smell of leather permeating the car's interior.

"You told Nick what our goal is here. Right? Nick?"

The boy answered with a noncommittal groan, barely looking up from his puzzle.

Arvo glanced at Christine.

"Don't worry. It'll be fine. Besides, we don't even know for sure if we'll find anything."

"Sam told me they'd located a potential match for this machine the kid saw. Which sounds like the same one that nearly ran us off the road a few weeks back. My contacts at the King of Spades and at the Cycle Shop in town tell me that a bike like that one has been seen at Roadsters. With the River Run going on today, we'll see a lot of bikers out. It's our best shot. And we have to throw everything we have at it."

Arvo felt the butt of his gun digging into his side. It was well hidden under the leather jacket, which, he realized, had been the perfect accessory for the trip. Paired with a vintage set of Ray-bans Christine had brought for him, he looked like Steve McQueen, Christine told him. "A mature Steve McQueen," she said.

"Better than the dead one, I guess," he answered.

Christine seemed looser than he'd ever seen her in quite some time, though it annoyed him he found her sexy in the leather and denim.

He needed to break out of some ruts himself.

Once they made it just past Frontenac, they parked in downtown Battle Landing, which was nothing more than a street that dead-ended at the river, and contained a gas station, Laundromat, and a barbershop. They found the small side street that led up the hillside, and as they walked along it, a few motorcycles roared past, telling them they were going in the right direction.

"This road would be awesome for skate boarding. I should have brought my board," Nick suddenly piped up. The tone of his enthusiasm was striking. And the fact that it was the most he'd spoken the entire day. The boy almost got ahead of them in his eager inspection of the hilly road, and Arvo and Christine hurried to catch up. Arvo was out of breath from the steep climb.

"Hang on," he panted. "Let's stop here and make sure everyone understands what we're here to do."

"Identify. Verify. Then leave," the boy said.

"Yes. That's it. We're just passing through, a couple of tourists taking a little walk along a country road. The wife," Arvo gestured towards Christine, "likes bikes. The kid," Arvo gestured, "is fond of them too."

"Nice machine there, mister." Nick chirped in a speedy cadence.

"You don't need to say anything. In fact, don't even talk. Trust me, it's better." Arvo said, worrying now that the kid was not the most reliable performer. "If either of you spot anything, you look at me. Do not, I repeat, do not say anything, go after anyone, or in any other way call attention to him. Or us."

"Just a casual stroll through the countryside," Christine said, "on a beautiful spring day."

"With our mouths shut." the boy added, yawning.

They rounded another curve in the road, and suddenly Roadster's was right in front of them. A long row of motorcycles lined the front of the bar, and many more parked alongside the building. Other bikes pulled up. The River Run was in high swing, and bikers were eager for a beer or two with their pals, and a cruise along the winding road, with occasional stops to help sandbag the low-lying areas.

A biker couple, his hand in her back pocket, hers in his, led the way into the bar

"Don't try that on me," Christine said, as Arvo began to reach for her.

He continued. "Official business," he whispered in her ear. "Makes us look more convincing."

She batted his hand away.

The boy stepped inside, just ahead of them, while Arvo and Christine were distracted by their whispered argument.

"Welcome to Roadsters," the bartender said to the boy. "Are your parents here? You can't come in here—oh," she said, changing her tune. "That's them. Come on in, close the door please?"

Arvo greeted the bartender, a woman with deeply-lined skin, the texture and color of turkey jerky. She'd drawn on eyebrows to take the place of the ones that had been over-plucked, and she peered at him and "his family" with a pair of tiny deep set eyes, all the while mopping the bar with a damp, dirty towel. "What can I get you, sir?" she asked brightly. "Tap beers are two for one during the River Run."

Arvo ordered tap beers for himself and Christine, whom he sent off to claim an open table.

"What brings you to Battle Landing? You from the city?"

Arvo answered in the affirmative, trotting out the story he'd just restated to Christine and the boy a few minutes earlier. The small talk gave Christine and Nick time to scan the room, getting acquainted with the biker crowd. Arvo didn't dawdle for too long. He was afraid they could create a spectacle, since clearly they had not been seen inside Roadsters ever before.

"Did you see anything you liked out front?" Arvo asked the boy, setting a beer in front of Christine and sounding for all the world like a father trying to relate to his son.

The boy looked at him, gesturing to his closed mouth.

"You are allowed to say 'yes' or 'no.'"

"No."

Nick glared at him, still pointing to his mouth.

"Yes?" Arvo said, groaning. "Go ahead, speak."

"Can I get a coke or something?"

"Of course. But do not move from this table, " he warned Nick.

"Keep an eye on him," he said to Christine, who was making slow progress drinking her beer out of the glass. He knew she must have hated the idea of all the hands that had touched the glass before it got to her.

The bartender caught Arvo's eye as he came up to her to order Nick's coke. "Kids," she said shaking her head. "I got a boy that age at home. Not into bikes like your boy, and apparently your wife, too."

"Yeah. At this age, you don't know what to do with them. The kid or the wife." He gave himself points for the banter, though he knew it wasn't his best material.

"At least your boy came out with you and the wife. Mine won't go anywhere there's no wireless."

"We don't have that problem. This kid loves to go places. He is constantly in motion. He's been that way since he was a toddler.

ADD," Arvo whispered. "Anyway, we promised him if he did well in school this week, we'd take him out cruising. He loves bikes."

"Well, you came to the right spot," she said, handing him the Coke and taking his payment for it.

"Looks like it. Say, you wouldn't happen to know if anyone has one of those imported jobs, the really speedy ones. Of course the kid is interested in the fastest ones."

The bartender looked at him with interest, and glanced over at Christine and Nick.

"I can't say that I'm surprised." She leaned in. "You're not going to let him get one of those, are you?"

"Oh, no. Of course not. We're just rewarding good behavior, as I said, with the carrot of looking, but not touching."

"I'm pretty sure we get a regular down here with that sort of bike, though I haven't seen him in a while. I think it's some sort of modified Honda. I don't know, these guys are more up on that sort of thing. I'm just here tending bar. But of course winter tends to slow things down. I wouldn't be surprised if the guy showed up today, what with the River Run going on. Tends to bring everyone out."

"Well that's good news," Arvo said a little more cheerfully than he thought he should. "For the boy I meant."

"If I see him come in, I'll let him know you're interested," she said.

Arvo thanked her and headed back to the table with Nick's Coke. When he returned and shared what he could of the bartender's news, Christine glanced at her nodding, as if to thank her. The bartender was having a long conversation with a big man at one end of the bar, and happened to be pointing at Arvo, just then.

"Oh, oh," she said under her breath.

"What?" Arvo said, casually sipping his beer.

"Something seems strange about the way she was pointing you out to that big guy. Do you think they're onto us?"

"Nick, come with me. We'll take a walk outside." He and the boy got up, passing the bartender again, "he's like a kid in a candy shop," he remarked brightly.

This time the bartender didn't seem as interested in his banter.

"We've got all of two minutes left," Arvo said quietly to Nick, "before I think we need to make our exit."

He walked the boy around the side of the building, a few of the bikers eyeing them with suspicion. "My kid likes motorcycles," he said a little too loudly. "Hope you don't mind if we check out your rides."

He wondered if he'd used the right word.

"See anything you like, son?" he asked.

"Not exactly, *Dad*."

They were about to head back inside when the unmistakable sound of a custom street bike came roaring up the hill, fast. Even the other bikers sat up to take notice.

"Sounds like the bike I remember," the boy said.

"Me too," Arvo agreed.

Out of eyeshot, they watched as a one-of-a-kind modified import, a Honda, pulled in and parked, its helmeted driver dismounting and going inside. They followed him in and rejoined Christine, who followed the direction of their eyes.

"That might be the guy," Arvo whispered.

"That's definitely the bike," Nick said.

The driver stepped up to the bar, removing his helmet, and providing the three with a view of the back of his head. Arvo made rapid mental notes, judging the suspect's size and weight, noting the driver's close-cropped hair. He was about to place his order when the big guy called the Honda rider down to the far end of the bar. The bartender joined the other two, and together the three had a hushed conversation, looking once or twice in Arvo's direction.

Arvo caught a quick glimpse of the guy's face. He looked both confused and menacing. Arvo quickly could see that the fellow was not Matthew Arndt. But he bet the guy knew Arndt.

Arvo smiled, raising his glass as if in greeting. What he wanted to do was punch the son-of-a-bitch in the face. But he kept his game face on, thinking it was still possible the guy thought he, Christine, and Nick were all a happy family out for an afternoon drive.

The biker put his helmet back on, and headed for the door.

"He's going to get away," Nick said, a little too loudly, beginning to get up.

The rider began to move faster, and then the big guy stood up too, alarmed.

The rider ran out and leapt onto his bike, and that proved too much for Nick, who ran out to catch the man driving off.

Then he did what Arvo feared he might. He grabbed the nearest bike, and jumped on it, chasing after the speedy biker in no time flat.

Arvo looked for the biggest, fastest bike among the rest of the machines out front. He flashed his badge. "Police business," leapt aboard the machine he chose, and in no time flat Christine got on behind him.

"You are *not* leaving me by myself with these people."

"Then make yourself useful." He handed her his phone. "Call in."

Christine made a quick 9-1-1 call, frantically explaining what was happening, but it was hard for the operator to hear her. They turned onto the highway, hitting a patch of uneven pavement and the cell phone bounced out of her hand.

Now there was nothing more for her to do but hang on tight, and pray. They quickly gained on Nick, passing him, but he had no problem keeping up with them. All three bikes sped south on the highway, and within moments they entered the most dangerous part of the roadway. They were below Frontenac, where the river narrowed, squeezed into its channel by high bluffs on both sides of the river. Bluffs edged close along the narrow, winding roadway, and there were signs along the way warning of sudden curves, passing lane restrictions, and the occasional rockslide.

One sign gave Arvo some hope. He pointed as they sped by. "Patrolled by helicopter."

"Let's hope the boys are on duty today," he shouted back to Christine.

"What's the plan if they aren't?" Christine shouted back.

Arvo answered by pointing to his gun, ready to shoot out the suspect's motorcycle tires, if they could get close enough.

That was the protocol, but that changed the moment Arvo felt a bullet whizzing passed. It came from behind them. Nick whizzed by and pointed. The big guy was behind them, gaining ground quickly. Too quickly.

Arvo and Nick gunned their engines and flew past signs warning of road construction ahead. "Oh, great," Arvo shouted. Ahead of them on the road, signs said "ONE WAY TRAFFIC AHEAD." Twenty feet later, a road construction worker held up a sign that said "STOP."

Arvo and Nick blasted through, the big man close behind. Just ahead of them they saw the suspect, narrowly dodging the one-way caravan headed their way. Arvo took one look at Nick and in a flash their decision was made, Arvo shouted, "Hang on," and he slowed to drop along the gravel shoulder to the left side of the oncoming traffic, Nick expertly took the right.

The big man on the Harley pulled onto the freshly paved lane, the one without the traffic, and made steady progress, closing in on both Arvo and Nick until he was close enough for them to see the big smile on his face, and the gun pointed directly at Christine. The smile didn't last beyond two obstructions he hadn't noticed, directly in his path: the end of the fresh pavement and an oversized Caterpillar road paver, the latter of which he hit head on.

Nick and Arvo met up shortly after, returning to the right lane just at the end of the construction, Arvo slowing down long enough to drop Christine off. "Go get help from the construction people. Make sure the highway patrol is on the way. Now *go!*"

Nick was waiting just ahead, and Arvo quickly caught up. "You're done. You need to go and stay with Christine."

"You need backup," the boy said. "And all you have is me. Plus, I want to get this bastard as much as you do."

Arvo sped off and the boy stayed close behind. Another gunshot flew by, this time fired by the suspect. Arvo took aim and fired, but the suspect took a curve, fast, and he just missed.

One glance at the speedometer told him more than he wanted to know. They were racing along at over a one-hundred miles an hour and he was sure the suspect was accelerating far faster than that.

And then in a blink, they lost him. Both Arvo and Nick slowed down, and then stopped.

"There!" Nick pointed, as they saw the suspect heading back in their direction from some distance away.

"Why the hell is he coming directly for us?" Arvo shouted, the question answered a moment later.

The State Highway Patrol chopper appeared from behind the bluff. The biker swerved and headed down a gravel road towards the river, and Arvo and Nick took off after the guy, turning as fast as they dared to take the same gravel road.

Signs along the way, which everyone breezed by, warned that the river crossing in that area was closed due to high water. The suspect sped past the signs, turning to fire another shot, and as they approached the crossing, they could see that the rushing water had overtopped the bridge, though parts of the roadway were still clear. Arvo fired once, hitting the motorcycle's rear tire. The man almost lost control of his machine, but kept going.

The suspect fired back, and this time his aim hit its intended target. Arvo heard Nick scream, and as Arvo turned to see if it was the boy who got hit, he realized that the world instead was turning around him, almost like it had on the swing bridge, but faster, and more sickeningly. As it rushed at him, it pressed so hard against him that he could no longer breathe, spiraling him so deep inside the dizzying vortex that he forgot his panic momentarily and wondered if he was about to die, or already had. He sensed he could break free but did not know whether it would release him, or spell his doom. Living the way he had was just like this, like drowning, every moment of every day. Who wanted to go back to that? Actually drowning, though it would solve all of his problems permanently, wasn't necessarily the better option.

He did not know what to do because he was a man who for so long had held fast to a life that only made him ill. He was damn sick of it. But the boy was waiting for him, somewhere beyond the dizzy visions he faced. He had to be sure the boy was safe.

He grabbed for something, anything, taking hold of a tree limb. He stood with difficulty, a pain shooting through his leg, overwhelming spasms in his lung as he struggled to breath. He turned and saw the boy was safe.

Looking the other direction, he saw the man and his huge machine were not far away from him. The man was taking aim at him again, then suddenly the cyclist staggered in the swirl of rising floodwater. A moment later, both the man and his machine were swept off the bridge by the crest of one of the highest floods ever recorded in the area.

Arvo thought he felt the water flowing over him as well, and he was unafraid. He welcomed the cool waters. He knew the river meant him no harm, though he would have been glad to be carried away to a cool and peaceful place where nothing spun around him, ever again. He would never be able to explain that feeling to anyone. He could swear the river had asked him, and it was only when Arvo made his decision known that the boy was given the chance to grab Arvo by the shoulders and drag him to safety.

IT TOOK MANY DAYS FOR ARVO to recover from his grave injuries: a collapsed lung from a bullet that grazed his heart, deep abrasions and a near concussion from being thrown off the motorcycle. He had nearly been swept away by the floodwaters, too, but through some miracle the river relinquished its grip on him, depositing him and another important object not far away from Nick. Christine and a substantial number of highway patrol squads arrived not long after, and the chopper landed nearby, quickly carrying Arvo to the nearest hospital.

Along with Arvo, the river had given up the suspect's gun. The suspect's body was never recovered.

It wasn't long before a new legend began to be told along the shores of Lake Frontenac, the largest lake in the Mississippi. Locals claimed that the Lake Monster had surfaced that afternoon, taken one taste of each man, and quickly judged which man was beyond redemption. It spat up the one with the wounded soul, and dragged the soulless one back to its lair beneath the lake. The Lake Monster was never seen again.

The long time of healing for Arvo did not mean the investigation went on hold. Far from it. Sheriff's offices from two counties, Nokomis and Mendora, rapidly teamed up to fast track what turned out to be a massive corruption and contracting scandal. The corporate crimes were definitively linked to the murder of Karl Lutz, when the recovered motorcyclist's weapon was determined to be the one that killed Karl.

It took a well-coordinated effort to arrest the many people involved, a number of whom held prominent positions at RoadCon, MinnFreightways, and the phony organization, River Valley Business Association that had hired the killer.

J.T. Sanders himself arrested Matthew Arndt, and later told Arvo that the guy had the most unusual looking skin he'd ever seen.

"Hereditary hemochromatosis," Arvo told him some time later.

"Hered—wha?"

"Iron overload. Say it three times fast. It's kind of tongue twister."

After Arvo was well on his way to recovery, Bill Ruud dropped by his hospital with other news.

When Arvo saw he was holding the editorial page, he looked pained.

"Do you need more meds?" Ruud asked.

"I won't if you keep that opinion page outside the door."

"That's just it. Listen."

"Do I have to?" Arvo begged.

"Yes." His boss said. "I am ordering you to listen. It's rather old news, printed the day after you were brought to the hospital."

Dear Editor,

I want to offer my gratitude to the brave men and women of the Mendota County and Nokomis County Sheriff departments.

The bravest of them, Detective Arvo Thorson, lies at this moment gravely wounded in a hospital bed. It was his persistence, at risk of his own life that is finally bringing to justice my son's killer.

We often judge too quickly when we are presented with questions we do not understand. These mistakes of judgment are particularly easy to make during a time of personal crisis. I know, having hastily judged Detective Thorson when he spoke with me as part of the investigation into my son's death. I hope one day, once Detective Thorson has completely recovered, that I will be able to personally express my family's heartfelt gratitude for all that he has done, and express my deepest apology for having wrongly judged.

He is a true hero.

At that point, Arvo asked Sheriff Ruud to hand him the newspaper. He reread the entire letter, more than once, and he was still astonished when he read the name of the writer, even though it could be no one else.

Sincerely,
John Lutz

TWENTY-SEVEN

I HEARD YOU WERE FEELING BETTER," Christine Ivory said. She
stood in Arvo's hospital room doorway, and it didn't take him
long to realize something about her that had changed.

And it wasn't the simple fact that her hair was growing out,
and the purple was gone. She looked at peace.

"Are you feeling well enough for a visit, from me?" she asked.

"Of course, come in," he said, his voice not quite back to
normal from the ordeal.

Christine came inside and sat in the chair that had been pushed
close to Arvo's bed. "That's interesting," she said, spotting a
handmade get-well card in his hands. "What a beautiful design."

"It's an original," Arvo told her. "Designed by a local artist."
He showed her that it was three-dimensional, and that when
opened, a small diorama sprang up. "See? It comes with toys." Arvo
displayed the tiny hand-carved animals that fit perfectly into the
little display.

"I've never seen anything like it. Do you know where it came
from?"

Arvo looked toward the doorway and gestured with a nod of
his head. "There's the artist herself."

Jade stood in the doorway with two steaming cups of coffee.
Arvo motioned her to come in, and she set the cups on Arvo's tray
table, and kissed him on the cheek.

"You must be Christine," she said. "Arvo's told me about you."

Christine's eyebrows arched.

"I mentioned we used to work together," he said, knowing that
Jade might have sensed more than that, but he kept the details to a
minimum.

She held out her hand, and Christine took it. "I'm pleased to meet you. I hear that no one compares to you in your line of work. You've done amazing things with children."

Christine thanked her, and Arvo could see that Christine accepted that compliment as a sincere one.

"So, you're an artist?" Christine asked.

"An aspiring one," Jade said. "For now waitressing pays the bills."

"Well you're obviously very talented. This card is really charming. I'm sure you could sell these at boutiques."

"I do. But this particular piece is a one-of-a-kind. Kind of like Arvo," Jade said, looking at Arvo with a warm smile.

"Christine is probably wondering what someone with such great taste and talent as Jade sees in a one-of-a-kind guy like me," Arvo said with a grin.

"What can I say? I like a guy in a uniform." She gave Arvo another kiss.

Christine's look told him she knew she was on the outside of an inside joke. She stood up from the chair and looked as if she was about to leave. "Well," she said. "I was just stopping by to look in on you. Make sure you are on the way to recovery. I hear there's another commendation, or medal, or both, waiting for you when you get back to work."

"What about you?" he said. Would she be waiting for him?

"That's the other thing I dropped by to tell you. I've had a great job offer. J.T. hooked me up with someone in Nokomis, and with both of you giving me such glowing recommendations, I was offered a job. I'll start there in a few weeks."

Arvo didn't consider the news surprising, but it was hard not to feel shocked that she truly was moving on.

"So I came by to say goodbye. By the time you get back, I'll be officially off the Mendota County payroll."

Jade excused herself. "You're not leaving are you?" Arvo said to her. One woman saying goodbye was almost more than the wounded detective could take. Two would kill him.

"Of course not. I'll stay as long as you like. I just need to step away for a moment."

Clearly the woman did have good taste to know when it might be best to let the detective have a final word with the social worker.

"She seems really smart. And nice." Christine said.

"She is." Arvo said, quickly adding, "You're smart, too, Christine."

"But not very nice."

"I left that part out as a joke."

"We both know that it's no joke." She sighed and held out her hand. "So, it's goodbye?"

"Why so hesitant in your farewells?" he said, his voice stronger. "Given how things have gone with us, you should be celebrating that you are finally going to be free of me. So say it like you mean it, Christine. I want a goddamned goodbye." He smiled, but felt a few tears stinging his eyes. Things would not be the same in Mendota County without Christine around, as irritating as she could be.

"Then goddammit. Goodbye, Arvo Thorson," Christine said, this time without the question mark in her voice. She pumped his hand, and when she tried to pull it away, he held onto it, then pulled her close for a long, last embrace.

THE END

ACKNOWLEDGMENTS AND SCATTERED NOTES

A MINNESOTA MOTORCYCLIST WAS CLOCKED speeding along at 205 miles per hour one afternoon in September 2004. A Minnesota State Patrol airplane pilot tracked the cyclist racing along Highway 61 in southeastern Minnesota. Although no official records are kept, it was probably the fastest ticket ever written in the state. The motorcycle was a modified Honda.

My apologies to acquaintances with hereditary hemochromatosis. Most, 99.999 percent, are not criminals. I could not, however, resist the temptation to have my crook caught "red-handed" and the tie-in with Minnesota's famous iron ore, in the form of taconite, was also perfect. I love you and support you.

Lake Pepin is the large lake in the Mississippi that inspired the "Lake Frontenac" of *Broken Down*. Its fabled lake monster is named Pepie.

Likewise, a real swing bridge serves as the inspiration for the book's bridge. The Rock Island Swing Bridge was built in 1895. The double-decker bridge provided a river crossing for both automobile and rail traffic for just over a century. The bridge fell into disrepair but is today preserved and refurbished as a pier, and connected to the Dakota County trail system. Sadly the swing span is no longer in existence.

Thanks once again to my beta readers—Melissa Doffing and Lindsay Taylor. I look forward to reading your new novels and seeing them on the bookshelves in the near future.

DISCUSSION POINTS

1. The river plays a central role in the book. In what ways is it used in the story? Find examples and share.

2. How do environmental issues, such as land use, historical preservation, and natural resources, impact the small town of Somerset Hills and the story?

3. What do we know about Arvo's and Christine's demons? Are their strengths and weaknesses complementary? Are they better off apart?

4. From the beginning of the book, only the reader knows that Nick is not the murderer. Can you think of other books, or movies, where an innocent person is accused of murder?

5. Does Nick understand that he is under suspicion? What convinces Arvo that Nick is not responsible?

6. How has Arvo changed, or grown, since Washed Up? Or not?

7. For readers who have not read Washed Up, how did the book work as a standalone novel? Do you get a full picture of Arvo and Christine's history within Breakdown?

8. The book is written from two somewhat limited points of view: some chapters are told entirely from Arvo's point of view and other chapters are told from Christine's. How would the book be different if it was told only from one point of view?

9. Arvo's biggest blind spot revolves around his relationship with his ex-wife. How does his character evolve in coping with his blind spot?

10. What do you think will happen to Arvo and Christine next? Does their relationship seem finished? Why or why not?